Jack 'Fitzy' Fitzpatrick gets the promotion of his career to regional vice president of sales at his publicly traded company as his gambling addiction increases exponentially. Fitzy is trying to win a twenty-eight million dollar healthcare software sale, the biggest of his career. At the same time, he is putting his career, wife, and son at risk as he battles his gambling addictions of sports betting, craps, blackjack, and proposition bets. Jack travels back and forth from Boston and Nevada, as he navigates the steps of winning a complex multi-million dollar sale, is in-debt, is being threatened by a big time Boston bookie, and being followed by the FBI. All while trying to keep his job, not go to jail, avoid getting murdered, and saving his marriage. See if Jack makes the right 'Decisions' as he uncovers a company secret.

"A robust fictional story that intertwines sales, business, and gambling.......",
Matthew Smith, CEO, 3C Software

"A great read – this new author weaves a tale like a savvy veteran.",
John Kelly, Vice President, Arbor Commercial Mortgage

" 'Decisions' should be called 'The Ninth Habit'. After I finished the book, I reread it again.",
Kerry Ringham, General Manager, Sheraton Hotels

"What a compelling novel, Shaun Priest paints a gut wrenching story of the inner turmoil of being a gambling addict.",
Larry Enright, General Manager, Perferx Optical

"What a story. I could not put it down and I recommended it to my management team......",
Chris Hintz, President, CPT

SHAUN PRIEST

DECISIONS

SHAUN L. PRIEST

WWW.SHAUNPRIEST.COM

Cover Design by Shaun Priest

ISBN-13: 978-0983807315 (Shaun L. Priest)
ISBN-10: 0983807310

For Christine,
I Love You Unconditionally.

SHAUN PRIEST

Acknowledgements:

Decisions took several years and legions of family and friends to go from an idea to a published book. There are many people to acknowledge, who without their support this book would never be in print today. The first is my wife and two children. For their enthusiastic support: "Daddy is an author", to "Yes, I will put the kids to bed so you can work on your book," to simply, "We are proud of you." I want to especially thank my dad, who was my first editor on both grammar and content. My father put countless hours into *Decisions* and was my sounding board on each storyline and every change. Together we hashed out the content, I would write the chapter, and then my dad did the detail work reviewing each and every word. I am grateful and proud of my dad. My mother, who before she even knew what the book was about, told me "Your book will be great." To my brother who read the very first completed draft of the book and made several fantastic recommendations.

To my many friends and family, who read the early drafts with excitement and offered sound advice. I tried naming each of you but each time I added another name I realized I left off someone else. You know who you are, and Thank You.

It takes a team to write and publish a book. I appreciate all of your hard work, insights, and time, from all who helped with *Decisions*, thank you.

Shaun

1

Flight to Reno, NV

"Sometimes too much drink is barely enough."
Mark Twain

Jack Fitzpatrick's wife, Colette, hangs up on him while he is tied up in the worst traffic jam he's ever encountered on 93 north. Friends call him Fitzy but instead of looking Irish, he looks like he walked off Laguna Beach with his sinewy 6'4" frame. Boston's Logan Airport is still ten miles away and he is about to miss the plane for Reno. He may not look Irish but it is taking all of his will to control his temper and not smash his cell phone against the dashboard. Instead he leans on his horn but does not feel any better.

Whose dumb idea was the Big Dig? Fifteen years and fifteen billion dollars and it's driving people to murder. Leans on his horn again. This highway project is as foolish as Betty Turner, his former sales executive. Betty quit this morning right in the middle of the biggest deal of Jack's career with CM Solutions. A twenty-eight million dollar contract to sell CM's healthcare computer system to Reno Regional Medical Center is at stake and she quits.

Of course, it had been Betty Turner's deal, too. Why would she quit? But she did, on the very day she was supposed to go to Reno to schmooze their senior management and to set the table to win the deal with Reno Regional, which is the only reason he is struggling to catch the plane.

He is also trying to placate his wife, Colette, who was planning his birthday party tomorrow night but now he will be in Reno. As the northwest regional Vice President of Sales for CM Solutions, he can't let this deal go under. True, he had wanted to get rid of Betty Turner from the first day he'd met her; she was a pain in the arse because she had expected to get his position and, in revenge, dragged her feet on his every suggestion. And even his boss, Kevin Blair, wanted to fire Betty but he couldn't because there are not many sales women at CM and both of them knew Betty would sue their asses if she was fired. With her dyed blond hair, fake boobs and fake smile, no-one wanted to take Betty on in court. So, Jack and Kevin had made Betty's life at the company miserable by doing the one thing seasoned sales people hate most, making cold calls, every day. True to her nasty nature, she had quit at the worst possible time. *Bitch.* Not like his wife who is all woman. Colette is the opposite of Betty, natural brown hair, real boobs, and rock hard stomach, packed into a 5′7″ frame. Colette's only drawback is her ferocious temper, which has been directed at him since he had told her earlier in the day she had to cancel his birthday party because he has to go to Reno with Betty quitting.

Earlier in the day, after walking in the door of his house, to pack for Reno, Colette immediately accused him. 'It's your fault she quit.'

Mistakenly, he pushed back, 'Take it easy,' and she simply blew up, 'You just don't want me to throw a birthday party for you.'

He stormed upstairs after her, 'I'm sorry, babe, you know I love you but we need this deal. I will call everyone to let them know why I had to cancel the party.' He unsuccessfully tried to get her to calm down which made him even later for catching his flight from Logan. Finally he had to leave the house, which is why she just hung up on him again.

Still stuck in the stop-and-go traffic, he leans even harder on the horn while dialing home again. Even with a temper, compared to Betty Turner, Colette is Miss America. With her rock hard stomach, making love seems like doing it with a Greek Goddess.

"I'll be home Saturday and we can celebrate just the two of us," he jokes on her voicemail but he is not happy. *Woman, I'd rather go to Reno than celebrate my birthday, anyway.* For starters, Jack doesn't like being reminded he is 31 years old and the second reason, equally compelling, he is deep in debt and Colette's parties are always very nice but very expensive, plus being a gambling connoisseur, he can play the tables and make some extra cash while in Reno, even though he shouldn't.

Before he gets to the airport, he makes a business call to another hospital in Reno to see if they will meet him. If he is going to fly 2,000 miles he might as well have two meetings instead of one.

Of course when you're late, you get a full body-search at airport security. On a dead run he sprints across the airport to catch his plane which is finishing boarding, and congratulates himself for being in top physical condition. Playing basketball is his third preoccupation, after his family and gambling. His legs are as hard as a pro's and he weighs the same as he did when he played college basketball at Kennesaw State. And at the end of his run is a first-class seat with a double VO and Ginger.

He settles in his seat and orders a double from the pretty stewardess, who gives him a second look. Relaxing, he mentally prepares for the Reno meetings. Betty had been working on Reno Regional Medical Center for 18 months and if Jack closes the deal, he will get half a percent of the contract price, a very nice $140,000 commission check.

He gets a second double VO and Ginger. *If I can make a little run at the tables, I can get my ass out of debt.* In the last year, Colette had remodeled his Tudor house in Bridgewater. He bought himself a seven series BMW and a cute little Saab convertible for Colette, and maxed out his credit cards. The worst blow was losing ten grand at the Foxwoods Casino in Connecticut just last month. *I really need a good run at the tables this week.*

He frowns, on his last trip to Vegas, he lost over fifteen grand at the craps table. Jack told his wife he only lost two grand and she was so mad, she bought a new couch for two grand. The irony is if he wins, Colette spends the winnings and if he loses, she is upset and spends his losses to make it fair. As Colette likes to say, "I may have spent two grand on a couch but at least we have a couch. You lose two grand in Las Vegas and we have nothing."

He refocuses on the Reno deal, because even though he loves to gamble he knows he has better odds winning the sale than winning at the craps table. He opens his laptop to review Betty Turner's notes in their sales management data base. This visit will be a pre-demonstration meeting, so CM can prepare the on-site demonstration in two weeks. Ordering two more double VO and Gingers, he reclines his seat and goes over his pitch to Reno Regional's Chief Financial Officer and the Chief Information Officer.

Make'em love Fitzy, he smiles to himself and promptly falls into an alcohol induced sleep. He dreams about throwing winning dice as big as couch pillows. With all the VO, he wisely catches a cab to check in at his hotel and falls immediately into a deep sleep.

First thing the next morning, he takes four Advil for his hangover and calls Colette. He reaches her when she is feeding their thirteen-month-old son, Harrison, his breakfast. Harrison is the spitting image of his dad with his bleach blond hair and easy smile. Colette is in a lot better mood. "Don't worry about calling everyone. I called them last night to cancel your party." Jack is ready for battle, and he is disappointed, because she is being so nice. He is always amazed at how quickly she gets mad and how quickly she gets over it. Colette keeps talking, "Want to know what I bought you for your birthday?"

Still feeling the effects from the alcohol and the flight yesterday, he quickly frowns, "I said before. I do not want anything."

"You are pretty grumpy birthday boy, so how about you guess", she jokes with no response from Jack. "Okay, I will just have to make you guess. How about a riddle? 'What is greater than God, more evil than the devil, and if you eat it, you will die.'"

He wants to stay mad at her but he just can't. "I told you the riddle and it is, 'nothing'", he says while laughing.

"I may not have bought you anything but I have decided to give you your gift in the bedroom when you get home." With her beautiful laugh, "If I'm up to it."

Getting into the teasing, "I'm counting on it. Plus, I will need it after a couple of days in Reno."

"Stay away from the tables."

"You can bet on it. I am taking the prospects out to dinner tonight, so no gambling, then I fly back tomorrow." They talk for a while then Jack says, "I am going to head down the hotel gym before my meeting, so give Harrison a kiss from me and a big wet one for you."

The call with Colette pumps him up and he starts getting the vibe of successful meetings, and, hopefully, there is a little positive vibe left over for the craps table. Slinging a towel over his shoulder, he heads off to give his abs and pecs a full court press.

2

The Old North Church

"Most of the important things in the world have been accomplished by people who have kept on trying when there seemed to be no help at all." Dale Carnegie

Earlier in the evening in Boston's historic North End, right next to the famous Old North Church, two FBI agents are in a cramped one bedroom apartment on Salem Street. The exact church on April 18, 1775, Robert Newman, the church's sexton, hung two lanterns in its steeple to warn that the British troops were coming 'by sea', thereby sending Paul Revere and William Dawes on their famous 'midnight ride' to Lexington and Concord to warn Samuel Adams and John Hancock; 'The British are coming; The British are coming'.

It is a muggy Wednesday night in June. With his coke bottle glasses, small frame, balding scalp, and oversized off-the-rack suit; twenty year FBI veteran Agent Tim Stephenson walks into the apartment and smirks, "If Skinny does not show up in ten minutes, I am going home." Sandy Marino, better known as 'Skinny', is the owner of Al Sacerdote Ristorante across the street from the FBI's apartment. Skinny is an oxymoron because Skinny weighs north of three hundred pounds.

The younger agent, 'Ringer', in his ripped shorts and old Boston Red Sox T-Shirt is at a wobbly foldout table full of electronics, "Skinny is probably waiting for you to go home so he can have a nice big plate of lobster ravioli without you watching him."

"He better not know we are watching him. I am sick and tired of the BPD tipping him off," as he scratches his growing bald spot.

"I personally broke into his place, so I guarantee they do not know we are listening to him," Ringer says as he wipes the sweat off his head with a dirty towel.

Under Stephenson's geekish exterior burns a fire to do anything to get Skinny, from illegal phone taps, to false arrests, and fake charges. He has gotten close to getting an indictment on Skinny three times and every time something happens. He is tired of getting burned by Skinny and by the Boston Police Department.

"Is anything going on in the back room?" Al Sacerdote's luxurious back room, not open to the public, is where Skinny and his crew get together.

"Still no sign of Skinny, but some of his flunkies are playing poker in the back room," Ringer quickly responds.

"I am surprised those guys are smart enough to play poker. Who is playing?"

"The usual misfits, with Carl D'Auria as the senior guy."

Stephenson paces in front of the window overlooking Al Sacerdote talking to himself and the agent, "Carl D'Auria is a made man from Providence. There is no way he came up here just to play poker." He glares at the younger agent, "Why don't you have a complete list?"

Ringer throws him his notebook with his notes. "This is not easy with those guys swearing all the time and calling each other different nicknames on different days. Too bad I didn't put a camera in there too. Now shut up, so I can get your list." Ringer is just out of college and is Stephenson's protégé, a.k.a. whipping boy. Their apartment overlooks the restaurant's front door because it is Skinny's entrance, but the low level guys typically come in through the back of the restaurant. "I count eight people in the back room with two guys called Bunar and Stevey, who I have never heard of."

Stephenson glares at him, "Well get more information on those guys?"

"Why are your panties in a bunch tonight? Maybe you should go home so I can get some work done". Stephenson does not tell Ringer their boss wants to take out the illegal wire taps.

Throwing Stephenson a headset, "You need to listen to this. D'Auria and this guy Bunar are getting into it."

As he puts on the headset he hears the first voice say with a slow thick Boston accent, 'Cocksucka hands off my cash, now'

The second canary voice quickly responds, 'Bunar, I do not know who you think you are, asshole, but that is my money.'

The first voice calmly, 'You foldad, that means that you lose and I win, now sit your arse down, so we can play anothar hand.'

The second voice gets louder, 'I did not fold. I put my cards down. Bunar you are new to our game, so back off.'

The first voice, 'I said sit down before Stevey and I start shoving cards up your arse.'

There is a loud crash, the canary voice yells in a high pitch, 'You are not so tough with a gun is pointed at you'

The first voice very coolly, 'Put the gun away.'

"What should we do?" Ringer yelps.

"Nothing, we are not going to blow our cover because two low level Mafia guys have trouble playing poker together. Now shut up so we can listen."

The canary voice yells, 'I am tired of your shit already and I just met you.'

The first voice yells, 'Stevey, No!'

The FBI agents hear three quick gun shots. "Should we go over there?" Ringer yells as both agents look out the window as four people run out of the front door.

"Relax, make an anonymous call to 911 to get the Boston Police in there. My goal is to get Skinny, not these low level guys, and I do not want the local police to know we are watching Skinny."

"What if someone is shot?"

"I do not care if these guys shoot each other over a poker game."

After six long minutes the police arrive and through their police scanner and wire taps, the FBI agents quickly learn, the back room is empty except for one guy who was shot in the chest but is alive. An ambulance arrives to take George

Mullane to the emergency room. The agents scan their notes, and Mullane is one of D'Auria's guys from Providence.

"Should we call the Providence FBI?" Ringer asks.

"We are not telling anyone we have an illegal bug in Al Sacerdote's not even the Providence FBI. I am going over there to question Mullane before he dies," Stephenson says staring at the junior agent. "I would have you come with me but not with you dressed like that."

Ringer ignores the comment on this attire. "What are you going to tell the BPD?"

"I was in the area, and I heard about the shooting over my radio."

Scurrying down the creaky back staircase Stephenson almost falls on the slick old hardwood. To keep up with the act, he gets in his car and drives around the corner to Al Sacerdote's. Police cars are everywhere. Showing his identification three times he makes his way to where the EMTs are working on Mullane. He quickly learns Mullane is alive and is telling the police he was by himself when his gun accidentally went off. The police laugh because Mullane cannot find the gun he shot himself with and they have found two additional bullet's in the wall.

Stephenson quickly flashes his badge and asks the EMTs to leave him alone with Mullane. He is surprised how big Mullane is even while on the stretcher and a hole in his chest. Without introducing himself, "So who shot you?"

"As I told the police, I shot myself while cleaning my gun. Who are you?" Stephenson does not answer the question.

With no one else near him Stephenson whispers, "I know you work for D'Auria and Skinny will want to know why he shot you. We both know you did not shoot yourself and Skinny will be pissed you got shot in his place." Mullane is trying to figure out if Stephenson is on Skinny's payroll. Listening to the wire taps, Stephenson believes D'Auria had the gun, so he presses, "Why would D'Auria shoot his own guy?"

Mullane quickly responds, "Carl did not mean to shoot me. You need to tell Skinny it was an accident. He was just threatening Bunar when his guy tackled Carl and that is when I got shot."

Stephenson internally smiles and keeps pushing, "Who is this Bunar?"

"All I know is that he is from Southie and that Skinny likes him."

"What does Bunar do for Skinny?"

"He runs numbers from Southie and because of him I got shot. That is it. Hey, how come you don't know who Bunar is?" Stephenson does not answer the question and walks away as Mullane tries to sit up, "What's your name?"

3

Reno Regional Medical Center Meetings

"If past history was all there was to the game, the richest people would be librarians."
Warren *Buffett*

Reno Regional Medical Center, with 500 beds, is Reno's largest hospital. Memorial Hospital is its closest competition, and although Memorial is significantly smaller than Reno Regional, RR is currently upgrading its maternity suites to keep up with Memorial, which updated its maternity suites two years ago. Jack reflects, *Airports and hospitals always seem to be under construction.*

As he walks into the recently remodeled lobby, he smells money. All the glass and chrome, with a monumental urn of cut flowers as the centerpiece of the space, the lobby tells Jack he's in a progressive institution and won't mind spending big bucks for a high-end computer system. A 1970's lobby, on the other hand, might mean a hospital will be looking for a cheap solution to its technical problems. He can sell in both situations, but it's always preferable to go where the money is. His research has also told him Reno Regional is not only profitable but has an endowment of $100 million in donations from the local casinos.

Handing the volunteer his business card, he asks for direction to Cheryl Scharff, Reno Regional's CFO's office. He also asks the volunteer for Cheryl's secretary's name, so he can address her when he gets to Cheryl's office. Being nice to secretaries is vitally important because they manage their bosses' schedules and grant access to the decision maker. Additionally, they know who and where the power players are. Jack has paid his dues when it comes to selling and is well aware of his killer instinct, his ability to size up a prospect within minutes and to lay it on when he has to, and when to hold back.

Entering Cheryl's office, he turns on his practiced 1000-watt smile. "Good morning, Sonja. I have a nine a.m. meeting with your boss, but I'm afraid I'm a little early."

Looking at his business card, the plump young woman behind the desks smiles, "No problem, Mr. Fitzpatrick. I'll just show you to the board room where the meeting will take place. Peter Galetta, our CIO, and Michelle Parks, our Clinical

Information System project manager, are attending, too. Would you like a cup of coffee?"

Score one for me. As he settles down at the 25 foot long oak board room table, he presses his luck with the CFO's secretary. "I haven't met Ms. Scharff before. How should I proceed?"

The secretary is quick with a reply. "Just be direct. Cheryl doesn't like beating about the bush."

Minutes later, the three executives walk in together. Jack sizes up the female CFO. She is dressed conservatively, in a grey suit and plain white blouse. Seems 50-ish. The CIO is fat, and probably older than he looks. Maybe late 40's. But it is the project manager who really interests him. Late 20's, black suit, short hair, glasses, very dignified and elegant. *No wedding ring. Michelle Parks may be Lady Luck.*

Quickly after the standard polite preliminaries concerning air travel and comfortable hotel rooms, Cheryl gets down to business. "I'm glad you had a good night's sleep, Mr. Fitzpatrick. Now let's get moving. I have another meeting in thirty minutes. Our goal today is to make you aware of our expectations for the demonstrations which, as you know, will take place in two weeks. And by the way, we were expecting Betty Turner, not you. Why the change?"

Prepared for the question, Jack takes the secretary's advice giving Cheryl it straight. He also goes informal and uses her first name. "Cheryl, Betty abruptly gave her notice yesterday. We were disappointed this happened, but I am our Northwest Vice President and I will personally be involved with Reno Regional during your vendor evaluations." Pausing for a moment, he observes the slight change of expression on the CFO's face as he addressed her by her given name. *A mistake*? Quickly, he cements a grave expression on his own countenance, "If we are fortunate enough to be selected as Reno Regional's business partner, you will receive our absolute top-flight attention. I was always scheduled to appear at the demonstrations, as you know."

"I didn't know", the CFO says, which sets Jack back, but she seems satisfied by his remarks and unruffled by his form of address, which causes him to think with relief, *maybe she's beginning to trust me.* "Shall we begin?"

During the course of the meeting, Jack gains a lot of information. Cheryl Scharff is smart and tough. She hands him the agenda:

Reno Regional Day 1 Clinical Information Demonstrations
Attendees: Reno Regional Clinical Information System Steering Committee

- 7:00am to 7:30am: Reno Regional Overview
- 7:30am to 9:00am: Vendor Company Overview
- 9:00am to 10:00am: Vendor Scripted Demo
- 10:00am to 10:30am Break
- 10:30am to 12:00pm: Vendor Scripted Demo (cont.)
- 12:00pm to 1:30pm: Lunch
- 1:30 pm to 2:30pm: Physician and Nursing Information System Demo
- 2:30 pm to 3:00pm: Laboratory Information System demo
- 3:00 pm to 3:30pm: Break
- 3:30 pm to 4:00 pm: Radiology Information Systems demo
- 4:00pm to 4:30 pm: Pharmacy Information System demo
- 4:30 pm to 5:00pm: Wrap up/ Questions and Answers

Reno Regional Day 2 Clinical Information Demonstrations
Attendees: Departmental Teams

- 7:00am to 8:30am Physician Out Reach
- 8:30am to 10:00am Physician Computerized Order Entry
- 10:00am to 10:30am Break
- 10:30am to 12:00pm Nursing Information Systems
- 12:00pm to 1:00pm Lunch
- 1:00pm to 2:00pm Laboratory Information System
- 2:00pm to 3:00pm Radiology
- 3:00pm to 4:00pm Pharmacy
- 4:00pm to 5:00pm Wrap up / Question and Answer

Her agenda, typical for a vendor presentation, has a BIG problem on Day 1, the 'Scripted Demo". A type of demonstration which demands a lot of information and preparation from the vendor in terms of its capacity to produce, and is designed to discover if the vendor can actually handle what is needed by the buyer with its current system.

"When can we expect a copy of your scripted demo?"

"We sent it to Betty Turner over a month ago. It is very detailed," Peter the CIO quickly answers.

Betty is still screwing me. He replies calmly, "I'm sure she passed it on to our demonstration specialists. Still, could I have my own copy to look over?" *Bitch, not only did she quit before making this trip; she also kept the script from me. What else has she kept from me and CM?* Jack is beginning to feel a queasiness in his stomach.

More and more, he sees Betty Turner has set him up for failure on this project. Several other items have apparently been sent to her without any transmission of information to Jack. The queasiness begins to rise to his throat. *Stay cool; you know how to handle these people.* "It is becoming obvious Betty did not pass on select pieces of your information to CM and I don't know why. I do know we are very excited to have this opportunity to work with you." Takes a deep breath to keep the queasiness down, "I also know you have been through an intensive selection process and you have narrowed your vendor selection down to two, CM and MacroHealth. I am prepared to personally manage this partnership if we are fortunate enough to earn your business." He gives another of his Crest white-and-bright smiles to Cheryl, who seems mollified, but has still more requests.

While Jack takes notes furiously, Cheryl talks non-stop. Apparently, she is the key decision maker and after listening to her personal goals and her business goals for Reno Regional, he is definitely not prepared for the demo session in two weeks. And even though CM is a lot smaller than MacroHealth, CM has newer technology and higher client satisfaction. He is confident he can win the deal IF he can get RR with the program but he will have to bust his ass. Cheryl has mentioned in her laundry list of necessaries, as if he needs more updating, Michelle Parks, the project manager, will fill him in. Looking at the attractive Michelle, who has demurely said not one word during the entire meeting. *It would be a pleasure to work with her, even if she isn't one of the real players.*

And so the meeting ends on an upbeat note, only slightly marred by Cheryl's inability to have dinner. As Jack's bile settles back in its proper place around his liver, he closes with, "We are excited to be working with you and we are looking forward to our meeting because our clients and our software are our sales people." He notices Michelle smirks at his obvious sales line. Cheryl Scharff shakes his hand on the way out and she doesn't seem as tough as she had at first. *Remember to send a nice CM polo shirt to Sonja.*

The tension of the meeting has been allayed, feeling more secure and assured. He also hears the casino beckoning, always a respite to business bullshit. After a couple of phone calls, one to the wife, where no answer qualifies as a call from the road, and one to his boss, Kevin Blair, to bitch about Betty and to find out who the bitch is working for now. No luck on finding her next employer, but Kevin promises to find out. He does tell Kevin it is not a rumor and Reno Regional's project manager is a hottie. His final obligation for today is finding a restaurant for dinner tonight. He takes the hotel concierge recommendation and makes dinner reservations at the Wild Moose. He heads for the casino floor.

The action is not as lively at 11 a.m. as it is at 11 p.m. but it is still a casino with the slot machines chirping, the busy red carpet, no windows to the outside, no clocks on the wall, just lines of green tables for the customer's pleasure, with the constant 'ding, ding, ding, ding, ding' sounds of the slot machines.

Reluctantly he avoids the craps table, even though craps is his favorite game, but the craps table is empty and he prefers a full table when he plays. He goes for blackjack. He has gotten $500 from the ATM machine, five crisp brand new 100-dollar bills instead of the typical twenties, a ploy the casinos use to get more chips cashed all at once. Jack gets his frequent gambler card, so the casino can track his gambling habits and he can receive free hotel rooms and meals courtesy of the casino. He knows they are not really free but enticements to get him to gamble more.

He spots a half full table and surveys the blackjack players before sitting down at third base. Third base is the last player to take a card before the dealer. Many players are superstitious about playing third base and who is playing third base at their table. Opposite him on the far left is a very young woman who annoyingly keeps asking the dealer what her total points are, who wins, what the face cards count as opposed to the point cards, when she should stay and when she should draw, and if she should split or double down. *She should have purchased a cheat sheet.* Cheat sheets are a great tool for amateur players, the cheat sheet advises a player on every move from hitting and staying to more complicated double downs and splits.

But the 20-year-old has a disarming attractiveness. She will certainly be no opponent and her companion doesn't seem too swift either. There are two other middle-aged men in the middle, checking out the twenty year old. Jack notices the dealer has a goatee, *he could be a lucky dealer.* Feeling pretty good about the table until being dealt a pair of eights and the dealer has a queen for his up card.

Always split Aces and Eights. Sixteen is a shitty hand, gotta split these suckers. The cutie to his right has drawn a nine and an eight. She's gotta stay even with the dealer showing a face card. She asks, "What do I do?" Before the dealer can answer Jack winks, "No question, you got to stay."

On Jack's turn, he splits the eights and tosses in another twenty-five dollar chip. The dealer smiles a tight smile and deals to him a ten on the first eight. With a deliberate wave of his hand, he signals he will stay on eighteen. On the second eight hand, he gets a five for thirteen. Taps the table for another card from the dealer, nine for twenty-two, *Busted,* and in one single move takes his chips and cards. In slow motion, the dealer flips over his down card a ten for twenty. "Shit", announcing his bad news to the table. The dealer rapidly scoops up all the cards and chips. The middle aged guy to his left pats on him on the shoulder laughing, "Welcome to the table."

Down a quick fifty but not defeated. Like any other experienced gambler, he knows only too well the best way to get out of a losing streak is to get into a winning streak. It's like physical exercise—you have to stretch and warm up. He has often started out betting $25 a hand and ending the night playing multiple hands for a thousand plus.

This day, however, Jack's winning streak does not materialize but neither does a losing streak. He is having trouble latching onto the ebb and flow of the game. He's stubborn, though, and hangs in long after the pretty young woman and her advisor have left the table and the dealer has changed too many times to count. In no time, it is 3 p.m. and Jack has lost three hundred dollars, *not bad.* It's time to head back to RR for his meeting with Michelle.

But the afternoon is not lost. In the lobby of the hotel, he runs into an old friend and client, Howard Black. Howard is the CIO of Memorial Hospital, Reno Regional's only competition. When Jack was a CM sales rep, Howard was his very first sale. Joking, "How come you have not returned my call?"

"It hasn't even been twenty-four hours, CM's customer support does not call back quickly," Howard jokes back.

Howard can be a great resource for RR, so Jack asks him to get a drink. Howard resists and explains he is coming from a luncheon meeting at the hotel, so Jack corners him in the lobby about what is going on at Reno Regional. He quizzes

Howard so penetratingly about Reno Regional, finally Howard cries out in protest. "Give me a break with all this bullshit about RR, Fitzy. Do you know Memorial's board has just approved twelve million for a physician portal program? Your sales skills are slipping, my man. You must have just lost at the tables."

Twelve million, wow, another fact left out by Betty. He cranks up his spiel. "Let me take you out to breakfast tomorrow morning and talk about this, Howard. You've known me a long time. I've listened to your dumb golf and doctor jokes for years. You owe me."

The meeting is set and Jack freshens himself up in the hotel lobby's gilt-edged men's room and heads off for his meeting, *date,* with Michelle Parks, the project manager, whom he plans on snowing until she caves. Michelle is as gorgeous as she appeared in the morning, calm and fresh. Conscious of his rumpled jacket and casino-pale complexion, he tries to pay attention as Michelle goes over the hospital's selection process in great detail, and nods a lot in agreement, but he is really staring at her breasts, which move enticingly under the black suit.

As they wrap up their meeting, Michelle says she is looking forward to their dinner at eight. He is half listening wondering how she would look naked. Nonetheless, he asks one more question.

"If you had to pick a vendor today, which one would you pick?"

Michelle gives him a quizzical look as if the question is inappropriate, but replies, "Unfair, Jack. And lucky for me, I'm undecided. Otherwise, I'd be out of a good dinner tonight." She gives him a final dazzling smile. *What I need is a good, long nap before dinner but no time; it is time to gamble.*

4

Dinner at the Wild Moose

"I hope to break even this week. I need the money."
Veteran Las Vegas Gambler

It is now 5 p.m. and Jack is in the hotel elevator, ready for a long, hot shower and a refreshing nap. At the fifth floor level, he reaches into his pants pocket for his key and finds over $100 in chips. *Too good to waste,* he presses the down button. In the casino, he sits down at the same blackjack table he had lost at earlier and, playing at $25 stakes, suddenly finds himself up over $500. Great but it is a quarter past seven. If he is to get to the Wild Moose at the Mountain Casino before his guests, he must leave immediately. A shower is out. He asks the bald dealer in the oversized shiny tuxedo shirt, "How far by cab is it to the Mountain Casino?"

"Less than fifteen minutes", the dealer answers quickly, knowing he can come up with some bullshit for being late, and he will stay for one more shoe, six beautiful decks of 52 cards, before giving up on his mini-winning streak. Since Reno Regional's main player, Cheryl Scharff, is opting out of the dinner, if he's a little late, it's no big deal. Jack stares at the shoe, a red box chained to the table enabling the dealer to work quickly and accurately, while he briefly entertains the idea he is possibly making a mistake here, staying.

He ups his bet to $250 a hand and holds his own, up $1,500. It is now 7:45 and the dealer is into another shoe. No way he is going to be on time to meet his dinner guests. He plays one hand for half his winnings. He gets a six and a four for a total of ten. The dealer is showing a nine as his up card. Figuring the odds, puts up another $750 and draws a seven. To his horror, the dealer then flips over a jack. Within fifteen seconds, Jack has gone from being ahead $1,500 to being without a single chip.

Annoyed with himself for the lack of gambling discipline plus feeling dirty and disheveled, he sprints up to his room and manages to wash his face and hands, throws himself into a clean shirt and blazer, and is out on the hotel's front steps and in a cab in less than ten minutes. He feels out of control again. *Why did I stay at the damn tables,* he wonders to himself, but loud enough for the cabbie to reply, "My thoughts exactly, buddy." He takes out his cell, calls The Wild Moose and tells the headwaiter to inform his guests, he will be there in 15 minutes. But by the time the cab arrives at the Mountain Casino it is 8:30, and Jack dashes through the lobby without even noticing the antler chandeliers and animal busts all over the restaurant.

Slightly breathless, he approaches Peter Galetta and Michelle Parks, who do not seem to be at all offended by their host's lateness or his lame excuses about the home office interrupting him at a bad time. The CIO is on his second glass of a bottle of Chateau Neuf du Pape. Relaxing a bit after thinking to himself Galetta has good taste in wine, accepts a glass himself and surveys his prospects. When there is pause in the small talk he tactfully asks Peter Galetta his feelings about CM versus the competitor, MacroHealth. Jack gives Peter his full attention and listens. He discovered the hard way early on in his sales career that listening is more important than talking. Peter, now on his third glass of wine, confides CM's software is better than Macro's, but CM's a smaller company and it could be bought. Jack ignores the comment on CM's possible buyers, but encourages the CIO to confide further. *In vino veritas.* It turns out Galetta used to work for a hospital using MacroHealth software and found its support system was poor and expensive.

With Peter's revelations at dinner and the three really great filet's grilled to perfection rolling along, Jack turns his attention to the project manager. Michelle confirms she is not married. She grew up in Mission Bay near San Diego. She maintains the dignified manner of his previous encounters with her, and unlike her coworker, has barely finished one glass of wine. Nevertheless, something about her gives the notion she is sending him sexual vibes. She laughs at all his jokes, for one thing, and looks him boldly in the eye when she speaks. Peter Galetta orders another bottle of the burgundy.

One of the many rules in sales is not to get plastered in front of clients. Another rule is to keep drinks flowing to the clients but stop if they start to get drunk, because in the morning they will be humiliated and could be defensive. Michelle appears to be a social drinker, but Galetta drinks enough for two. Galetta must be a big drinker because he is handling himself fine. Jack would have preferred a bottle of Sam Adams but keeps mirroring his prospect by drinking the Chateau Neuf du Pape.

During dessert, a baked alaska with raspberry sauce, the subject of gambling arises naturally, because the Mountain Casino is three times as large as the casino at Jack's hotel. He says nothing about his earlier $1,500 loss at the tables. Smart clients realize it is their money via commissions, the sales rep is throwing away.

Instead, he asks his guests what games, if any, they play. Peter, appropriately remarks, he'd rather drink good wine than gamble, and then, with a wistful look at the half bottle of Chateau Neuf left, "I need to head home before I am over served because I got an early meeting tomorrow. Plus, my wife will have my head if I stay out past midnight."

Awkwardly, in spite of hoping Michelle will stay on, asks if he could see Michelle to her car. To his surprise and delight, she responds she has tomorrow off and will help him finish the bottle. Right away, asks her about her interest in gambling and learns sometimes she plays blackjack when friends come to town. Her apologetic smile is irresistible and so is Jack's mental picture of her body. Michelle also confides she loves to watch crap games, but finds them overwhelming with all the betting options and the shouting.

Never one to resist an opportunity, Jack launches into the basics of the game, speaking slowly and carefully, as if to a child. While pouring Michelle the last of the wine, he says, "Well, you know the initial player, or shooter, rolls the dice to establish an initial number. There are only certain numbers that can be rolled initially—four, five, six, eight, nine or 10 for the point. Once the point is established, the shooter simply keeps rolling until he hits the number again and wins or rolls a seven, or craps, and loses. But...," leaning a bit closer to his beautiful companion, "if the shooter rolls a seven or 11 on his initial roll he wins and if he rolls a two, three, or 12 he loses."

Michelle complains, "Too many numbers to remember. Can you write them down on your palm?" Jack laughs while noticing she has not drawn away from his face, now intimate with hers.

"Sure", he jokes, "but don't let the other players see you cheating." Suddenly, a great idea comes to him. "How about we go downstairs and play craps together. I'll be your tutor."

She agrees readily as Jack looks at his watch. It is now close to midnight and with his early morning meeting with Howard Black of Memorial Hospital, he should have said no. *How often do I get the chance to go out with a beautiful woman who is not my wife?*

For some reason, the craps table at this hour has only four other players. Jack and Michelle decide to play at a low level table with a minimum of $5.00. When the craps stickperson pushes him the dice, he passes his turn so Michelle can roll.

He can tell the very act excites her. She blows on the dice and rolls an eleven, winner. The table claps as the dealer pushes the dice back to hear "Roll again, my dear, you're good luck." She hesitates then blows on the dice again and rolls an eight. On the very next roll she rolls an eight, winner.

Two winners in a row by an attractive woman, the table cheers as two more players join their table. Now inspired, Michelle blows on her dice, and rolls a seven, winner. Jack and the other six other men clap and whistle. They egg her on. "C'mon, babe, show us your stuff. You've got the wind at your back." Another guy yells, "Winner, Winner, Lobster Dinner". Michelle is swept up in the moment and sings "Luck Be a Lady" and rolls again. This roll delivers two fives, a hard ten. She accepts a Coors Light from the waitress. Her next roll is a seven for a loser, but she doesn't seem to mind, she's hooked.

"You make this game seem easy." Her high spirits infecting everyone, including the dealer, wearing a funny Tyrolean hat and lederhosen. A crowd starts to form around the game. Soon, twelve people are playing, the noise is high-decibel, and the table is getting hot. It is after one o'clock, Jack is up about $500 and Michelle is up, too. He notices everyone at the table is fascinated by the woman in the black suit rolling and winning, laughing a lot and generally giving a high-class tone to the game.

Jack feels the effects of all the alcohol with the wine and then several beers, which turns out, is Michelle's drink of choice. She seems to be perfectly in control. With Michelle and the table hot he ups the bets on Michelle's rolls and puts down an additional $500 on top of his earlier bet of $100. Michelle gives him a direct stare, "What do I get if I win?" To his alcohol-induced mind, her flirting seems to have intensified. She rolls an eight.

Jack encourages her to keep going. She rolls another eight. He is up over three thousand, and has crossed some imaginary line from prospect vendor to intimate. He picks up his partner and spins her around, drunk and full of himself. *Maybe I'll ask her back to the hotel room. But would that be sexual harassment of a prospect?* Michelle quickly pulls back and pats him on the shoulder, "Easy Partner." The move could have been awkward but Michelle has him blow on the dice for her next roll.

The rest of the early morning passes in a blur of beer, winnings and the rush comes with winning. Jack has forgotten about his upcoming appointment, his wife, and even Michelle. With a drunken focus, he is pushing the winning streak.

Michelle, however, seems no more flappable than at the start of the evening. When at five a.m., she finally suggests breakfast, pulling them back to reality and away from the table. They find a coffee shop and Jack orders two carafes of coffee for himself alone. With the alcohol wearing off and the dry mouth and headache starting, he has lost, completely, any sexual feelings he had for the woman he has spent almost 12 hours with.

"This is the most fun I've had in years", burbles Michelle. "I hardly ever go out." She brandishes her winnings and seems ready to start all over again. Jack, his eyes as red as routes on a road map and stinging like hell, contemplates the energy level between himself and a young twenty-something. He needs Visine, a hot shower, and more coffee.

But Michelle cannot be persuaded from her monologue. He likes her old, quiet self better. "I love the game of craps", she says, "It's better than my job and I thought nothing could take the place of working with computers. I'm really a nurse, you know, but computers don't talk back like patients." She chuckles. "And I like gambling with you best of all."

Jack buys a bottle of Advil and downs four. As he and Michelle go their separate ways, promising to return to the craps table when they meet again in two weeks, he realizes he no longer has his blazer.

Getting into his cab, his exhaustion reminds him today he is 31 years old, and getting too old to stay awake for 24 hours. His stomach rumbles and his head aches as if he is riding in the trunk.

Jack contemplates this quick trip to Reno. *Some okay business, but some really good casino action. Ten hours, a clear four grand and a bitch of a headache. Great time.* He remembers his meeting with Howard Black in two hours. He puts out of his mind entirely that he has been implicit in spawning yet another gambling addict.

5

Bunar Visits Skinny

"I would be a billionaire if I was looking to be a selfish boss. That's not me.", John Gotti

Agent Stephenson is in the middle of a morning meeting at the Boston FBI Field office in downtown Boston with his boss and one of the FBI's attorneys. The meeting is about removing the illegal wire taps and is not going well. Stephenson scratches his bald spot before saying in a frustrated voice, "If we keep this just between the three of us and Ringer, there is no way this will backfire on us. But we need to keep this between the four of us; a lot of people like to tip Skinny. Look, we know who shot Mullane because of the taps."

The FBI head, "Tim, no one, including me, cares about Mullane. We are all in deep shit if the BPD or Skinny finds the taps."

Still scratching his bald spot, "The Boston PD could not find a bug up their ass."

"Take it easy on the BPD. They could take all four of us down. Ringer is a valuable resource. I am thinking about re-assigning him to get him away from this mess."

"No way, I need him."

A secretary interrupts the meeting because Agent Ringham has an urgent message for Stephenson. Looking at the message, he states, "Ringer just got a new tip on Skinny and I got to go. Give me a couple more weeks." He does not wait for a response.

The comfortable AC of the FBI office is less than three miles from the heat at the FBI Al Sacerdote apartment, which should be called Al Inferno apartment with the summer heat. Ringer is sucking down bottled water and quickly learns Skinny is waiting on Bunar.

With a smirk, "So, did I interrupt anything important at HQ?"

Taking off his standard grey suit jacket, Stephenson lies, "Nope."

Ringer, with a head set over one ear, says, "We got a few minutes." Ringer enthusiastically explains his plan to arrest Skinny on RICO and racketeering charges on the Mullane shooting.

But Stephenson is not buying. "First, the Boston Police have no plans on following up on the Mullane shooting because Mullane is sticking to his story he shot himself and no one cares about him. Second, the bugs at Al Sacerdote's are illegal, so they will not hold up in court. Third, you cannot arrest a restaurant owner for someone getting shot in their restaurant, especially when they are not even there." Stephenson jokes, "Maybe we can arrest Skinny the next time his driver gets a speeding ticket."

Ringer, "Watch yourself or I will get another agent on this stake out. I am up here busting my ass 14 hours a day listening to bullshit, so I got a lot of time to come up with ideas."

Stephenson is holding onto this case and Ringer by a thread and backs off. "You are a rising star, so keep thinking. Just think it all the way through."

Ending their conversation, the agents hear Skinny say in his smokey voice, 'Bunar take a seat. I want to talk about the unfortunate incident.'

'I hear D'Auria's guy is fine and the police are not pressing charges,' Bunar says with a thick Boston accent.

'I am impressed. Have you heard D'Auria blames you?' Silence. Ringer looks at Stephenson and shrugs his shoulders. Finally Skinny continues, 'I warn you about D'Auria and you say nothing.'

'I am not surprised but he is the one who fired the gun.' Bunar responds with a laugh.

'This is serious. You are moving into the big time and you do not want D'Auria seeking revenge. On your behalf, I contacted him and he agreed as long as you pay him his two grand in poker losses, he will not blame the shooting on you.'

'That is bullshit. He shot the guy not me and I am not paying him shit.'

'Now you're fired up.' Skinny laughs, 'Well don't worry about the two grand; I paid him.'

Ringer looks over at Stephenson, "I love it when Skinny sounds like Tony Soprano." Stephenson, just glares at him to shut up.

'I did not ask you to do that. I can take care of myself.'

'I know you think you are an independent guy but we all need to look out for each other. I need you running books in Southie and you need me looking out for you.'

'I pay you to look out for my bookie business but I do not need you to look out for my personal business.'

'D'Auria after you becomes my problem. I did this for you and that is that. Now get back to Southie taking sports bets on the Celtics.'

There is a long silence before Bunar says, 'Thanks for taking care of this, but in the future, I can handle guys like D'Auria'

'I know you are a tough guy and you are used to running your own show. One of the many benefits paying me each week is I can offer you advice in addition to protection. You will also learn it is not about how tough you are physically but how you position yourself. I know you are learning because you have hired Stevey to do collections for you. You are still tough enough to do collections but your time is more valuable taking bets. In this case, your time is more valuable having me taking care of D'Auria then doing it yourself, which could create bigger problems for all of us. Bunar I like you, now get out of here.'

Stephenson is staring at his notes when Ringer hands him a manila folder. "How did you know I was thinking about Bunar?"

"After the shooting you asked me to get information on Bunar and Stevey."

They review Justin Bunar and Steven O'Rourke's police records and notes from FBI contacts in Southie. Bunar's record is very small with only speeding tickets and one drunken disorderly. Stevey's record is as long as the Boston Marathon. Stevey has spent time in jail for attempted murder and is a suspect in another murder case. From their street contacts they learn Bunar is an up and comer, who is running a very profitable sports book out of an Irish bar in Southie. Before running a sports book he was a Southie High School football star who turned down a scholarship at Boston College. His right hand man, Stevey, played football with him in high school. Stevey is simply dumb muscle but he has not been arrested since he started working for Bunar.

"Let's focus on Bunar. Based on the conversation with Skinny, it sounds like he is a mafia outsider who Skinny is trying to bring on the inside. Bunar does not have a record, so maybe we can get him to turn on Skinny." Stephenson walks out of the apartment without saying another word.

6

Memorial Hospital Meeting

"I found out that if you are going to win games, you had better be ready to adapt."
Scotty Bowman, National Hockey League Head Coach

With his head still pounding, he takes a quick shower to wash off the gambling and booze from last night. He is up almost five grand and is tempted to keep gambling at his hotel and blowing off the meeting with Howard. The Memorial deal can put him over the top and if he blows off a meeting to gamble, it could mean he has a gambling problem.

He is deciding what to tell Colette about last night. There are three major issues with his behavior last night: one, he drank too much; two, he gambled too much; and three, he spent too much one on one time with a beautiful woman. All three would land him in the doghouse, especially without calling his wife last night. In Jack's mind nothing happened, but Colette would not see it that way. Traveling three weeks a month, Colette knows sales people have a reputation for extra marital activities. She also knows her husband likes to drink and is very outgoing. He basically agrees with Colette, but he has to remind her he loves her and likes to tell her 'I take my appetite with me everywhere I go but I only eat home.' Colette does not like this analogy because, he should only have an appetite for her.

He apologizes for not calling yesterday, saying the meetings just kept running into each other until it was too late to call her. He also does not want to give many details about last night besides a quiet dinner with some prospects, male and female. Colette wants to talk, but luckily she has to take Harrison to the doctor to check his ears. Harrison's ear infections save Jack from an interrogation about last night.

He rushes through getting ready, grabs a Mountain Dew from the hotel refrigerator and heads down to check out. It never fails when running late; the elevator is slow, there is a line to check out, with only one person working, and a line to catch a cab. Jack is definitely going to be late, so he calls Howard. Getting Howard's voicemail, tells him he will be fifteen minutes late and jokingly adds due to unforeseen winnings at the casino.

On the cab ride over Jack is checking to see how he looks for a guy who had a bunch of beers last night and has not slept in 36 hours. Looking in the rearview mirror, then at Jose Martinez's picture on the back of the taxi seat, "Jose, how many hours sleep do you think I got last night?"

The cab driver laughs with a Spanish accent, "Do you want me to tell you what I would bet or how you think you look?"

Jack jokes back, "Both".

"Zero hours for the wager because this is Reno and if you had eight hours sleep last night you would not ask. For how do you look, good."

Howard is sitting behind his desk tapping his watch. "You could not pull yourself away from the blackjack table to meet with your favorite client."

Because of their relationship, "It was craps and you are my favorite client but Reno Regional will give you competition." Jack knew the Reno Regional comment could backfire on him so he lessened the blow with, "Even after RR signs, you will still be my favorite client, plus when they do become a CM client, I will have even more visits to Reno to meet with you too."

"The only reason I am your favorite your client is that you like that Reno has gambling."

Transparently and professionally he rolls the conversation into the deal, "The opportunity to gamble is a big benefit but you are my first client with CM, therefore, you will always be my favorite. Now how can we help you with your Physician Portal project?"

Howard goes into detail on the project. Howard also says there are other vendors bidding on the project. Jack asks who and all Howard will say is MacroHealth. They meet for almost two hours.

Mentally and physically exhausted, he takes a cab to the airport and daydreams about Michelle. Knowing Michelle is out of the office he leaves her a voicemail, thanking her for the great time last night and that he is looking forward to CM's demonstrations in two weeks. Thinking about all of the follow up work he has to do from this trip, *I should do a lot of work on this flight but man I need a nap.* Because he travels a lot Colette is not a big fan of him taking naps on the weekends.

Colette figures her husband should be able to catch up on his sleep while traveling because he does not have to get up with Harrison in the middle of the night. She also figures he does not get to see the two of them as much, so he should want to spend time with his wife versus taking naps. Jack likes to play golf and basketball on the weekends, so he is reluctantly in agreement on the naps, unless he is really tired.

At the airport he calls Colette to see how Harrison did at the doctor's. Getting her voicemail, *They must still be at the doctor's.* He is not worried about his son because Colette is just a worrier. With his hangover, the sleep is very uncomfortable. By the time he lands at Logan airport it is after eleven p.m.

7

Colette and Foxwoods

"You cannot beat a roulette table unless you steal money from It.", Albert Einstein

Jack pulls into the driveway to their house in Bridgewater, Massachusetts after midnight. It is a growing town south of Boston, which has the rare distinction of having both a prison and a college. They live in a two-story tudor on a side street about a mile from downtown and a mile from the local state college. Homes are very expensive in the area but they got theirs for a steal about two years ago.

The good news is they got a great deal on the house; the bad news is the house was built in 1927 and needed a lot of work. Jack likes to joke with his wife, saying she is a full time Mom and part time general contractor. The house is under constant construction. They have added a detached two-car garage, gutted the kitchen, and finished the basement.

Jack is up to his ass in debt and the winnings from last night will help pay some bills, including a recent gambling loss at a casino in Connecticut. He is always thinking about ways to get out of debt, like sell more deals, spend less, and win gambling.

Pulling into the garage, he is not surprised to see the painter's ladders stacked up neatly next to the garage but, to his surprise, the kitchen light on. When Jack is not home, Colette typically goes to bed early. Walking from their detached garage into the house, he sees Colette in her night shirt sipping coffee.

Jack gets excited, assuming Colette is staying up to give him his birthday bedroom present. Starting to get turned on, he is thinking he needs a release after the sexual innuendos with Michelle last night.

Walks in and gives her a big hug. He is about to tell her how much he misses her but sees she has been crying. *How can she know about last night with Michelle?* Colette can see his confusion, asking him if he checked his cell phone voicemail. Jack shakes his head no.

Throwing a pink invoice at him, she screams "What the hell is this?"

Confused, he bends down to pick up the piece of paper off the floor. Bending down, he recognizes it before it is in his hand. It is a bill from Foxwoods for his ten thousand dollar marker. Last month, he went to Foxwoods with Billy Nestler. He was drunk and on a bad losing streak. Between craps and blackjack, he lost the two thousand he brought in cash plus his whole ten thousand dollar marker. *Why do the damn casinos let me set up lines of credit?*

"Oh that," with a fake funny laugh.

Her face no longer crying is full of rage, "You keep bitching to me we do not have any money because of all of my home improvements and you go out and lose ten thousand."

Lying, "I am getting a big commission check at the end of the month and we will be all set." There is a long shot chance Memorial or Reno could come in this month but even Jack would not take that bet.

"How can you say we will be all set, when you lose ten grand gambling?"

Offering a weak olive branch, "I have been traveling and I miss you and Harrison, so I will not play golf in the morning."

Colette keeps getting louder. "What the hell is, 'I love you. I will not play golf?' This is about you losing ten grand, asshole."

So much for the olive branch. He tries to give her a hug and she aggressively pushes him away. They have only been fighting for a minute and he is already exhausted. "Let's go to bed and we can talk more about this in the morning."

"No dice, Kenny Rogers, I want to talk about this now. What else have you not told me? Did you lose in Reno this week? You need to ask Kevin for a new territory"

Trying a subject change, "How was Harrison's doctor appointment?"

"He is fine, now answer my questions. What else have you not told me?"

Jack still does not answer the questions and reassures her he will be getting commissions this month and Colette starts to calm down. Just wanting to go to bed, "Can we discuss this in morning?"

Colette reluctantly agrees, "As we both know, you are sleeping in the guest room and just because you can pay the bill, does not mean you are off the hook. We will talk about your gambling problem in the morning." As they are walking up stairs, Jack has a quick thought to ask for his bedroom birthday present but instinctively knows now is not the time.

8
Jack and Colette

"I was nauseous and tingly all over. I was either in love or I had smallpox." Woody Allen

In the morning, Jack hears Colette and Harrison playing downstairs. He looks at the guest room clock, 10:07. Not believing he slept this late, especially with Colette so mad at him, he rolls out of bed preparing for the Collette assault.

He asks why she did not wake him up. To his surprise, she was up anyway, and he could use the rest after being on the west coast.

With a smile, "Are you sure you have a plan to pay off your gambling debt?" Jack nods and gives her a hug. With a friendly push back, "You need to stop gambling."

Still hugging Colette, "I will". *Maybe this will blow over.*

Sure enough, Colette wants to believe her husband and she dives into their weekend schedule. Harrison has a birthday party at one of their neighbor's today and she wants all three of them to go. Jack agrees because he likes doing things with his family; the birthday party will have beers, plus Billy Nestler, one of his best golfing and gambling buddies will be at the party, and the party will mostly likely go into the evening. Colette says on Sunday after church she needs him to watch Harrison, so she can go run some errands.

Jack reminds Colette she needs to be home by six on Sunday because of his basketball game. Colette mocks, "I know." She continues, "I really wanted to have a get-together for your birthday but you were traveling on Friday, today Harrison has the neighbor's birthday party, and God forbid I ask you to give up one night of basketball."

Jack played division three basketball at Kennesaw State and plays basketball on a traveling team every Sunday night. This is his second year with this team. The team is from his sports club in Bridgewater. The different gyms in the area put together their best team and play each other. He is his team's best player, and they lost in the finals last year. Being six feet four inches, he plays center for the sports club team, but back in college played shooting guard. He really loves playing basketball for a lot of reasons: the competition helps him stay in shape, gets his mind off work and the family and it reminds him of his college days and being the basketball star. It also does not hurt that the guys usually get together for beers after each game.

Colette starts to lay into Jack, "You gamble, you travel five days a week, you play golf on Saturday morning, and you play basketball on Sunday nights. By my math that only leaves Saturday afternoon and Sunday morning for Harrison and me."

He does not want to get into it with Colette and takes the high road, "I am happy to give up playing basketball this Sunday, but I do not want a birthday party."

"I want to do something special for your birthday."

He grabs her around the waist, "How about a 'birthday bedroom present' when Harrison takes his nap this afternoon?"

"Until you pay of your gambling debt, your 'bedroom birthday present' is on hold."

"How about a dinner just the two of us this week?"

"I will ask my mom if she can watch Harrison Sunday night."

Smiling, "How about we see if your mother is available during the week."

"So you are playing basketball on Sunday?"

His smiles even bigger, "I did not play golf today and the basketball playoffs are in a couple of weeks." He pauses then adds, "I still want to have dinner with you, just during the week."

Colette smirks, "Before I ask my mother, what days are you traveling next week?"

Somehow Jack's smile keeps getting bigger, "I am not traveling next week, so any night is good. How about hoops on Sunday?" Before Colette can answer, "I will not go out for beers after."

Colette gives him the look, "Why do you always get your way? Sure you can play but consider playing basketball tomorrow night your birthday present."

Giving Colette a big hug, "You are the best. What time are we going to the neighbors?"

"Three this afternoon."

Jack offers, "How about I take Harrison on a run and you can have a couple of hours to yourself before the party." He runs a couple of times a week, usually putting Harrison in their jogging stroller. Most of the time, Harrison falls asleep during the run.

Realizing Jack is getting his way but wanting some time to herself, Colette reluctantly agrees.

Jack risks bringing up Foxwoods and gives her a thousand dollars of his winnings from Reno. He walks over to his wallet on the kitchen counter and hands Colette ten one hundred dollar bills.

Colette frowns, which doesn't surprise him, "You just need to stop gambling. Just because you won this week means nothing. I need you to stop gambling. Every time you win you end up giving your winnings and more back to the casinos, just like Foxwoods. And don't think I do not know how much gambling it takes to win a thousand dollars, never mind losing ten grand."

Not wanting to go down this path because he was gambling with Michelle, he changes the subject, "Why don't you get ready to head out, while I get ready to go running with Harrison?" He gives her a hug and a kiss, and heads upstairs to change before she can respond.

While running, he tries to come up with a plan to pay Foxwoods.

9
Neighborhood Party

"Words are easy, like the wind; Faithful friends are hard to find." William Shakespeare

Jack, Colette, and Harrison head over to the birthday party. He will get some flak from Billy Nestler about missing golf but he is looking forward to telling Billy about winning in Reno and Michelle.

Not at the birthday party two minutes, Billy comes up to him with a Miller Lite and a smile. Billy, with his graying goatee and muscular frame, starts right in on him, "Fitzy, I hope you got your beauty rest this morning. Just in case you did not get enough sleep this morning I brought you this," Billy pulls back the Miller Lite with one hand and gives him a baby pacifier with his other hand. Both Jack and Billy laugh.

They met about three years through the country club. Billy and Jack hit it off immediately. Billy has two young kids, likes to play golf, drink beers, and gamble. They frequently sneak down to the Foxwoods casino in Connecticut together to play blackjack, craps, and every now and then a texas hold'em poker tournament. Billy was with him two weeks ago when he lost the ten grand. Billy grew up in Raynham, the town next door, loves to bet on college football, plus he knows a bookie in Boston, who will take any size bet.

Pulling Billy into the back yard away from the other guests, tells him about Colette finding the ten grand marker from Foxwoods. Billy's wife is friends with Colette, so Jack does not want him to get blindsided by his wife.

Telling Billy about winning in Reno and gambling with Michelle, Billy's advice is very straight forward on Michelle, "Fitzy, you are crazy, you have a great wife, a great kid, and why you would want to mess up a twenty-eight million dollar deal by trying to start something up with one of their employees."

"I agree but I did not come onto her and I cannot tell if she is coming onto me."

Billy giving a crazy look, "It sounds like you both were coming onto each other."

The risky plan Jack came up with while running to pay off his debt involves Billy. Jack is going to try and extend his gambling winning streak from Reno. The plan is to bet big on NBA playoffs games and use the winnings to pay off Foxwoods and some of his other debts.

Jack's favorite sports betting strategy is to bet the same amount on three different games. He figures he will win two out of three games and there is the big upside, he could win all three games. The downside is he may lose two out of three, but he always assumes there is no way he can lose all three games.

Jack asks Billy to place three bets of ten grand on three different NBA playoff games tomorrow with his bookie. Believing he is guaranteed to make ten grand on the bets to pay off the Foxwoods Casino plus there is upside of winning thirty grand in cash. Billy is surprised by the size of the bet. Billy says, "Who died and how much money did you inherit?"

"Nobody died. I am feeling lucky and I need to pay off Foxwoods."

"Are you sure you want to lay down a thirty grand bet? If you lose you will have to pay Bunar by this Wednesday and you will still owe Foxwoods."

"Why Wednesday?"

Billy explains that bookies takes bets all week and they pay and get paid by Wednesday. Billy asks again, "Are you sure?"

Frustrated, Jack snaps, "I would not have asked you to use your bookie if I wasn't sure." He hands Billy a ripped out page from the Boston Globe with the three NBA games with his winners circled.

"Okay but you realize if you lose all three games you will actually owe the thirty thousand plus the ten percent vig for a total of thirty three thousand." Billy explains to make money, bookies take an additional ten percent on the losing wagers, called the Vig. The reason games have spreads is because the bookies want fifty percent of the bets on one team and the other fifty percent on the other team. This way for example if one hundred thousand dollars is bet on each team, the bookie is guaranteed their ten percent Vig or ten grand on one game. There is another gambling theory that the Vig just adds to the bookie's profits because gamblers will keep gambling until they lose.

Jack gives a heated, "Yes. You make it sound like I have never gambled before. Plus, in reality I am only betting ten grand because the worst I can do is lose two out of three. And yes, I know if I lose I owe that amount I lost plus the ten percent Vig."

Billy's biceps tense up, "I just want to make sure you have thought this all the way through and you know Bunar will want his money by Wednesday."

To break the tension, "So does this Bunar have a first name or is he like Cher, Madonna, and Kramer?"

Billy laughs, "Yes, Justin." Billy then starts telling another lame story about when Bunar was a freshman in high school playing varsity football. Billy knows Bunar because they were childhood friends until the ninth grade when Bunar moved to South Boston. Billy goes back to preaching to Jack, "Bunar is becoming a big time bookie in Boston. He now has guys tougher than him collecting the money."

"I know Bunar will want his money if I lose but I am not planning on losing."

"Bunar and I go way back, so he will know it is not me betting the thirty grand. I will have to give him your name. Even though Bunar and I are friends he will want his money."

"Be sure to tell Bunar he better have my money on Wednesday when I win." With phase one of Jack's plan complete, they head back inside to the party to be social.

Jack, Colette, and Harrison head home when Harrison starts to get cranky. Walking home, he is feeling frisky after a few beers and making the big bets. He whispers, "Bedroom birthday present" and grabs Colette's firm waist. Colette had a few drinks too and she tells him if he can wait until Harrison goes to bed the forecast is looking good for him.

Jack wakes up early Sunday morning with Harrison so Colette can sleep in. He is in a great mood because he got his birthday present from his wife last night, he could win up to thirty grand today in NBA playoff games, plus, as a bonus, he has a basketball game tonight.

While taking care of Harrison, He goes into the family room to turn on ESPN to get the updates on the three basketball games. At noon the Boston Celtics at the New Jersey Nets with the Nets favored by three; at four in the afternoon is the Atlanta Hawks at the New York Knickerbockers or better known as the NY Knicks with the Knicks favored by six; and at eight tonight is the San Antonio Spurs at the Las Angeles Lakers with the Spurs favored by four. Jack has the bets on the Celtics, the Hawks, and the Lakers.

Jack is feeling pretty confident, but he usually likes to bet on the home team in basketball. Statistically he knows home teams win about sixty percent of their playoff games. But today he only went with one home team. Also, he typically bets with the point spread because basketball games can be blow outs where the point spread does not have an effect on the betting but today he went with three underdogs. He is betting with his heart too, which scares him. He lives in Massachusetts and has become a Celtics fan. Being from Georgia, he has always been a Hawks fan.

First piece of bad news; the Lakers best player is hurt and will most likely not play today. Jack shakes it off because he is feeling lucky and starts playing with Harrison while getting ready for church.

Getting home from church, he heads right for the television to get the score of the game. The game is tied halfway through the fourth quarter. As Jack is sitting down, Colette yells from the kitchen, "What are you and Harrison going to do today while I am running errands?"

Jack wants to watch the basketball but he is also looking forward to hanging out with Harrison, so he responds, "Hang around the house for a little bit and head over to Billy Nestler's."

Not knowing he has bet on the games but knowing Jack, "Did you bet on the games with Billy?"

Jack smiles and gives Colette a hug and tells the technical truth, "Nope". His bet is with Bunar.

Colette advices him, "Then why don't you take Harrison to the playground before heading over to Billy's?"

"You better get going because you need to be back by six so I can head off to my basketball game."

With Harrison in his crib, Celtics are down by two with two minutes left on the clock. Because Jack is getting three points on the game, if the Celtics win or if they lose by less than three points he wins; if the Nets win by more than 3 points he loses; and if the Nets win by three points they tie and there is no bet.

With 17 seconds left in the game, Harrison starts crying. Jack scrambles to put a pacifier in his mouth and turns up the volume. Glued to the television, the Celtics foul the Nets and the Nets make both of their free throws, so the Nets are now up four, and he is losing his bet. The Celtics get the ball and miss their three point shot with 5 seconds left. The Nets run out the clock and they win by four points. *Shit, down ten grand plus the vig.*

10

Sunday at Al Sacerdote's

"The only difference between me and a madman is that I am not Mad.", Salvador Dali

Stephenson scratches his bald spot, wondering what he is doing at the FBI apartment on a Sunday by himself. He could just read the transcriptions from the wire taps tomorrow morning, but he had nothing planned and Sunday's are usually busy days for Skinny, but nada today.

Sucking down a cold bud, he goes over his obsession with Skinny Marino, his frustrated attempts to get him arrested, the Boston PD's foot-dragging cooperation and the day of the shooting. Ringer likes the idea of arresting Skinny on the Mullane shooting but there is no real evidence. They have listened to the sound of poker bets and the shooting in Al Sacerdote's enough times to memorize the dialog. There is nothing to tie Skinny to the shooting.

He re-reads the Boston Globe story buried on page nine the next day. POLICE SAY PROVIDENCE MOBSTER SHOT SELF DURING POKER GAME IN BOSTON RESTAURANT. "Yeah, and I'm J. Edgar Hoover in a dress"

A creaky fan blows hot air in his direction as he opens another Bud. Wiping more sweat off his forehead, thinking about the tapes and this guy, Bunar, he decides Bunar is the key and the next step is to stake out his bar, McCracken's, and put in another illegal wiretap.

With the decision made, he contemplates retirement on a cool lake in New Hampshire with large-mouthed bass competing to jump on his hook.

Skinny does not show up. "Wasted afternoon unless McCracken's pans out," Stephenson locks up and heads home to his family.

11

Billy Nestler

"Never bet on baseball." Pete Rose

As soon as the game is over, Jack's cell phone rings in the kitchen. Knowing it is Billy calling about the ten grand, answers, "You at home?"

"Yup"

"I will be over in ten minutes." The call lasts less than 10 seconds. Jack hangs up before Billy can respond because he is livid he lost. He has two completely different thoughts. The first is negative, *Why did I bet on that game* and the second is more positive. *It was a very close bet, could of gone either way, and my goal is to win two out of three bets, so if I win the next two games I am back on schedule.* Throwing Harrison's stuff in his diaper bag, he heads over to Billy's.

Before Jack can close the screen door, Billy starts peppering him, "Fitzy what if you lose all three games? Do you have the thirty-three grand for Bunar in addition to the ten grand you already owe Foxwoods? Do you think both the Lakers and Knicks will win?"

Jack is reconsidering his decision to come over to Billy's. Maybe he should have listened to Colette and taken Harrison to the park. "Calm down. No more negative questions about losing the next two games or I am going home."

Billy nods and the two of them talk about how close the Celtics game was. Being from Massachusetts, Billy is a huge Boston Celtics fan. Being from Georgia, Jack is a big Atlanta Hawks fan, so they also talk about the Hawks chances versus the Knicks. The first half of the Knicks and Hawks is not going Jack's way with the Hawks quickly down eleven points. He has seen enough and takes Harrison home.

Jack gets home to an empty house and calls Colette on her cell phone. "I just left the store and I will be home in 20 minutes and you will not believe the sales. I got a bed, desk, and bureau for Harrison's room."

Jack is annoyed but responds with a smile, "Great but please no more stops. I need to leave for my basketball game as soon as you get home." *I may need to come up with thirty grand and my wife is buying furniture for my son who is still in a crib.* Jack is superstitious and does not watch the end of the second basketball game. He figures he watched the first game and lost. He puts on his basketball outfit and stretches out as he waits for Colette.

As soon as Colette gets home, he sprints out the door. Colette wants to talk about the furniture, but Jack gives Colette a kiss, "I miss you and you can tell me about the furniture for Harrison's room later."

Colette reminds her husband, "Remember you promised to come home right after your game instead of going out for beers with your buddies."

"See you after the game."

On the car ride to the basketball game, Jack is trying to decide if he should listen to AM Sports Radio to get a score or if he should just listen to music. He doesn't listen to the game because he will get the score after his basketball game.

Getting to the gym, Chip Savard, a short fat lawyer and shooting guard, is making free throws like layups. Chip cannot rebound, play defense, nor pass but he sure can shoot. Chip's wife is Kim Savard who works for Jack. "Fitzy, can you believe your Atlanta Hawks are down by thirty points to the Knicks?" Unknowingly, Chip informed him he lost the second game for another ten grand.

"You are shitting me?"

"Nope, I was listening to the game in the car." Chip can see Jack is upset with the news and says, "Fitzy, I did not know you cared that much about the Hawks." He jokes, "It is just a basketball game, it is not like you lost any money."

Jack likes Chip but because he works with his wife and his wife knows Colette, he does not talk about his gambling habits with Chip. Changing the subject, "How was your weekend?"

While Chip is talking about his weekend, Jack is cursing himself for his shitty plan to gamble to pay off the Foxwoods marker. If he loses the next game, he will be down thirty-three thousand to Bunar plus the ten grand for Foxwoods. He can worry about Foxwoods later because Bunar will want his money this week and he can just pay Foxwoods a couple of hundred bucks for now. He is trying to stay positive but *where can I come up with the money?* He has less than two grand left from Vegas; he has about a grand in the checking account, and his home equity credit line has about two grand in equity. He would be totally tapped out and still be short over twenty-five grand. Plus he still has all his monthly bills and is afraid to find out how much Colette spent on the furniture for Harrison. He never thought he would lose two out of the three games, and now he could lose all three.

Jack is thinking he could re-finance the house but he just refinanced six months ago to cover Colette's home improvements, their cars, and random gambling debts. It will take at least a week to refinance. The good news is home prices keep going up, so he may have some additional equity in the house if needed.

He is ready to play some hoops and blow off some steam. Fired up he has a great game, scoring thirty-five points, leading his team to victory. After the game, all of Jack's teammates say he played like a man possessed, being everywhere on the basketball court tonight getting rebounds, stealing, and diving for loose balls. Jack did not tell any of them he is down over twenty grand today and could lose another ten grand before the night is over.

After the game, his team is excited because they won and Jack had a great game. They all want him to go out for beers. With a winning smile, Chip grins, "Fitzy, the first beer is on me tonight."

Feeling pretty good because he had a great game but he made a promise to his wife, Jacks grins back, "Sorry guys but I am out".

"No dice man, I am buying."

Contemplating what to do, he told Colette he would come right home after the game but he had a great game, he is losing his gambling bets, and what will one beer hurt, responds, "You're on, but just one beer. Where are we going?"

Chip quickly responds, "I have never seen you stop after one. How about the Mexican place just down the road?"

Getting into his car, he is having a self debate if he should call Colette to tell her he is getting one beer. Jack decides not to call the wife.

They get to the Mexican restaurant just after nine. Jack figures he has a twenty minute ride home, games can go as late as nine-thirty, so if he leaves the restaurant after one beer he should be fine. The basketball game is on the television and the Los Angeles Lakers are down 7 points to the New York Knicks in the first half. He orders a large Dos Equis Amber draught beer with two limes.

When the team orders another round, Jack is right with them. He is now hoping Colette will be asleep when he gets home. No such luck. Waiting for his second beer and his cell phone rings. *Not answering that one.* Less than five minutes later his cell phone rings again definitely not answering now. Doing the math on when he will get home, if leaves the restaurant by ten p.m. he will be home by ten-thirty and hopefully Colette will be asleep.

Finishes up his last beer, checks the TV to see the Lakers are now down twelve in the second half, says goodbye to this team, and heads for his car. Jack gets into the car, checks the car clock and it is after ten-thirty. He is screwed if Colette is awake.

On the car ride home Jack is going back and forth, thinking about the thirty-three grand he owes Bunar. He is no longer worried about the ten grand to Foxwoods. He is thinking about a new plan to get out of debt as his cell phone rings two more times. He is thinking about answering to tell Colette he is on his way home but he does not want to get into a fight on the cell phone. Pulling the car into the driveway, he sees the kitchen light on. *No choice but to take my medicine like a man.*

Jack walks into the kitchen and before he can say anything, "How many beers and why didn't you answer my calls?"

He could make up a story about his basketball game going into overtime or he was just talking to the guys after the game but knows a lie at this point will only makes things worse. Jack does a good job not giving the truth. For example he bet on basketball games today, but he always seems to get caught when he lies. "I am sorry. We won the basketball game and I played well. The guys wanted me to come out to celebrate winning. Again, I am sorry."

This does not make Colette feel any better, "So what you are saying is your word is only good if you lose the game or better yet, if nobody went out after the game. How do I know you did not go to Foxwoods to lose more of our money?"

Back peddling, "Honey, you know I played basketball. I was going to call but I did not want to wake you up."

She gets louder, "Well if it is true, which I doubt, how come you did not answer my calls."

Knowing she made a great point, he tries to lie, "I left my cell phone in the car."

Colette keeps getting louder, "Jack you are really starting to piss me off. You never go anywhere without your cell phone. If you did leave it in the car, why didn't you call me on your way home? I just called you ten minutes ago and I know you were in the car."

Gives his first honest answer, "I knew if I spoke to you in the car we would get into a fight, like we are now, and I did not want to get into it on the cell phone."

Colette keeps on him, "So you knew I would be pissed about you going out for beers but you went anyway. How do you think that makes me feel?" Jack tries to give Colette a hug. Colette continues, "Don't try to give me a hug and answer my question, how do you think I feel? We just got into it on Friday, I forgive you on Saturday, and you are lying again to me on Sunday. Plus, what if I was hurt and you did not answer your phone?"

One of the ironies about Jack is 'honesty is the best policy' but he does not practice what he preaches. If he just called Colette to tell her he was going out for beers, she would have been fine, but because he did not call her, he is in the middle of this fight, so he tries apologizing again, "Honey, I apologize I should of either not gone out for the beers or called you."

Colette will not let go of her question, "Answer my question, how do you think I feel?"

Jack now just wants to get out of this fight and go to bed and says, "You feel second to drinking with my friends versus coming home to you." Trying to add something positive, "I love spending time with you but I figured you would be asleep by the time I got home so what would it hurt going out for a couple of beers."

"How can I trust you?" He tries a hug again but she pushes him away.

"Because I love you so much. Now let's go up to bed and get some rest."

Colette reluctantly nods but says, "This is the second time in two nights I stayed up waiting for you. Don't think you are off the hook."

Jack loves Colette's passion which has its pros and cons. The arguing combined with his passion for her turns him and on the way up the stairs to bed, starts rubbing Colette's neck, whispering in her ear, "How about I give you an early bedroom birthday present?"

Colette turns around, smirks, and says, "Fitzy, why do you turn me on so much? You should be staying in the guest bedroom again."

"Because I just played basketball for two hours and I have not showered yet."

"Fitzy, you are not romantic but you do turn me on." She walks into the bedroom, gets naked, passionately kisses him and whispers, "This does not mean you're off the hook."

12
Back to Work

"Work is victory." Ralph Waldo Emerson

Surprisingly, Jack has a smile on his face as he gets up for work. He is thinking about Colette as he heads downstairs. Starting a pot of coffee, turns on ESPN. He no longer has a smile on his face as he waits to get the score on the Lakers game. While eating his cereal, he officially gets the bad news, the Lakers lost by fourteen points losing all three bets.

As usual, he gets into work early on Mondays because they are his meeting days. His first weekly meeting is at nine with his sales team. They review the sales forecast, weekly call volume, industry news and what is going at CM. The second weekly meeting is at eleven with Kevin Blair and the other sales managers. This is a very similar meeting to the first but instead of Jack leading the meeting Kevin does. Kevin reviews forecast, industry news, and what is going at CM. Jack's third weekly meeting is at four with the sales, implementation, support, and development managers. At this meeting, each department head updates each other with what is going in their department and they address any departmental conflicts.

This Monday Jack is not preparing for the meetings but thinking about how he is going to come up with thirty-three grand by Wednesday. He determines the quickest way to get out of debt is to make more bets. His phone rings as he is working on his plan. Billy calls asking if he has the money for Bunar.

Jack tells Billy, "Call Bunar later this morning and tell him I am going to give you a thousand today, and I also want to make additional bets on NBA games this week"

He can hear Billy's frown, "Fitzy, I told you on Saturday if you lost you had to pay by Wednesday. Bunar is not going to care about a grand when you owe him thirty plus. Don't go down this path. Just pay the thirty-three grand, and stop."

Starting to get defensive, "Don't Fitzy me, if I can win a couple of games, I will be back to even."

"I can probably get Bunar to float the tab but he will not take the bets."

Pleading, "Just ask him to take the bets. How about I contact him directly?"

"I will ask him about the bets but I heavily recommend you put your tail between your legs, pay your bets, and go home. This is the big time"

"Message sent, message received. Just call Bunar, see if he will take the grand and additional bets. I will call you later today."

Jack gets back to thinking about CM business, a welcome distraction. He has some decisions to make at his nine o'clock meeting. His team consists of three sales account executives but because Betty Turner quit last week, has an open account executive position. The other two account executives on the sales team are Larry Goodrow and Kim Savard.

Larry Goodrow is in his early fifties, looks like a typical middle aged salesman, thinning hair, twenty pounds overweight, and dresses one decade behind, with an ex-wife and two grown children. With Larry, Jack knows what he is going to get. On the plus side, Larry is very bright; he has twenty plus years of selling software and services in healthcare; and has a lot of contacts at consultants, competitors, and hospitals. On the negative side, Larry is lazy and has a negative slant on everything. Larry basically likes working for him because he is treated with respect and isn't pushed too hard. One plus of Jack pushing Betty to make more cold calls is Larry saw the aggressive side of his boss and is now making more calls. Larry is very happy Betty quit. Even though Larry is typically negative, he was tired of Betty always complaining.

Kim Savard is in her late twenties, a little chubby but very attractive and recently married Chip. Kim is a rising star at CM. Kim has been with CM over five years. She started out installing pharmacy systems, moved to client support, and then to sales. Because of her time in implementation and support, Kim has a great understanding of CM's solutions and she really leverages her knowledge to increase her sales. Kim needs to work on her sales skills and confidence. What she gives up in sales skills and confidence she makes up in product knowledge, hard work and enthusiasm.

Even though it is illegal to say out loud, Jack's biggest fear is she will get pregnant and quit. Kim is his friend outside of work. In addition to Chip playing on his basketball team, Colette really likes Kim and the four of them get together every couple of weeks. Kim and Jack get along great and she really enjoys working for him. She is happy Betty quit too. Betty Turner knows they are friends outside of work and Betty was always trying to get to Jack through Kim. Betty would submarine Jack politically by telling anyone who would listen their friendship corrupted his ability to make objective decisions on the team.

Because there are only three of them, the meeting takes place in Jack's office. Unlike the top floor, Jack's office contains one plain desk and a small table with three chairs. Larry starts the meeting with a bang.

"So does anyone want to know where Betty is working?" Larry immediately has both Jack and Kim's attention.

Jack quickly says, "Don't mess with me, so if you really know spit it out."

"MacroHealth!"

To which Kim screams, "Holy shit, bad news for them and great news for us."

Jack asks, "Are you sure?" Larry explains, a buddy of his from MacroHealth called him this morning to tell him they had a new employee starting today who previously worked at CM and called to get some background on her. Larry asked the person's name and was told, Betty Turner.

"Hold on" Jack calls Kevin Blair, updating him on Betty. He asks Kevin to call his contacts at MacroHealth to confirm the information. Also asks if Betty signed a non-compete agreement. Kevin says he will check but they are more of a scare tactic than a legal document.

Larry knowingly asks who is going to manage Betty's territory and specifically Nevada until they get a new sales account executive. This is a potential hot potato because Nevada has two deals worth a total of forty million. Jack has been thinking about this issue over the weekend because he knows he needs help with both deals. He needs Kevin's approval but he is going to give Larry the state of Nevada and have Kim manage the Reno Regional. Kim should get along with Michelle at Reno Regional and Larry will get along with Howard at Memorial. Because this has not been approved, Jack tells Larry, "Give me to the end of the week and I will have an answer. Until then I will cover Betty's territory."

Jack wraps up the meeting then gets ready for his meeting with Kevin by updating his forecast and accounts. He is also putting together a plan to sell against MacroHealth because Betty is now working for them.

Jack is even more nervous about winning the Reno Regional deal for three reasons: Betty was managing Reno Regional, so she knows more about the account than anyone at CM Solutions, Betty knows CM's weaknesses; and if Betty is smart she will combine the two. He has to discredit Betty at Reno Regional. He has to build a strong relationship with Michelle and start a relationship with their CIO Peter Galetta. He will try to subtly tell Reno Regional they should be wary of an ex-employee bad-mouthing their previous employer. He will do a pre-emptive strike and let Reno Regional know Betty is at MacroHealth. He will also start telling Michelle about Betty.

The hardest part will be to set up Betty, so she discredits herself. Although a long shot, if Betty did sign a non-compete it could be illegal if she works the Reno Regional deal.

Jack sends a brief thank you e-mail to Cheryl, Peter, and Michelle at Reno Regional. The e-mail includes a link to a recent article on a CM hospital and that Betty Turner is now working at MacroHealth. Then he is off to his sales management meeting with Kevin.

Kevin Blair, with his salt and pepper hair and crisply trimmed beard, has been with CM over ten years. He is CM's Executive Vice President and Chief Sales Officer. Kevin is in his early forties and is CM's eleventh employee. Kevin has three kids, works very hard and seems to manage family and work. Kevin is not afraid to take a day off or skip a sales trip for his family. Jack really enjoys working for him.

Jack walks into Kevin's office at five after eleven because the weekly sales manager meeting usually starts at least ten minutes late. To his surprise the five other Regional Vice Presidents of Sales are already in Kevin's office. Tim Clossy, CM's Northeast VP of Sales, says with a smile, "Fitzy I hear you gave Betty our source code before she left." Jack immediately realizes everyone knows Betty is at MacroHealth, which is why everyone else is on time for the sales managers meeting. CM has one thousand employees but news travels very fast.

Kevin begins the meeting, "I have confirmed Betty started today at MacroHealth and she will be covering the Northwest for them."

Jack interrupts, "Did Betty sign a non-compete?"

Kevin had already contacted CM's human resources and legal departments, and is ready for the question. "Nope, Betty worked for us for over seven years and we only started having new employees sign non-competes in the last three years. I still called our attorney to see if there is anything we can do. Our attorney let me know everyone has a right to work, so unless we can prove Betty stole confidential information, there is nothing we can do."

"Obviously this puts the Reno Regional deal at risk, but on a positive note," Kevin leans back in his chair and smiles, "the bitch is gone." Of the six Regional VP of Sales at CM, Carolyn Lake is the only female and Carolyn is one of the boys.

Jack figures he needs some credit so he clears this throat, "Ding dong the witch is dead, or should I say Bitch is dead. Kevin, who helped rid CM of Betty?"

Not to be one upped Kevin responds, "Fitzy, does that make you Dorothy?" The room laughs.

Kevin takes back control of the room, "Seeing as Betty worked for you Fitzy, let's do your forecast first." Jack goes through his sales forecast with the sales management team and is excited to tell everyone about the opportunity at Memorial. Each of the Sales' VPs goes through their sales forecasts. Kevin pushes all of them to get deals done this quarter and to do whatever it takes. Kevin gives the corporate update and wraps up the meetings. As everyone is getting up to leave, Kevin asks Jack if he is available for lunch in a few minutes to review Reno Regional.

13

Lunch with Boss

"Sell the sizzle, not the steak." anonymous

Jack heads back to his office to gather his notes on Reno Regional so he will be prepared to answer Kevin's questions during their lunch. His message light is blinking on his phone. The message can wait until he has all the Reno Regional information for Kevin. He prints his notes, a copy of Reno Regional's 40 page proposal, and gets a copy of their 200 page request for proposal (RFP) from his file cabinet. Checking through his e-mails from Betty Turner, looking for her updates on Reno Regional, Kevin walks into Jack's office without knocking, "Fitzy you ready?"

"Sure, just let me check my voicemails before we go." On speaker phone, 'You have one new message and 27 old messages, please press one to check unheard message.' Hits one, 'Jack, this is Michelle....' Because Kevin is in his office, hangs up the phone without listening to the messages.

Wow, she called me first thing in the morning. Why is she calling me? Should I have listened to the entire message? Should I check my voicemail again? Does she like me? Staring into space, Kevin interrupts, "Who was that?"

Jack hears the question but he is not sure how to respond, "Ah, the project manager from Reno Regional and I will call her back later today."

Kevin is frustrated, "This is the biggest deal you have going, you need to listen to the entire message." Kevin pauses with devilish smile, "Isn't Michelle the hottie you were telling me about last week?"

Jack is taken back Kevin remembers his comment on Michelle. Not wanting to listen to the message in front of Kevin, he gathers himself, "I agree. I will listen to the message on my cell phone on our way to lunch. Let's get rolling. I assume you are driving." Kevin nods and they head to the parking garage.

Jack is surprised he is looking forward to checking his voicemail. As they get into Kevin's S600 Mercedes, 'Jack, this is Michelle and I just wanted to return your call and tell you I also had a great time on Thursday evening too.'

Before he can hang up his cell phone Kevin asks, "So what did she say?"

Not wanting to talk to Kevin about Michelle, "She just wanted to confirm the on-site demo. I will call her back after lunch."

"Reno is a very big deal for us. Do not screw around on this deal. I need this deal this month. When are the on-site demos?"

"Next week. The on-site presentations are Tuesday June 17th and Wednesday 18th. We will have eight of us doing the presentations."

"Who are the eight?"

Jack lists the clinical and financials sales specialists including himself and probably one more not specifically stating he wants Kim Savard. "The only one who has not confirmed is Dr. Carson Alvarez as usual. I checked and his schedule is open. Anything you can do to get him to confirm would be great."

"Assuming you are correct and his schedule is open, I will make sure he confirms."

Smiling, "Thanks, he does a great job of presenting but he is a prima dona and high maintenance. Because he is one of only five doctors at CM, he wants all of us to suck up to him except for you and the senior management team."

Kevin laughs, "I need this deal, so I will get him to come, and I am coming too. "

"Fantastic, nine is the number". Jack is thinking about Michelle again, hoping to spend more one on one time with her during his next trip to Reno. But with Kevin on the trip, he will have to be careful.

"Nine damn people. The travel expenses alone are going to cost us twenty grand and our total cost of sales for this deal is going to be north of a hundred-fifty grand with travel expenses and wages."

"Yup", Jack is used to Kevin complaining about the cost of sales and travel expenses. Because Jack is known for running up his expenses he does not want to have a travel expenses conversation with Kevin. Jack stays positive but slightly changes the subject. "Hey, I will also set up a meeting with you at

Memorial. Maybe I can set up golf with you, Memorial's CIO Howard Black, Dr. Alvarez and myself."

"That is a good idea but you better book the flights today, while we still have the week advance notice on the flights."

"Agreed, my priority this afternoon is the Reno site visit."

Kevin pulls into the Charlie Horse restaurant parking lot. The Charlie Horse is a popular local sports bar. Kevin did not ask Jack where they were going to have lunch because the Charlie Horse is their spot. The Charlie Horse is less than a mile from the office. On Thursdays after work a bunch of people from CM Solutions usually head over the Charlie Horse for drinks. On some Fridays Kevin takes the sales managers out to lunch, which typically includes adult beverages.

During lunch Kevin wants to focus on Betty, Reno Regional, and deals he can close this quarter. Kevin starts with Reno Regional. Jack figured Kevin would want to talk about Reno, so he opens up his file, and goes through his notes and the RFP.

After Jack gives the update, Kevin states, "As I see it we are currently in second place and we are totally at risk. Betty knew she was leaving us and she kept information from us, obviously not trying to win the deal for CM if she knew she was going to MacroHealth. Also, if she thought we would win, she would not have given notice until after the deal. I need you to focus on this deal and I am relying on you to win the business this quarter."

Jack nods *Yea Right. We are in second place and Betty is going to be screwing us the whole time and there is no way this deal will sign for any company this quarter.*

Kevin wants to review the rest of Betty's sales forecast. Jack guesses Betty has been looking for at least three months because the rest of her forecast is pretty light. They discuss their plan for filling the position. Jack gets Kevin to agree to his plan of looking internally first while posting the position externally on monster.com.

Kevin asks to assign Kim Savard to Reno Regional because he wants her to go on the trip. Jack is surprised, but because he wants Kim to come, he moves on.

Jack is thinking, *Am I going to put myself in a bind by putting Kim in contact with Michelle? What if Michelle tells Kim about their gambling evening? What if Michelle really does like him and starts asking Kim about him? Will Kim tell Colette?* He has been looking forward to seeing Michelle next week but will now have to deal with both his boss and his wife's friend, Kim, in Reno with him.

The rational and business side of Jack's brain starts to take over. He needs to win the Reno Regional deal and having a physical relationship with Michelle will most likely only hurt his chances of winning the deal. A professional business relationship and a personal friendship will help his chances. Also, he really does love his wife and having a physical relationship will not help his marriage in any way, shape, or form.

14
Calling Michelle

"I've looked on a lot of women with lust. I've committed adultery in my heart many times.", Jimmy Carter

Back in his office, Jack shuts his door and starts pacing around his desk, deciding if he is going to call Michelle. The question is rhetorical because he has to call her back. The Reno Regional deal is too important and he has not done anything wrong with Michelle. *What am I going to say? Do I only talk business? Do I ask personal questions? Do I try to lead Michelle on to win the deal? Do I ask her about the mountain biking trip? I feel like a high schooler calling the head cheerleader.*

He calms himself down and goes with the rhythm of the conversation. From a business perspective he will confirm the on-site presentations and will try to find out which way Cheryl Scharff would vote today. He will also ask about mountain biking. Jack is surprised at his nervousness as he is dialing the phone. *Pull yourself together you are not asking her to the prom.*

Jack gets Michelle's voicemail, he hangs up and will try again in a few minutes. He should be better prepared for the call with Michelle so he puts together bullet points on what he wants to cover:

- *Mountain biking*
- *Confirm Dates and Attendees*
- *CFO / Cheryl's Vote*
- *CIO / Peter's Vote*
- *Who are the primary decision makers*
- *When is MacroHealth going on-site?*
- *Who is the lead doctor, so he can introduce Dr. Alvarez*
- *Try to set up a dinner*
- *Betty Turner*

Before calling Michelle again, he calls Howard Black at Memorial and leaves him a voicemail to see if he is available for golf on Thursday, June 19th. He calls Kim to tell her she is coming to Reno. She quickly responds, "Great, Kevin already told me." Jack is confused, Kevin must have told Kim right after their lunch. Moving on, he reviews the time-line, history and players at RR.

He starts pacing around his desk as he gets ready to call Michelle again. Jack gets out his notes. After three short rings he hears, "Michelle Parks, how can I help you?"

He pauses, and for a split second thinks about hanging up, "Michelle this is Jack Fitzpatrick with CM Solutions, how are you doing today?"

"Fitzy, why are you being so formal?" Michelle tries to mimic him, "'This is Jack Fitzpatrick how are you today?'"

Thank God she cannot see me blushing, "You are right." He goes with a personal question to break the ice, "How was mountain biking?"

Michelle goes on for 10 minutes about how great mountain biking was. Jack is taken in by her easy going nature and asks her more questions about mountain biking. He refocuses and looks at the list of items he wants to cover, "I am looking forward to seeing you again next week. Are we all confirmed on the dates and times?"

"Yes, but before I officially confirm you need to promise to play 'craps' with me again."

"That is easy enough, we are confirmed for the demonstration and for 'craps." Looking at his notes he confirms and crosses off 'When MacroHealth is coming on-site after CM.' After more light business talk, he asks about Betty, "Has Betty Turner called you yet, because she went to work for MacroHealth?"

Michelle gets a gossip tone in her voice, "Nope, but I bet she will. What is the story?"

Great, Michelle has taken the bait. "Not too much to tell because I just found out this morning." Jack starts a subtle smear campaign, "I was not surprised based on the amount information Betty held back on me about you guys. I was lucky you, Cheryl, and Peter were so nice to me last week." He flirts, "But on a very positive note, I got to spend more time with you because Betty did not give me all the details on Reno Regional."

Michelle not to be outdone, "I bet you say that to all the girls."

Jack is starting to go down a path he does not want to go but he cannot help himself, "I only say that to the pretty girls." He can hear Michelle blushing on the other side of the country. He switches back to business to let both of them off the hook, "So, what did Cheryl say after our meeting?"

"Honestly, she said she was disappointed you were not more prepared for the meeting."

"How do you think Cheryl would vote if she had to vote today?"

"I think she is leaning towards MacroHealth. We are using MacroHealth now, even though she is not a big fan of theirs, at least she knows what she is getting."

Shit. But at least he knows where he stands. It is better to know you are losing a sale because you can do something about it versus thinking you are winning. Jack makes different decisions whether he is winning or losing a deal. Now that he knows which way Cheryl could vote, asks about the CIO, Peter.

"I saw Peter this morning and we talked about the great time we had with you on Thursday night. He enjoyed the wine and conversation."

He presses, "Does this mean he would vote our way?"

Michelle pushes back, "Fitzy you are pretty aggressive this morning."

He is about to say 'Morning?' before realizing the time change from Boston to Reno. "It is a Monday afternoon on the east coast and I am already tired from being in meetings all day."

He looks at his watch, then his list one more time. The remaining item is a dinner. "Back to the agenda, I would like to invite all your committee members out to dinner on Tuesday evening."

He can hear her perk up, "Great, and I better sit next to you."

He stays focused on business, "I am planning on sending each member an e-mail to welcome them to our presentation and invite their significant others to the dinner." One reason Jack offered to send an e-mail is he does not have the attendees e-mail addresses and he would like to start a dialog with each member of the committee.

"That is a good idea. Do you have their e-mail address?"

Smiling, "Nope, if you could e-mail them to me would be great."

Jack follows the Colombo style of sales by asking one more question before hanging up. Colombo was a TV series in the 70's staring Peter Falk as an apparently incompetent detective. He would interview the guilty party. The guilty person would answer his easy questions and Colombo would get up to leave and the person would think they are off the hook but the last question would set them up, like 'Just to clarify where were you Friday night at 11p.m.?' Jack has a habit of asking one more question just before hanging up.

"Who is the main doctor on the committee?"

Without hesitation, "Dr. Harold Mainer our Chief Medical Informatics Officer and an internal medicine doctor too."

Because he got all the information he needed, he wraps up the call. "Thanks, I will follow up with you later this week and I am looking forward to winning on the craps table again too. "

He jumps out of his chair and yells "Bam". He really likes Michelle, the call went very well, and in the up and down world of sales, he is starting to feel better about winning the Reno Regional deal. He is surprised he is giddy like a little schoolboy.

15

Bunar's Money

"Money is a terrible master but an excellent servant."
P.T. Barnum

Jack looks up this week's basketball games on the internet. There are three more NBA games this week he wants to bet on. There is one on Tuesday, one Wednesday, and the last one on Thursday. He calls Billy, "Its Fitzy, did you talk to Bunar?"

Billy hesitates, "I have good news and bad news. The good news is Bunar will float your debt but the bad news is he will only float twenty-five grand, so you owe him eight grand today."

He needs to figure where he is going to get eight grand. "Okay, I will call you back in fifteen minutes."

How do I get to eight grand? Jack may have won in Reno but he only has two thousand in cash left, so where can he get another six grand. His credit cards are maxed out. He could simply answer one of the new credit card offers he gets in the mail but won't help him today. He could call the credit cards to get another extension. He has another two thousand open on his home equity line of credit but he does not want to use it. He still has this week's NBA games on his computer screen. Grins to himself calling Billy.

"Billy here is the plan. Call Bunar and tell him I will give you one thousand tonight and I want to bet on three more games this week at twenty grand per game."

"Fitzy, you are nuts. One of my favorite sayings is 'When you are digging a hole, stop digging!' And you are heading down a very deep and dangerous hole, my friend."

"Don't I always come through? I was just on fire in Reno. So I had a bad gambling day yesterday. I will win it back this week."

Billy reluctantly offers to pitch the plan to Bunar and writes down the three bets for twenty grand a piece. On Tuesday Jack bets twenty grand on the Boston

Celtics beating the New Jersey Nets; on Wednesday another twenty grand on the Los Angeles Lakers over the San Antonio Spurs; and on Thursday another twenty grand on the New York Knicks over the Atlanta Hawks. Sticks with his favorite bet of betting on three games and plan on winning two and if all goes right winning all three. If he wins all three he will be up twenty-seven grand, if he wins two he will be down a manageable thirteen grand, if he loses all three he will be down almost a hundred grand but it is impossible he could lose all three games or six bets in a row.

Billy repeats them back to make sure he does not get them wrong. "I will call Bunar for you but I am not going to guarantee he will take a thousand versus the eight thousand. I disagree with this but you got balls."

"I know you will take care of it. Let's meet around six at the Charlie Horse for one beer and I will give you the grand."

Jack has to head home to get the money, so he calls Colette, "Honey, Billy called me to meet him for a beer after work. I am going to head home, change, and get a quick beer with Billy."

"You better call Billy back right now and tell him you are not going to be able to meet him because my mother is going to watch Harrison tonight. I am going to take you out to 'Jimmy's Harborside' for your birthday dinner in Boston. Now you know the surprise, I need you home by five-thirty."

Jack cannot push the wife any further, "Great, I will be home by five-thirty. I have got to go. I love you and thanks for setting up dinner tonight."

Jack is now trying to figure out how to get Billy the grand tonight. He figures there is no way he can do it. He has to make a couple of more calls for work and will be lucky if he is home by 5:30. "Billy, there is no way I can get you the grand tonight."

"Fitzy, you are shitting me. I called Bunar. He is pissed you are only going to pay him a grand. I had to beg Bunar to take the grand tonight and take another sixty grand in bets this week. Plus, Bunar is sending one of his guys to the Charlie Horse to get the money and to meet you. Bunar wants someone else besides me to say you are good for an additional sixty grand in bets."

"Colette made dinner reservations in Boston tonight and I am already in the dog house for going out for beers last night after hoops."

"That is not my nor Bunar's problem."

"Billy can I borrow the thousand from you and pay you back tomorrow? I have the money."

"Yes, I will 'loan' you the money but that does not solve the problem of one of Bunar's guys wanting to meet you."

Think, Think, Think. "Can you call Bunar back and tell him you got the grand from 'me' but we are not getting together?"

"Fitzy you got balls of steel. I will call Bunar but you owe me big time again."

"Thanks man, I have got to go because I am going to be late getting home."

Jack makes a couple more business calls before leaving the office after five-thirty. Sprints home to change and head off to dinner with Colette. He runs into the house and kisses Colette as he heads upstairs to change, "Honey, I apologize I am running late. I will be back down in 2 minutes and we will head into Boston. I am really excited you and I are going to get some one-on-one time tonight."

He is halfway upstairs when Colette stops him in his tracks, "Who is Bunar?"

How can she know about Bunar? He uses his sales skills and acts quickly by going with partial truth, "He is a friend of Billy's, why?"

"Because he called you about twenty minutes ago and left you this message," Colette mimics a deep man's voice, "'Tell Fitzy I am available to have lunch with him tomorrow in South Boston'. This Bunar guy did not sound friendly at all. What the hell is going on?"

Jack is trying to think of his response, while dissecting Bunar's message. Obviously Bunar is sending him a message. He knows his phone number and wants to meet in person. He lightens up the mood, "You know Billy. He has been talking about this seafood restaurant in South Boston you can only get into with connections and his connection is Bunar."

He thinks he is off the hook, but Colette fires off a bunch of questions, "Why would he call you versus Billy? Why did he sound so mean? You never told me you and Billy were setting this up? I am not sure if you should hang out with Billy? What are you up to Jack Fitzpatrick?"

He explains to Colette she is over reacting as he is going to go upstairs to change because they are running late. As soon as Jack gets up stairs he shuts their bedroom closet door and calls Billy on his cell phone, getting his voicemail, whispering as loud as he can, "What the hell are you doing giving Bunar my home phone number? I will call you later."

Jack and Colette have a great evening at 'Jimmy's Harborside' restaurant in Boston on the water. He relaxes, recognizing how much he loves Colette, especially when they are out of the house. At home Colette worries about keeping a clean house, what Harrison is doing, what is going on with the neighbors, etc., but out of the house they really enjoy each other's company. Enjoying himself so much, he doesn't worry about Bunar nor the sixty grand riding on this week's basketball games.

At home, Jack is glad Colette did not get him an actual birthday present, but he is excited Colette offers another bedroom birthday present.

16
Morning in the Office

"A small debt makes a man your debtor, a large one your enemy." Irish Proverb

Jack has a smile on his face as he gets ready for work. Two birthday bedroom presents in a row. The smile goes away as he remembers lunch with Bunar today.

At work, he calls Billy first thing. "Billy what are you doing giving Bunar my home number? He called me at home last night."

"Calm down, what did you expect me to do, and you are in the phone book anyway."

"I am calm now, but you should have seen the look on my face when Colette said 'Who is Bunar?'"

Laughing, "Did you crap your pants?"

"I was close but I figured Bunar is smart and a pro, so I played it cool and brought you into the mix by truthfully telling Colette, Bunar is your friend. So back to this lunch, I assume you are going with me?"

"Thanks for dragging me into your web with your wife, and I am not going to lunch with you. Bunar told me he wanted to see you alone."

"Kinda scary."

"Big Jack Fitzpatrick is afraid. Calm down. If you pay your debts you have nothing be scared of, plus I told you not to bet."

Gathering his composure, he puts his sales hat on, "I am not afraid but give me some background on this guy, so I can know what to expect and how to work him."

"Fitzy, this is serious shit and do not treat Bunar like some simpleton. Just have lunch and tell Bunar you will pay your debts and get the hell out of there."

Jack presses, "Tell me something about this guy I can use. Does he have kids? Does he like playing basketball? Has he lived anywhere besides Massachusetts? I want to try and bond with this guy, especially if I have to push out my debt a month or two."

"Do not push this guy. He does not have any kids, he does not play basketball, and has only lived in Raynham and Southie."

"Okay, Okay, okay, I am nervous about our meeting but I am also excited. It kinda feels like a movie."

"Fitzy you are killing me. Just go meet with him and pay your debts. I need to get back to work. Call me from your cell phone after the lunch."

"Hey before you hang up, I need you to e-mail me directions. Where is this place?

"The place is on East Broadway and I will e-mail you directions in an hour. I need to get some real work done."

Jack also needs to gets some real work done so he can earn some commissions, ie cash, to off his debts. He does some basic follow up on the Reno Regional and Memorial deals. He figures he has to leave in an hour to get into South Boston and to the restaurant by noon.

Jack's phone rings as he is getting ready to leave. The caller ID says it is Michelle calling from Reno Regional. He is surprised he is excited to get another call from Michelle, "Michelle Parks how are you doing?"

A coy Michelle, "Fitzy, how do you know it's me?"

Playing along, "It is my sixth sense with you."

"You better bring your sixth sense with you when we play craps again in two weeks."

Jack and Michelle have an enjoyable conversation about nothing. Looking at this watch, tells Michelle he has to go to a meeting and they will talk later this week.

In a great mood after talking to Michelle because she called just to talk. There was no real reason why she called.

His heart is beating fast as he drives into South Boston to meet with a bookie he owes over thirty thousand with only a grand in his pocket. His adrenalin is in overdrive: he had a great dinner with his wife; he is flirting with a sexy lady in Reno; and it is exciting to go see a bookie. *I am the shit.*

From the outside, people see Fitzy as a successful, nice, funny, church going, and conservative guy. He is all those things, but on the inside, loves the thrill of the chase and riding the line between getting caught and getting away with it. The chase is going on in three areas: winning the biggest deal of his career, flirting with Michelle, and betting with Bunar.

17
Lunch with Bunar

"Here's a toast to your enemies' enemies!"
Irish Toast

Jack heads into South Boston with its own long and storied history of over 350 years. Back in 1634, Governor Dudley of Massachusetts Bay Colony ordered three cannons to Castle Island, which makes it the oldest continuously fortified site in America. During the Revolutionary War, the fort was under the command of Lt. Paul Revere. South Boston's rich history isn't in Jack's thoughts.

Today, South Boston is known as 'Southie'. 'Southie' is a peninsula village community bordering Downtown Boston and the Atlantic Ocean, is densely populated and known for triple deckers and row houses. 'Southie' is the heart of Irish Boston. 'Southie' was a haven for Irish Immigrants in the early days of Boston. There is a small bar on every corner. Because of the growth of Boston, today you will see more diversity but 'Southie' still has the Irish neighborhood pride. Jack drives slowly through 'Southie' looking for the Irish Bar called McCracken's.

Jack nervously drives by the front of the meeting place, McCracken's on East Broadway in South Boston. He cannot find a parking spot and has to park two blocks down from McCracken's. Sitting in the car, he prepares like this is a sales meeting. He needs to negotiate the deal on how much he owes Bunar. He takes three slow deep breaths to calm himself down.

McCracken's is the first floor of a triple-decker house. Jack opens a big black hardwood door and walks into a dark long skinny bar. The bar has a full-length mirror behind the bar, opposite from the bar. There are Irish symbols all over the place from shamrocks, to Irish sayings, to crests. It is lunch hour but he counts only eight people including the old skinny bartender and a pasty attractive waitress dressed in all black.

It is obvious which one is Bunar. He is sitting in the back at a big circular wooden table. There is a Guinness draught beer in front of him and he is reading the newspaper. Seated with Bunar is a very large and muscular man. The muscular guy is dressed in a very tight white shirt and jeans. Bunar is dressed in a golf shirt with a Guinness logo. Jack is the only one in the bar wearing a tie.

It must also be obvious who he is because Bunar waves him over to his table. He says to the big guy, "Stevey, why don't you help behind the bar". Stevey stares at him then walks behind the bar. Jack sits directly across from Bunar. Without getting up, Bunar reaches across the table to shake Jack's trembling hand.

Jack clumsily hands Bunar the one thousand in cash.

Bunar calmly puts the cash in his pocket, "First, relax. Second, I assume this is the grand Billy told me about."

Still shaking Jack nods.

"Relax, let's talk a little before we get to the business side of our lunch, how is Billy doing? I have not seen Billy in months?

They have small talk about Billy and his family. Jack is thinking the conversation is going well and Bunar is nice enough guy.

"I appreciate you coming into the city to see me. I would like to discuss a little business. You obviously know Billy is a good friend of mine. A friend of Billy's is a friend of mine but now you want to start betting twenty grand a game? You and I need to build a business relationship."

Bunar has Jack's undivided attention, "Agreed."

"As with any business relationship, there needs to be a level of trust and a set of expectations from each party. From me, you need to know I will pay you if you win a bet, and from you, I need to know you will cover your losses. To manage my side, there is a certain size bet I will not take because the bet is too large and I cannot pay out the winnings."

Jack is dying to ask Bunar what size bet is too large for him, but he isn't bold enough with Bunar or at least not yet. He is also thinking for a guy with only a high school education, he is smooth. *Maybe I should hire Bunar to replace Betty on my sales team.*

"From you, I need to know you can cover your bets." Bunar then pauses for what feels like five minutes. He very coldly continues, "Fitzy, when you only offer to pay me one thousand of a thirty-three thousand debt, I start to get worried." He strategically pauses again, "Because you and I are now business partners, you need to increase my confidence level by paying me another two grand in addition to the thousand in the next hour or I am not going to take your additional sixty grand in bets. Also, if you do not get me the two grand today, I am going to have to make some tough decisions on how I start motivating you to pay me sooner rather than later."

Jack went from the excitement of being in a scene from a movie to the cold reality this is not a movie. At the same time, he is very impressed with Bunar. He does not want Bunar to think he is some loser who cannot cover his gambling losses.

Jack gathers himself, "I agree both parties need to live up to their responsibilities in a business relationship. I will pay you the two thousand today. I am going to step outside and make a few calls."

Bunar nods then Jack heads outside to call his American Express credit card to see if can increase his credit line by two thousand and get an immediate a cash advance. American Express agrees to the increase and lets him know there is a bank right around the corner that can do the advance today.

Jack goes back inside to update Bunar. Bunar flashes a big smile, "Fitzy, I think this is going to be a profitable relationship for both of us."

Laughing, "I like your positive attitude."

18

Bunar's Tough guy

"One pain is lessened by another's anguish."
William Shakespeare

As Jack leaves the bar to go the bank, Bunar calls Stevey back from behind the bar. Stevey is six feet four inches and 280 pounds of hard muscle. Stevey and Bunar played high school football together. Stevey is not too bright but is loyal in doing what Bunar asks him.

Stevey obediently sits down. "The guy who just left owes me over thirty grand. He is going to the bank to get me two grand for his gambling losses."

With a stupid laugh, "Bunar you going to let a first time loser only pay a little of his bill. You going soft on me?"

Grinning, "First, he is a friend of Billy Nestler's. Second, if he comes back with one penny less than the two grand, I want you to slash the right front tire of his black 7 series BMW out front with the following license plate." Bunar slides a napkin across the table with a license plate number.

With his stupid laugh, "No Problem."

19

Flat Tire

"There are only two forces that unite men -- fear and interest." Napoleon Bonaparte

Because the bank is so close, Jack walks. He goes up to the teller giving her his American Express card. She kindly let's him know there is a 2.5% service charge of $50 from them and another $50 fee from American Express. He has no choice, taking the nineteen hundred in cash. Walking back to the bar, he hopes Bunar will take the $1,900 after he explains the $2,000 cash advance has cost $100 in fees. All this on top of 20% interest rate on the cash advance from American Express.

Jack's hands are shaking as he walks back in McCracken's. *Use your sales skills before this guy breaks your leg.* Sliding the bank envelope across the table, "As with any relationship there is some give and take." Jack Pauses, "Because of the unforeseen bank charge of a hundred, there is only nineteen hundred in the envelope."

Bunar coolly says, "Fitzy this is not a good start." Bunar gives Stevey a quick look. Jack does not see the look nor does he see Stevey walk outside of the bar. "What does a tire cost on your car?"

"I do not know. Ah, maybe two hundred bucks."

Bunar lightens up, "No worries, I will cover the hundred and I will take your additional sixty grand in bets."

I got skills, now get out of here. "Great" Jack starts to get up to leave.

"Sit down, I invited you here for lunch. I recommend the Sheppard's pie."

"I need to get back to the office, can I take a rain check?"

Bunar pauses until he sees Stevey walk back in the bar, winking at him, "No worries, we will have lunch next time."

Man that was close. I better win the sixty grand. Jack hops in his car and pulls out. As soon as the car starts to move, he knows something is wrong. He pulls into a parking lot. Walking around the car sees the front tire is flat.

"Shit!" looking at his watch. It is after one and he needs to be back in the office by two p.m. He will change the tire himself, taking off his tie and shirt not wanting to ruin them. He figures he cannot do too much damage to the black pants.

Jack gets the full size spare tire out of the trunk and starts changing the tire. He is sweating and getting dirty as he is changing the tire. He looks for the nail or rock in the tire to determine if a garage can plug the tire. To his surprise he cannot find the nail. He notices a small hole in the side of the tire. A chill runs up his spine, as he comprehends he did not run over a nail and Bunar slashed his tire for short paying. *It must be because I was a hundred dollars short and is why he asked how much a tire costs on my car.*

A cold sweat runs down his back because he never told Bunar what kind of car he drives and he parked two blocks from the restaurant. Sitting on the pavement, he realizes he is now in the big time, like Billy warned. In the past he has run up gambling debts with his with his buddies, and he will keep doubling the bet until he eventually wins, ending up even. Jack does the same thing with them when he is on the winning side.

Jack realizes the strategy of doubling your bets will not work with Bunar because every time he loses, Bunar will want to get paid. Even though he makes well over six figures a year, he is not financially strong and is in a lot of debt. He calms himself down by whispering, "If you can win two out of three this week, you will stop gambling and pay off the debts", louder with a confident smile, "There is no way I can lose 6 bets in a row."

Filthy from changing the tire, he cancels his two o'clock call and heads home to take a shower. While driving home he works on a story for Colette regarding getting a flat tire. Calling home, no one answers. He speeds home hoping he can shower and get back to the office before Colette gets home.

20

Colette comes home

"My attitude toward men who mess around is simple: If you find'em, kill'em." Loretta Lynn

Colette is pulling into their driveway after running errands. Colette is surprised to see Jack's BMW in the driveway. She gets Harrison out of the back then heads into the house. Colette puts Harrison in his playpen calling out, "Jack you home?"

Nothing.

Colette is getting nervous. She does not hear the water running upstairs. Her husband does not come home unannounced in the middle of the day and why is he not answering. Screams, "Jack!"

Still Nothing.

Colette carefully walks around the first floor looking for him. She slowly starts to walk upstairs but goes back to the kitchen to grab their black carving knife. As she walks up the stairs, she hears the shower running.

"I bet the bastard has a woman with him." She hears the shower, "Fitzy you are in for one big surprise, when I catch you." Holding the knife, she could be the next Lorena Bobbitt.

She takes a slow deep breath before bursting into the bathroom, "What is the best way to catch 'Mr. Salesman" in the act?" To her surprise Jack is all alone but she has worked herself into frenzy and she is ornery.

He is washing his hair and does not see Colette come in their bathroom. Colette starts slamming her hand against the shower door.

He jumps and lets out a loud and quick "Ahh!" Jack is extra jumpy after his meeting with Bunar.

Jack quickly spins around and sees Colette at the shower door, "You scared the shit out of me. What are you doing scaring me like that?"

Colette has a mean look on her face and says, "You scared the shit out of me by not telling me you were coming home in the middle of the day to take a shower AND I was even more scared because I yelled out your name downstairs and you did not answer."

After his lunch and flat tire with Bunar, the last thing Jack needs is a fight with his wife. "Why don't you come on in and wash my back?"

Colette is in no mood and shakes her head side to side. "Harrison is downstairs and you still have not answered my questions as to why you are taking a shower in the middle of the afternoon."

"I got a flat tire in Southie today. I changed the tire myself and I was filthy. I did not want to go back to the office all sweaty and dirty. I called the house and when you did not answer, I needed to take a quick shower before going back to the office. Let me finish up and get dressed."

"This is why we need Triple A!"

"We do not need Triple A. We need to stop spending. Even if we had Triple A, I did not have the time to wait around for them. I was trying to get back in the office in time for a call."

Colette gives Jack a stone cold look, "You better not be up to anything. I am going back downstairs to take care of Harrison."

He quickly finishes his shower, gets dressed, and goes downstairs. Jack does not want to talk about his lunch because he obviously does not want to tell Colette about the bets and he told Colette that Billy went to lunch with him too.

As soon as Jack comes down the stairs Colette says, "So tell me about your lunch with Billy and his friend Daniel Boone?"

Jack takes a quick look at his watch and says, "It is Bunar and I am running late. Let's talk tonight."

Colette lays a little guilt trip on him, "You work all the time, you finally come home in the middle of the day and you are just going to rush in and out. You need to at least play with your son for five minutes before going back to work."

Jack takes another look at his watch, with the Memorial and Reno Regional sales opportunities, his bets with Bunar, and the normal bullshit at work, he really needs to get back to work, but loves his son and Colette is right. He works too much. "You are always right."

He throws Harrison into air and carries him into the family room and plays with him on the floor. Colette comes in from the kitchen and the three of them play together. Colette is staring at him, "Jack Fitzpatrick, what are you up to?"

Jack acts surprised, "What are you talking about?"

Colette sarcastically restates his questions, "'What am I talking about?' I am talking about the weird call from Daniel Boone yesterday, then this lunch in Southie, then you come home in the middle of the day and you do not tell me. If you have a girlfriend Fitzy, I will divorce you and take you for everything you got."

Jack winks, "No worries."

"No worries ……. No worries…….. No worries, you have got to be kidding me."

He interrupts, "Let it go. We can talk about it all tonight, I really need to get back to the office." Jack stands up and gives both Harrison and Colette a kiss on the tops of their heads and is out the door.

21
Back in the Office

"My main focus is on my game." Tiger Woods

As soon as Jack gets in his car, he calls Billy to tell him all about the lunch with Bunar from the trip to the bank to the flat tire. Billy tells him, "Bunar is not like the guys at the country club. When you lose, Bunar wants his money. He probably only gave you a flat tire because of me. You need to pay off your debts ASAP and go back to the country club and the monthly trips to the Mohegan Sun casino in Connecticut and get away from Bunar, McCracken's, and Southie."

"No worries. I will win a couple of bets and I will be fine. Hey, I told Colette you went to lunch with me today so be sure to tell your wife you had a great lunch today in South Boston and I got a flat tire."

"I will, but please do not include me in your future lies, Fitzy."

"If you think about it, if you didn't know Bunar, I would not be in this mess."

"Whoa, you would have just found a different bookie and you probably would have gotten a couple of broken fingers versus a flat tire."

"Billy, I am just busting your balls. I will do my best to keep you and I out of future Bunar encounters."

"Fitzy you got balls of steel. Your world is about to crash down around you and you are making jokes." Jack hangs up on Billy has as he expert squeezes his BMW between two cars then he speed walks into the office.

Stay Focused. One thing Jack realized a long time about himself is he gets more done when he is busy. When he has a lot to do, he focuses and just starts cranking through tasks on his todo list. When he has little to do, he figures he can do it in the future, so he waits to get things done.

One bad habit most sales people have is calling people they know or like versus the people who are most strategic to the sale. It is very hard for a sales person to call someone they do not like or does not like them. Jack learned this the hard way. A couple of years ago, he was selling to an account where the Chief

Information Office (CIO) was retiring and they were promoting an internal director to replace him. He really liked the outgoing CIO and they got along great. The internal director didn't like him, so he just kept calling on the CIO. In reality the CIO was retiring and was a lame duck, who did not have decision making power and the internal director was making the decisions. To make a long story short, he lost the sale.

The first call will be to Cheryl Scharff the CFO at Reno Regional. Jack gets Cheryl's secretary, and leaves a message. The next call is to Reno Regional's CIO, Peter Galetta leaves him a voicemail. *Do I call Michelle?* He really likes talking to her but she can wait.

He needs to work on the Reno Regional deal, so he works on the e-mail from Michelle with all the attendees for the upcoming on-site presentation. Jack sends all of them an e-mail thanking them for meeting with CM stating he is excited to meet them, and to let him know if there is anything specific they would like to cover.

Jack focuses on Dr. Harold Mainer. Most likely, the decision will come down to Cheryl the CFO and Dr. Mainer. Knowing doctors can be pains in the asses, especially when it comes to dealing with salesmen, he makes an internal call to another pain in the ass doctor, CM's own Dr. Carson Alvarez. Dr. Alvarez likes to be called doctor, to tease him, "Carson this is Jack Fitzpatrick. Do you have a few minutes?"

Carson sarcastically responds, "Fitzy what do you want?"

Carson is trying to suck him into an argument. Jack knows like any good salesman, he has to sell internally as much as externally, so he turns on the charm but he still refuses to say 'Dr. Alvarez'. "Carson, I really appreciate you will be coming to our on-site presentations at Reno Regional. I wanted to update you on Reno Regional and let you know I am also working on setting up a meeting for us at our client, Memorial in Reno."

Carson starts to loosen up, "I got about fifteen minutes before my next meeting."

Jack spends about ten minutes updating Carson on both accounts before dropping the big question. "There is a Dr. Harold Mainer who will be very influential in Reno Regional's decision. Can you please put a call in to him introducing yourself and telling him you will be at the meeting?"

Carson is a bright guy understanding Jack wants him to make a cold call to Dr. Mainer. "So Fitzy, what you are telling me is you want me to do your job and cold call this doctor."

Jack knows he is caught, "Yes, if you can build a relationship with Dr. Mainer it will only help our chances of winning this twenty-eight million dollar deal."

Carson and Jack both know Carson does not want to make the call but he has to, "So Fitzy you call me Carson, but because this is a twenty-eight million dollar deal you call their doctor Dr. Mainer versus Harold. I will call him later this week and as usual. You owe me."

"I do owe you and I will try to make it up by getting us to play some golf in Reno. Memorial's CIO belongs to a beautiful golf course." Jack makes a note to follow up with Carson on Friday to make sure he called Dr. Mainer.

He has done enough on Reno Regional so he focuses on Memorial. The first call is to Memorial's CIO Howard Black. CM has a huge advantage at Memorial with being the incumbent vendor plus he has a strong relationship with Howard. Ironically his biggest challenge could be that very often when a company starts a major project they want to replace their current vendor and Jack needs to build relationships with other employees and doctors at Memorial besides Howard. He also knows to win Memorial is going to take almost as much work as Reno Regional.

Before calling Howard Black, writes down his objectives for the call:

- *Find out who is on their selection committee*
- *Is he using a consultant*
- *If he has assigned a project manager*
- *When he wants to make a decision by*
- *Confirm he has $12M for his budget*
- *Try to set up golf with Dr. Alvarez, Howard, and their key doctor*

"Howard this is Jack Fitzpatrick with CM Solutions"

"Fitzy, why are you so formal?"

"Habit and in case you are having a problem with CM. I do not want to answer the phone all buddy-buddy."

"Buddy-Buddy. Anyways, I always have problems with CM and you can still say 'Hey Howard its Fitzy'. Now why are you calling me today?"

Looking at his notes, "Do I need a reason to call my number one client?"

"I assume any client with a twelve million budget for a physician portal is your number one client."

Jack checks the $12M budget item off this list, "Seeing as you brought it up, how can I help you spend your budget with CM?" He does not wait for an answer to the question. "Or specifically, how can I educate you and your committee on the benefits of CM?" Again, does not wait for an answer. "And even more specifically, who is the key doctor on your committee?" This time pauses and waits for an answer.

"So which question do you want me to answer?"

Jack stays on the doctor question. "Just the doctor because I committed you to take out myself, Dr. Carson Alvarez with CM, and your key doctor on the selection committee to golf on me on Thursday, June 20th. I assume you are available for golf on me, and seeing as you have a budget of twelve million, feel free to make a morning tee time at your golf course."

"You forgot to ask if I was available."

Jack jokingly gets official, "Mr. Black, are you and a distinguished member of Memorial Hospital's medical staff available on the morning of Thursday, June 20th for a round of golf?"

"Now that is a lot better and yes, I am available. I will follow up with you next week."

Jack checks the golf invite off this list. He has four items remaining. Because Howard did not name a specific doctor for golf, he will only ask one more question, "Now we established golf next week, are you looking to make a decision before or after our golf game."

Howard is smart enough to know what was just asked, so to bust Jack's stones, "Fitzy, why don't you just come out and say 'When are you going to choose a vendor?'"

"Why don't you just tell me when you are going to choose a vendor, i.e. CM Solutions?"

Howard pushes back. "Everything I tell you I will tell your competition MacroHealth. Second, you better not assume you will win this deal because MacroHealth is telling me a lot of great things about their software and they tell me I will like their price even better."

Jack is excited because he thought he was about to wrap up the call and Howard just brought up the competition. "Is there anyone else besides MacroHealth you are looking at?"

"Right now no, but I am not against looking at three vendors."

Jack likes that he is only looking at two vendors because at face value his odds are fifty-fifty. If he was looking at three vendors, the odds would drop. He goes back to focus on MacroHealth and the timeline. "When is MacroHealth coming on-site?"

To Jack's total surprise, "Actually, they had a clinical team on-site two weeks ago."

Shit. Why didn't HE tell me last week when I was in Reno? Why didn't CM know they were looking at vendors months ago? Did Betty Turner know this information and keep it from CM? Has Memorial already chosen MacroHealth as their vendor? Why didn't Memorial invite CM on-site? Is my relationship really strong with Howard Black? Is Howard Black really the decision maker? He is confused.

"Fitzy you still there?"

Jack responds with the truth, "Yes but I am blown away MacroHealth has been on-site to present, and I had no idea. I have a bunch of questions for you, like how come we weren't invited on-site."

"All I will say is we want to make a decision by the end of June and we like MacroHealth. I need to get on another call."

Jack is still dumbfounded, "Can we schedule another call first thing tomorrow morning?"

"Sure how about eight am my time"

Jack says yes without even checking his calendar. Pushing his chair back from his desk, puts his head between his legs. He could not be having a worse day. He gets his tire slashed and a deal he was counting on for commissions, he is now losing. MacroHealth already going on site is very bad for Jack. 'Ahhh' *I gave Memorial Hospital as a reference to Reno Regional Medical Center and because MacroHealth knows Memorial is looking at them and no doubt they have told Reno Regional CM's reference is looking at MacroHealth.*

Jack gets up and starts pacing around his desk. He needs to win at least one of these two deals just to keep his job and pay off his gambling debts. Focusing on why he is losing both deals and keeps coming back to Betty Turner. *Did Betty know Memorial was evaluating MacroHealth when she interviewed with them? Did Betty submarine CM at Memorial and Reno Regional before leaving? Should he call Betty? Should I tell my boss? Should I have our lawyers threaten MacroHealth?*

Switches to positive thoughts, how CM can win one of these deals? How can he leverage his supposedly positive relationship with Howard Black? How can Jack leverage CM strengths in both deals? Who in CM support can help him at Memorial? Does he have any chance at Reno Regional? Should he go with scorched earth at both deals, so they both go to no deal?

Scorched earth is typically a tactic in politics, where a politician goes so negative it affects him too, so in the end all that is left is scorched earth. In sales this tactic is used when you are losing and you say if I am going to lose you want your opponent to lose too. An example would be to tell Memorial and Reno Regional all Physician portals do not work or there is a new technology on the horizon they should wait for before making a decision. This means CM Solutions and MacroHealth both do not win the business. The hope would be in a year when Memorial and Reno Regional start to look at Physician portals again, CM will be better positioned to win their business.

He totally underestimated Betty Turner. Now he has to decide if he wants to update his boss Kevin. Jack likes keeping Kevin informed just enough to keep him off his back and so Kevin is not blind-sided. Because he told Kevin they had a great chance of winning Memorial and he now believes they are losing, he will call Kevin and give him the bad news and to protect himself.

22

Meeting with Kevin Blair

"I don't believe in this business of being behind, better to be in front." Mel Brooks

Jack walks down to Kevin's office to give the Betty news in person. He gets right to it. Telling Kevin MacroHealth he has been on-site to present, Memorial wants to make a decision by the end of June, and CM has not officially been invited on-site yet.

Kevin starts yelling at Jack, telling him how important it is both of these deals sign this month. After Kevin calms down, "Betty is the reason we are losing both deals. I cannot believe that lazy bitch is now beating us in two deals and one is our own damn client."

Jack being Betty's manager should have been more on top of both deals, so he does not say anything. Jack knows the last thing he wants to do is interrupt to Kevin and upset him even more.

After what seems like an hour, Kevin surmises, "Betty must have stolen something from us. I have no idea what she stole but there is no way she is can be beating us at both Memorial and Reno Regional. When she worked for us all she did was complain. Come on Jack think, what did Betty steal from us?"

Jack did not like Betty but he did not think she would steal corporate secrets, "All I can think of are the usual stuff sales people take when they leave like client lists and marketing literature. She was not a developer so she could not have taken any code. She was not in finance, so would not have our financial data."

Kevin interrupts, "She did have access to our audited financials." Because sales prospects often want to know the financial stability of a privately held company, they often ask for audited financials.

"Our audited financials look great. I know she probably did take a copy of our financials with her, but this cannot be the reason we are losing. Can something in our financials hurt us?"

Kevin pauses, "Nope, but I know she stole something from us. How good are your relationships with Reno Regional and Memorial? Can you ask them what information on CM Betty has shared with them?"

"I will definitely try. I thought I had a good relationship with Howard Black at Memorial but when I met with him last week, he did not tell me MacroHealth has been on-site. At Reno Regional, I am building a relationship with Michelle Parks and I think she will tell me but I am not sure if she is in the know."

Kevin tries to motivate him, "That is better than nothing, please contact both of them today. Also, I need you to keep thinking about what Betty could have stolen from us."

"Are we losing any other deals to MacroHealth, we were winning before Betty quit?"

Kevin answers, "Not yet, but I am watching very closely."

"Keep me updated and I am going to head back to my office to call Reno Regional. I have a schedule call with Memorial tomorrow morning and I will ask Howard Black then."

23
Calling Michelle

"When you're prepared, you're more confident. When you have a strategy, you're more comfortable." Fred Couples

Back in his office he prepares to call Michelle Parks. One nice thing about Reno Regional being on the west coast, Pacific Time, is Jack can call them all the way up to eight at night because they are three hours behind eastern time. Preparing to call Michelle, writes down the topics he wants to cover on the call.

- *Betty Turner*
- *Betty Turner*
- *Betty Turner*
- *MacroHealth Update*
- *Confirm they are also set for CM's presentation*
- *Set up Dinner*
- *Betty Turner*

"Good afternoon Michelle Parks"

Jack needs to have more than just a personal conversation, "Michelle this is Fitzy how are you doing today?" They have a five minute conversation about gambling, mountain biking and nothing important. He slowly transitions to business, so he can get to Betty and MacroHealth. "So is Reno Regional all set for our meetings?" Michelle updates him on the meetings next week. He then moves onto MacroHealth, "Seeing you are all set for CM next week, are you ready for MacroHealth the week after?"

"Fitzy how did you know MacroHealth is going the week after you?"

Jack laughs, "Because you, Cheryl, and Peter told me when I met with you last week."

"Oh yea and we are all set for MacroHealth."

This is the transition Jack was looking for, "Isn't MacroHealth coming on-site this week for their pre-meeting?"

"That's right, they come tomorrow"

Jack gets to Betty, "Since Betty Turner went to work for MacroHealth, do you know if Betty Turner is coming on-site tomorrow?"

"Actually, yes she is."

Jack tells Michelle CM Solutions is concerned Betty may of told MacroHealth confidential information about CM Solutions and MacroHealth is also competing at Memorial, "Is Betty contacting you?'

"Yes but Betty prefers to talk to Cheryl versus Peter and myself." This is good news because it creates an opportunity to get Peter, Reno Regional's CIO in addition to Michelle to vote for CM. The bad news is Betty is connected to the CFO, who is higher on the corporate ladder and could be the ultimate decision maker.

"Has Betty said anything to you regarding CM that is confidential or very negative?"

To Jack's extreme disappointment, "Nope just the opposite she was positive and mostly talked about MacroHealth. She called me on Monday to tell me she was now working at MacroHealth and even though it may be awkward in the beginning with her switching companies, she is very excited to be working at MacroHealth. She also said CM is a good company with good solutions but she switched to MacroHealth because they are a great company with great solutions."

Jack is impressed Betty took the high road. He wonders if she knows he is building a strong relationship with Michelle but he figures Betty is just focusing on Reno Regional's CFO, Cheryl. Wanting to shake Betty's creditability with Michelle, "Did you know MacroHealth is trying to get Memorial to convert to them and they were on-site last month?"

"Nope."

Whispering, "I think Betty is playing all four sides."

"Four sides?"

"CM, MacroHealth, Memorial and Reno Regional." Jack speaks even softer, "Obviously Betty knew she was leaving before last week and she was going to MacroHealth, so when Betty was working at CM, she was most likely working both you and Memorial to choose MacroHealth."

"It is funny you say that. Last month before she left CM, she mostly wanted to talk about personal things and the only business thing she would say is CM has great products in development."

Jack keeps pushing. "Maybe she is setting us up so she can say the majority of our products are in development versus production. Everything we are presenting next week is in production, so Betty may be trying to be negative on our current products."

It is always a fine line in sales to talk about future products or services. You want prospects to see a vision for the future, while at the same time not being so positive on the future they want to postpone purchasing today for the future or showing future products makes release weaknesses in your current products. Even worse, you sell them futures so they think they are getting something that is in production but doesn't exist today.

Jack is deep thought when Michelle says, "Fitzy, you still there?"

"Yea, normally we just want to focus on what we are selling but now I have a wild card with Betty."

"Well obviously you have a lot on your mind, I am going to get going and I will give you a call tomorrow after the MacroHealth presentation."

As a reflex, Jack looks at his notes prior to ending the call, "Hey, are we all set for us to take out everyone on the committee to dinner on Tuesday?"

"Yup and I have picked a great restaurant."

Ends with a little flirting, "Great, we need to make sure we break away from the group to play some craps together."

"Are you sure you do not want to play alone?"

Playing along, "Why would I want to play with anyone else beside you?"

Michelle slowly says "So are you saying you want to 'play' with me?"

He sees the trap but cannot help from walking right into it, "I definitely want to 'play' with you and you only."

"Fitzy, sounds like a plan and you better not stand me up."

"I cannot wait. I will give you a buzz later on this week."

Putting his hands behind his head, he leans back in his chair with a big smile. *Your world is crumbling around you and you still got time to flirt with a beautiful woman, you got skills.*

The next call is to Peter Galetta, Reno Regional's CIO to build a working relationship. Betty may have the CFO but Jack is not going to give up. Getting Peter's voicemail, leaves him a message. Feeling pretty aggressive and sales momentum, he gives Cheryl Scharff a call too.

To Jack's surprise he gets a hold of Cheryl. Expecting voicemail, he is not prepared for the call. Looks at his notes from his call with Michelle he sees Betty Turner multiple times on the list.

- *Betty Turner*
- *Betty Turner*
- *Betty Turner*
- *MacroHealth Update*
- *Confirm they are also set for CM's presentation*
- *Set up Dinner*
- *Betty Turner*

After introducing himself, he just blurts out, "So I hear Betty Turner is now at MacroHealth?"

Cheryl quickly responds, "That's right and you already sent me an e-mail with the news. Are you calling to tell me something I already know?"

Back peddling, "I thought you may find it interesting Betty is at MacroHealth. Obviously, she knew she was going to MacroHealth when she was calling on Reno Regional as a CM Solutions employee."

"Jack, I am not sure the reason for this call. Yes, I know Betty is at MacroHealth and as I told you during our meeting last week, I want you to focus on your products not on MacroHealth. Is there anything else?"

In a voice that sounds like a little boy, who gets caught tattling on his sister, Jack responds, "No mam."

Cheryl says good-bye and the conversation is over.

Shit, laying his head on his desk. How could he make such a rookie sales mistake of not being prepared to make a call? Jack knows it is hard to get a hold of senior level executives and when you do you need to be prepared. Not being prepared just hurt him big time with Cheryl. Betty is probably telling Cheryl how young he is, and he just confirmed it.

It is almost seven in the evening. Exhausted, he locks up his office before going home. Plus he needs to get mentally prepared for the Boston Celtics versus the New Jersey Nets basketball game tonight. *I need a win by the Celtics tonight, BIG TIME.*

24

Dinner at Home

"That's not a lie, it's a terminological inexactitude. Also, a tactical misrepresentation." Alexander Haig

Jack gets home after seven-thirty. He can tell Colette is ready to talk about his lunch in South Boston. As soon as he sits down, "So tell me about this Daniel Boone you had lunch with today or should I say, Danielle Boone."

Exhausted, he tries to hold back his temper, "HIS name is Bunar and he is not a SHE."

"Does this Bunar have a first name?"

Jack needs to be on his toes because Colette is prepared for the conversation. "Yes Bunar has a first name, it is Justin but like people call me 'Fitzy', everyone calls him Bunar."

"So where did you have lunch with Billy and this Justin Bunar character?"

Jack knows she is recording everything he is saying in her mind, so she can test him later. Makes a mental note to remind Billy again he went to lunch with him and Bunar today at McCracken's. He stays close to the facts. "McCracken's in the heart of Southie. The food was great."

"I cannot wait for you take me there."

This would be a big mistake, "Honey, I would love to take you there but this is not the kind of place you take a lady. Even I would be a little nervous going there at night."

"Well it looks like you will have to take me there for lunch."

"Sounds great," knowing it is not going to happen.

"I am serious. You should take me there for lunch tomorrow."

"Tomorrow around lunch time I have a call with Memorial in Reno, Nevada."

"So you have time in your busy schedule to go with Billy and this 'Bunar' character but you do not have time for your stay at home wife."

Jack sees where this conversation is going and even though he is tempted to get in an argument he takes the high road, "Let's do this, I do not have time to drive up to South Boston tomorrow but let's have you and Harrison meet me at the Charlie Horse for a late lunch."

Colette puts in one more jab, "So you get great seafood in Southie and I get the Charlie Horse." Colette stills wants to have lunch with Jack. "I will take the Charlie Horse but I still want to have lunch with you at this McCracken's Seafood restaurant."

Sensing the storm is blowing over, he smiles to himself, *I am not planning on taking Colette to McCracken's but if I ever do, I sure hope there is seafood on their menu.*

Jack goes into the family room and turns on the TV to watch the basketball game, the game is already in the third quarter and the Celtics are up by five points over the Nets.

Colette asks him to come to bed. Even with twenty thousand riding on the game, he is so tired he needs to get some sleep. He can get the score of the game in the morning. Even surprising himself, with everything going on, he can still sleep. After kissing Colette goodnight, he promptly falls asleep.

25
Morning at the Office

"It is bad luck to be superstitious."
Andrew W. Mathis

Jack gets up at six a.m. He got almost nine hours of well needed sleep. Being superstitious, he does not turn on ESPN nor look at the morning paper. Fate will decide when he learns if the Celtics won last night. He leaves the house before Colette or Harrison are up.

In the office, there is a message on his phone. He left the office after seven last night and it is before seven in the morning. *Who would call me so late?* The message must be from Reno Regional or Memorial Hospital on the west coast.

"Fitzy this is Bunar and you owe me another twenty grand. That puts you over fifty grand." The Celtics lost. The voicemail continues, "Because I like you, you will only need to pay me five grand by four p.m. today. I did you another favor and I did not call your house but because I am a business man, I am going to send Stevey to your office this afternoon to pick up my five grand. One last thing, I told Stevey if you did not have the five grand to make a scene at your office. Knowing you will pay me the five Gs today, your outstanding tab will be forty-seven thousand." Bunar laughs, "Good luck on tonight's game." Beep, the message is over.

Jack is stunned.

So much for superstition, now he has to get five grand and not have Stevey come to the office. Even if he can come up with the five grand, he does not want a bookie's muscle coming to the office. *Who can I borrow five grand from and get the cash by 4p.m. today?* Billy was complaining about him borrowing one thousand. He could ask Billy to call Bunar to see if Bunar will hold off until after tonight's game but that was a disaster last time. *Where can I get five g's?*

Chip Savard is on his basketball team. The good news is Jack believes Chip can come up with the cash and will most likely let him borrow the cash; the bad news is Chip will probably tell his wife Kim who works for him. It gets worse because Kim is friends with Colette. But he has no choice and calls Chip at his office, and leaves a voicemail saying he will call again in an hour.

Looking at his watch, it is seven-thirty, and his schedule for today is loaded. He has an internal meeting with software development at nine about future product enhancements, the call with Howard Black with Memorial at eleven, lunch with Colette and Harrison, and now Stevey the bouncer at four. This is on top of hiring a person to replace Betty, managing the usual stuff from Kim and Larry, completing internal reports, and following up with prospects and clients. He needs to make cold calls to prospects, consultants, and potential partners but he is too busy. A big downfall with sales people when they get busy with urgent issues is they do not work on tasks which are important but not urgent like cold calling. Jack is a big fan of Stephen Covey and his books 'The Seven Habits of Highly Effective People' and 'The Eighth Habit: From Effectiveness to Greatness'.

My life is going down the toilet and I am thinking about Stephen Covey. Covey's books talk about managing your time. Covey says you can divide your activities into four quadrants:

Time Management	**Urgent**	**Not Urgent**
Important	**Quadrant 1** - Crisis - Pressing Problems - Deal Line Driven Projects - Never goes away but can make smaller	**Quadrant 2** - Prevention -Recognizing New Opportunities - Planning / Vision - Discipline and Control - The most important quadrant
Not Important	**Quadrant 3** - Interruptions - Popular Activities - Pressing Matters - Important for other people - Learn to say 'No' to other people	**Quadrant 4** - Useless Busy Work - Time Wasters - Useless phone calls - Useless meetings - Say 'No' to Quadrant 4 and say 'Yes' to Quadrant 2

Because he is under such stress, he is only working on Quadrant 1, Important and Urgent issues. He needs to work on Quadrant 2, Important but not-urgent issues, so he can get his ass out of trouble with his wife, Bunar the bookie, and win both deals at Reno Regional and Memorial. Memorial is important but not on his urgent list today, so he makes a note to work on Memorial, he also grasps if he loses two more NBA games he will owe another forty grand in cash he does not have.

While getting ready for his call with Howard Black at eleven, he calls Chip again before going to his nine o'clock meeting. He looks up Memorial in CM's contact management database to confirm how long they have been a client, how many products they have, and whether are there any outstanding issues. He wants to stress the positive length of Memorial's relationship with CM and be prepared for any negative issues.

When Jack looks up it is nine. He needs to call Chip before his next meeting. He hits Chip with the charm, "Mr. Savard, this is Mr. Fitzpatrick how are you this fine morning?"

"Fitzy what are you calling me for? It is only Wednesday, so it is early for you to be calling about our Sunday night basketball. So what do you want?"

Jack is glad Chip is getting to the point because he needs to go to his nine o'clock meeting, "I am glad you asked. I need a MONSTER favor. Are you sitting down?"

"Cut the bullshit. What do you want? I got a busy day."

He pauses for affect, "Can I borrow five grand in cash by three today?" Jack needs time to get the cash and get back to the office. Chip works south towards Cape Cod and, assuming Chip can get the cash, Jack will drive up to get it.

"You got to be shitting me. You know my first question is for what? My second questions is why me not your buddy Billy? My third question is what am I going to tell my wife, who, as you know, works for you?"

"I deserve the questions and I do need the cash." Answering confidently to sell Chip, "Question two is easy, I already asked Billy, he doesn't have the cash. The harder questions are why and Kim." Jack pauses and tells Chip some of the truth. "I thought I had a sure thing and I bet five grand on the Celtics last night. As you know they lost. I could not get a local guy to take the bet, so I used a bookie in Southie who does not know me and wants the cash this afternoon. I was so confident I would win that I never thought about coming up with the cash." Jack pauses to let his message sink in with Chip, and in a friendly voice, "So, can you help a brother out?"

"You know I want to help you and you still did not answer the Kim question. What do I tell her?"

Jack wants to find out if Chip can come up with the five grand, so he asks, "Before we talk about Kim can you come up with five grand cash?" It is Chip's turn to pause. Chip pauses for so long Jack says, "You there?"

In a reluctant voice, "If you give me a good answer on Kim, I can get you five grand cash today but it won't be easy."

Jack smiles, *One big problem down*. "Thanks man. Well, let's talk about Kim. First, I have not told Colette about any of this." Jack wants to lead Chip down his line of thinking, "I know it will be tough to not tell her you lent someone five grand but she works for me and she is friends with Colette. I will pay you back by the end of next week. Is there any way you cannot tell her?"

Chip pauses again, "Man you are putting me in a big bind. Not only do you want a lot of cash, you also want me to lie to my wife."

"I am not asking you to lie to your wife. I am asking you not to tell your wife something."

"You are killing me."

"Come on man. I know this is a big favor, but I need it."

"Okay, meet me at two at my office in Bourne."

"You are the man. The next time we get the wives together, I will pick up the tab and it will be our secret."

"You are playing with fire. FYI, I believe you owe a bookie, but I believe it is a lot more than five grand. I am glad I can help but watch yourself."

"No worries, see you at two. Can you e-mail me directions to your office?" It is too bad Chip does not work in Boston so Jack could hand deliver the cash to Bunar. But he will not be able to get the cash and drive to Southie before Bunar's muscle Stevey drives down to Bridgewater. He wants to call Bunar to see if he can stop Stevey from coming and hand deliver the cash to him. Instead Jack sends a quick e-mail to Billy, asking for Bunar's phone number. Looking at his watch, it is quarter past nine, he sprints out of his office to his next meeting.

Aside from being late for his nine o'clock meeting, it goes fine. He gets back to his office around quarter of eleven with enough time to check voicemails and e-mails. He checks e-mail first looking for the e-mail from Billy with Bunar's phone number but all the e-mails are spam or internal. He has only one voicemail from Colette reminding him they are on for lunch today and to call her for what time to meet. He calls her cell phone and they are on for quarter past twelve. This should give him just enough time to get to Bourne, which is only about forty minutes away.

Jack writes down his notes for his call with Howard Black:

- *Betty Turner*
- *Why didn't he tell me about MH when I was in Reno*
- *Has Reno Regional Called him*
- *Has Howard picked a MD to play golf*
- *Who are the primary decision makers on the committee*
- *When is MacroHealth going on-site?*
- *Who is the lead doctor, so he can introduce Dr. Alvarez*
- *Set up coming on-site*

He gets Howard on the first ring. They exchange pleasantries for a few minutes. Jack knows the relationship with Howard is not as strong as he thought it was, so he is no rush to jump right to business. He brings up Howard's favorite subject of golf. After Howard goes on for five minutes, he transitions to their golf meeting next week.

"Speaking of golf, are we all set for next Thursday to play golf?"

"Yes and after I dropped the MacroHealth bomb on you yesterday, I got some good news for you. Dr. Tony Heins will join us. Tony is an Internal Medicine doctor, Memorial's Chief Medical Officer, and is our physician sponsor for our portal project." *Finally, some good news.* He writes down Dr. Tony Heins name, checking golf off his list.

"That is great news. You will like Dr. Carson Alvarez who will be playing with us. Carson had a family practice before joining CM." Jack pauses, "Howard, I am not surprised you are looking at MacroHealth but I was surprised you did not tell me when I was in Reno."

Howard fumbles over his words, "Jack, 'ah'……. you are a 'ah' vendor and 'ah' I am hospital so you 'ah' and I 'ah' on different sides." He knows something is up but he has no idea what. Howard is a very smart guy. He does not butcher sentences. He is quiet looking at his list when it hits him. *This must have something to do with Betty.*

"Howard, we have known each other awhile and yes, you work for a hospital and I work for a vendor but we are on the same team. I want you to be successful using our solutions and you want to use our software to help your patients at Memorial." He drops the Betty bomb. "Based on our relationship, I am going to be direct. I do not know what exactly is going on but I know this has something to do with Betty Turner. Can you shed some light as to what is going on?"

There is a long silence. "'Ah' I know 'ah' Betty is with MacroHealth but is 'ah' about it."

Looks like Betty is spreading her poison to Memorial but not the right time to push Howard. He will wait until they play golf, in a more casual setting, to ask the tough questions on Betty Turner and MacroHealth.

Jack takes the high road, "Howard if you say so. Thank you for your time this morning and I am really looking forward to playing golf next week."

As soon as they hang up, he checks his e-mail again looking for Billy's e-mail. He gets the directions to Bourne from Chip but nothing from Billy. Jack calls Billy's cell phone.

Billy sees the caller ID and answers cautiously, "Fitzy what is up?"

"Have you checked your e-mail today?"

"Fitzy you do not realize how big of a request that is. What I can do is call Bunar for you."

Confused, "Are you saying you will not give me Bunar's cell phone number?"

"You do not know what you are getting into. Just tell me what you want to tell Bunar and I will call him."

Jack is furious, "You are right. I have no idea why you will not give me Bunar's cell number. The bastard called me at my office last night after I lost twenty grand on the Celtics game and said he is sending Stevey to my office today to get five grand."

"Do you have the five grand?"

He cannot believe he is having this conversation, "Yes, I got the five grand, which is why I want to call Bunar. To tell him I got the money and I will hand deliver it to him this afternoon."

"Okay, I will call Bunar and ask him."

Jumping on him, "I did not ask you to call Bunar. I asked you for his number, so I can call him. He has my home, business, and cell phone number, so I figured the least I could do was call him back on his cell."

"I will call Bunar." Billy just hangs up.

Jack does not understand what just happened. He called his best friend to ask the simple request of getting a cell phone number. Instead Billy refused his request and is calling Bunar himself.

Jack is just staring at the ceiling when his phone rings. Snapping out of his daze, looking at caller ID, seeing it is Billy, "What the hell was that?"

"What the hell was what?"

"You know, what I am talking about. Why didn't you just give me Bunar's phone number?"

"Fitzy try to calm down. As you are well aware, gambling is illegal in Massachusetts and the cops frequently shake down bookies. About a year ago the Boston Police raided McCracken's Tavern. Lucky for Bunar he does not keep his gambling records at McCracken's. When Bunar gave me this number he said to never give out the number."

Jack is still infuriated Billy would not give him the number but realizes it is a small problem. The big problem is having Stevey come to his office. "Okay but I am still disappointed you did not give me the number. What did Bunar say about having me hand deliver the five grand."

"No dice, Stevey is coming to your office at four today."

Jack is about to push back but, instead, pulls back, "Thanks for the effort," and hangs up. Looking at his watch, it is after twelve. He is going to be late for his lunch with Colette. Sprinting out of the office, he calls Colette's cell phone to tell her he will be five minutes late.

Driving to the Charlie Horse to meet Colette and Harrison, thinks, *Does Colette have any money he can use to pay down his debts?* When Colette's grandfather passed away he left Colette over a hundred grand. The account is in Colette's name and they have been saving the money for Harrison's college education. Colette gets statements each month and if things get real bad Jack can probably open one of the statements and figure out a way to borrow some of the money from Colette with or without her help.

Colette and Harrison are waiting for him. There is a half hour wait and they will not be seated until almost 1p.m. There is no way he will make it to Bourne by two. Jack is not worried about being late with Chip but he is worried about being late for Stevey at CM.

The three of them have a great lunch. Harrison is in a great mood and Colette is not pressing him about having lunch at McCracken's versus The Charlie Horse. It is almost two when Jack excuses himself to use the restroom. He goes outside to call Chip telling him he is running late and will not be to his office until after three. Chip tells him he has the cash but has a meeting and will be back by three-thirty. "Shit", if he gets the cash at three-thirty there is no way he will be back to the office by four. Jack asks if he can leave the cash in an envelope at the front desk.

"You are kidding. So you want me to leave you five thousand in a brown paper bag at the front desk? No way. What if the money gets lost or what if someone at my work opens the envelope and finds out I am giving you a wad of cash. Those are not the type of questions I want to answer."

Chip is doing him a huge favor. Backing off. "That would be kind of funny if someone opened the envelope. I will get to your office after three and I will wait for you in the lobby."

He heads back inside to finish up lunch with Colette and Harrison. When Colette accuses him, "What are you hiding?"

There is now way Colette knows about borrowing the money from Chip and acts dumb, "What are you talking about?"

"I saw you go outside and make a phone call."

Laughing, "I just wanted to check my messages at the office."

Colette does not laugh, "So you cannot check voicemails in front of me?"

Having been down the road of jealousy many times, he reassures her with a small lie, "Of course I can check voicemail in front of you, but I did not want to be rude and spoil our great lunch."

Colette is not buying it, "If you really had to check voicemail, why didn't you just tell me?"

He knows she is right. He is quickly going down the rabbit hole. He attempts to reverse tracks by falling on the sword, "You are correct; I just did not want to start a conversation about work."

Colette is not letting Jack off the hook, "So instead of talking about your work, you lie to me?"

Jack tries another tactic, "Can you please just let it go?"

"Jack Fitzpatrick, you are up to something, and I do not know what, but if you are messing around with another woman, I will find out and you will pay."

Jack is now getting annoyed. Even though he started this altercation by not telling Colette he was making a call, she is now going overboard.

Jack leans toward and whispers loudly, "I am sorry I did not tell you about the call but let's make one thing clear there is not 'another woman'." He goes for sympathy, "I have a lot going on at work since Betty left and I am under a lot of stress to close a couple of big deals."

Colette is wound up, "All I am looking for is respect and honesty."

Jack has had enough and waves over the waiter and asks for the check. Without looking at the bill, he throws his credit card at the waiter. "We were having a great lunch and it is now ruined."

"It is a big deal when you have weird guys named Bunar calling you, that you are taking showers in the middle of the day, and now making phone calls without telling me."

"Honey you just need to relax." As soon as Jack said 'relax' he knew he just poured gas on the problem.

Quickly responding, "Relax. Relax. Relax. You talk about your stress level. What about my stress level? I have to take care of the house, Harrison, and make sure everything is perfect for you. What about when you travel and I am home alone? What about….."

Jack interrupts her as the waiter brings back the credit card and bill. "Honey I know you have stress too. I am sorry I ruined our lunch. Let's pick up this conversation tonight." Looking at this watch, "I need to get back to the office."

After kissing Harrison, he tries to give Colette a kiss but she pulls back so he heads out to the parking lot shaking his head in disbelief.

26

Colette Follows Jack

"Husbands are like fires. They go out when unattended." Zsa Zsa Gabor

Colette watches her husband leave the restaurant and decides to follow him. Assuming he is going to the office, it will only be five minutes out of her way. Colette quickly gets Harrison ready and she walks out to the parking lot.

When she gets outside, she sees their BMW waiting to take a left hand turn. Colette's heart starts pumping because his office is to the right. Colette runs to her car and straps in Harrison. Like Magnum PI, she is waiting in her car for her husband to take the left, and then she will follow him.

With the traffic it takes a minute before Colette can take the left. By the time Colette takes the left Jack is gone. Colette drives down the road a couple of miles to see if she can see him but he is gone. So much for her Magnum PI skills.

Colette pulls over to the side of the road and tries to collect herself. Her adrenaline was flowing as she was trying to follow Jack, but as the adrenaline wears off, Colette starts to cry. Colette says to herself 'Pull yourself together; he probably just went to get gas or run an errand.'

As Colette starts to head home, she is debating to herself, should I go to Jack's office, and confront her gambling husband on his detour. Lucky for Jack, Colette decides to continue home so Harrison can take a nap. While Harrison is snoring, Colette calls both Jack's office and cell phone, when he doesn't answer, Collette knows the split second Harrison wakes up she is heading straight to his office.

27

Jack goes to Bourne

"Before borrowing money from a friend decide which you need most." Proverb

Going 90 miles an hour, Jack gets on route 24 south and then 495 South heading towards Cape Cod. Chip's office is in the picturesque town of Bourne, the Gateway to Cape Cod. The only way to drive to Cape Cod is one of the two bridges, the Bourne and the Sagamore bridges.

Chip's office overlooks the Cape Cod Canal. There are two schooners sailing down the canal. Jack wishes he could erase all of his problems and sail from Provincetown at the tip of Cape Cod to Key West at the tip of Florida.

Jack gets to Chip's office just after three. He is told Chip is in a meeting. While waiting on Chip, he checks voicemail, to his surprise he has a message from Colette saying she is sorry for lunch, and she wants to stop by his office this afternoon. His cell phone rings with caller ID let's him know it is Colette calling from home. He doesn't answer Colette's call.

Shaking, he now has to deal with Colette coming to the office in addition to Bunar's goon, Stevey. He could call Colette to tell her he has meetings this afternoon and cannot see her. But with caller ID, Colette will know he is on his cell phone. Jack could hit *67 which removes his phone number but that would cause more suspicion.

Jack calls the front desk administrator at CM and tells her to update his personal schedule to say he is in a meeting until four-thirty. This should help him if Colette comes to the office and hopefully with Stevey before he makes a scene. He is praying Colette does not come to the office and Stevey is late.

It is after three-thirty when Chip comes down with the cash. Chip hands him a bulky envelope. Jack is surprised at how big five grand in cash is. Jokingly whispers to Chip, "Thanks, should I take it out and count it here in the lobby?"

Chip chuckles, "As your attorney, I would not recommend that course of action."

"Thanks again. I owe you big time. I need to get going."

Chip gets serious, "Fitzy you take care of yourself."

He literally sprints to his BMW then goes 110 miles an hour on the highway to his office. The way Jack's luck is going he expects to get a speeding ticket.

Jack makes record time getting back to the office just after 4:15p.m. The good and bad news for him, is Collette cannot see the parking lot from the lobby. The bad news is he cannot see if Stevey is in the lobby causing a raucous. He looks for Colette's car in the parking lot, to his disappointment he sees her car. He parks away from her car and sneaks in through a back door of the building. He hopes Stevey and Colette are not in the lobby together.

Jack walks by the lobby, like he is on his way to a meeting, and acts like he accidentally runs into Colette and Harrison. At the same time he is looking for Stevey. "Hey Honey what are you doing here?"

"Did you get my voicemail we were coming over?"

"Nope, I have been in meetings. What is up?"

Slowly, "Well I just wanted to stop by after our lunch."

Jack sees Stevey walking up to the building. He immediately picks up Harrison, "Let's go up to my office."

"No, I just wanted to say a quick 'Hello'."

Jack looks behind Colette seeing Stevey walking and getting closer. Focused on Stevey, he has to get Colette out of the lobby. "Come on, you are here now and it is getting close to quitting time."

Colette does not move, "I will see you when you get home."

Stevey is now ten yards from entering the building. Holding Harrison, Jack turns his back and starts walking to his office. He says to Colette "Come on."

Colette reluctantly says, "Okay." Now he needs to get to his office in time to answer the call to come back down to the lobby. "Why are you walking so fast?"

"I am just excited to see you and Harrison."

Seeing Jack is holding Harrison and the bulky envelope, Colette offers, "Well if you are going to carry Harrison let me carry the envelope?"

"No worries, I can handle both."

Colette is now curious what is in the envelope. "Big envelope, what is in it?"

"Nothing just paperwork from my last meeting."

When the Fitzpatrick family gets to his office the phone is ringing. Putting Harrison down, he answers the phone, "Good afternoon, Jack Fitzpatrick."

On the other end of the phone the lobby administrator whispers, "Fitzy there is a very large gentleman in the lobby who says you need to come down to see in the next two minutes or there is going to be problem. I am afraid to ask him his name. Can you come down to the lobby?"

Jack says straight faced, "No problem I will be right down."

Jack tells Colette he has to do one quick thing and leaves his office with the big envelope. Walking into the lobby with a big pretend smile acting like Stevey is his buddy, "Thanks for coming to my office. Stevey, how are you doing?"

Stevey does not smile saying loudly, "Where is Bunar's money?"

"You are such a kidder." Jack walks outside in the hopes Stevey will follow him. Luckily, Stevey does follow. Handing Stevey the envelope, even though they are alone outside, whispers, "Here is the five grand Bunar asked for."

Stevey looks in the envelope and starts pulling out the cash. Jack begs, "Can you please not count it in front of my office? You can trust me. There is five thousand there." Seeing his boss Kevin Blair walking through the lobby on his way out of the building, he keeps begging, "Please put the money away."

In a disappointed voice Stevey says, "Bunar told me to make a scene if you do not have the cash. I was kinda hoping to make a scene."

"Like Bunar said, only make a scene if I do not have the money and as you can see, you have the cash. Can you please put the money back in the envelope?"

Reluctantly, "I guess so", just as Kevin walks out of the building.

Kevin stops, "Fitzy who is your very large friend?"

Jack does not know what to say to his boss. "A 'ah' friend of a 'ah' friend' who 'ah' wants me to join his basketball team. Stevey, isn't that so?"

Stevey just shrugs his shoulders and grunts, "Ya."

Jack does not want to introduce Stevey to Kevin but Kevin is not leaving. Kevin asks, "At your height and size you must be a center. How tall are you and good God, you must weigh over three hundred pounds? I personally would not want to go for a rebound against you."

Jack does not want Kevin to have a conversation with Stevey, so Jack answers the questions, "Stevey is over 6'4" and I would not wait to get a rebound against him either. Well Stevey must get going."

Kevin, "Nice meeting you," and he heads for the parking lot.

Jack begs Stevey, "You got your money, please get going."

Stevey sheepishly asks, "Can you help me get back to the highway? I was late because I got lost."

Jack smiles, *thank God Stevey is not too bright or today could have been a disaster.* He points the way back to the highway then sprints back to his office to see Colette and Harrison.

"I thought you were going to just be a minute."

"I was but I ran into Kevin on his way out of the office."

Colette pauses, "Where did you go after our lunch today?"

He thinks, *Could Colette know about my trip to see Chip?* He plays dumb as usual, "I do not know what you are talking about."

Colette is getting worked up and blurts out, "When you left the Charlie Horse you went left versus a right back to your office."

Laughing, "I had to run a quick errand and get some gas."

Colette stays on him, "When you were at lunch you said you had to get back to the office?"

"I did but I had to get a couple of quick things done." He walks around his desk to give Colette a big hug, "Honey, I must be putting the pressure of Betty quitting on you because you appear to be under a lot of pressure too."

"Nice try. You are up to something."

Calmly, "All you are seeing is the additional stress I am under. When I just saw Kevin, he asked about the deals in Nevada, Betty was working on." The stress is not a lie. He has a bunch of work, especially seeing MacroHealth is on-site at Reno Regional today, but he needs to be calm in front of his wife, "Let me pack up and we can head home together. Do you want to see if we can get a baby sitter on short notice so you and I go to dinner?"

"We just went out to lunch today. Let's just have you come home and I will make us something."

Jack packs up his laptop, done for today.

28

Betty Tells Reno Regional about accounting

"I take full responsibility for what happened at Enron. But saying that, I know in my mind that I did nothing criminal." Kenneth Lay, CEO Enron

Following Colette home, the pressure of work and his gambling debts is giving Jack a headache. He needs a gambling win tonight by the San Antonia Spurs when they play the Los Angeles Lakers. He owes Bunar forty-seven grand. If he wins tonight and tomorrow he will only be down seven grand. He can figure a way to borrow another $7,000.

Winning the RR deal will help. He calls Michelle Parks on his cell phone to see how the MacroHealth visit went to today.

They have harmless small talk before Jack asks about MacroHealth's pre-visit, "So, how did MacroHealth's pre-visit go today?" What he really wants to ask, *'Was Betty Turner at the meeting?'* but holds back.

Whispering, "MacroHealth dropped a big bomb on you guys?"

Michelle has Jack's attention. He cannot hold back on Betty, "Did Betty drop the bomb?"

Michelle keeps whispering, "Yup."

"So what did she say?"

Michelle pulls back, "Ah, I am not sure if I should tell you."

"Come on Michelle."

"You have to promise not to tell anyone?"

Jack cannot imagine what Michelle is about to say. Typically, vendors bash each other with stuff like: they have development problems, high turnover, and/or a dissatisfied client but all of this can usually be handled.

"I promise."

"You really promise?"

"I promise, come on what is it?"

Michelle pauses, "Betty has found deliberate accounting errors at CM Solutions and she is thinking about going public with the information."

CM is a public company. Jack has options in the company that have not yet vested. In the past, he has sold off his shares in CM to pay off his debts. The stock has done great with Jack making over $100,000 in the stock, since he joined the company. He has more options that will vest in December. With his 10,000 options valued at $45 per share and the stock currently trading at $50 per share, he will be up $50,000 in December. Even better, if the stock gets above $55 per share, he will have over $100,000.

Companies like CM offer their employee shares with an option price. For example with CM his option price is $45 per share. If the stock is above $45 per share, Jack will make the difference of $45 and the stock price. If the stock is below $45 per share, they are worthless or 'underwater'. Companies have options vest over time, so their employees will stay at the company until the shares vest which is typically over a number of years. Additionally, with options the employees care about the stock price because they benefit when the stock goes up.

Jack plays a little dumb, "We are a publicly held company, with top notch auditors." Michelle laughs so he says, "What is so funny?"

Michelle explains, "Cheryl, our CFO, said the exact same thing. Betty explained, CM being public means the stock will crash if they do not make their numbers every quarter. So CM is cooking their books to get and stay rich."

Jack is stunned. Does Betty really have something against CM or is she just doing this to spread FUD. FUD is the sales strategy of spreading Fear, Uncertainty, and Doubt. By creating FUD on CM Solutions, Betty is making MacroHealth look like the safe choice. He has been at CM for over three years and has never seen any accounting irregularities. Sure they backdate some contracts by a couple of days to put them in the previous quarter or hold deals back to put them in the next quarter but that is pretty standard in the business. Trying to get more specific information, "I am really surprised at this. Did Betty give any specific information?"

"Yes, she said CM is booking phantom deals and putting them on the books."

"Did she give you a name on the phantom deals?"

"Nope"

Jack asks another question, "Did she give any other specifics?"

"Not really but she gave a very compelling story. She said she liked working at CM Solutions and she wanted to give her notice as soon as she found out, but she needed a job, and she had to wait until she got a good job like the one she had at MacroHealth. She also said she is afraid to go public with the information as a 'whistle blower' because she is afraid it will ruin her life."

Betty may just be playing Reno Regional, "Michelle, I do not want to get into negative selling but Betty started this." Jack explains how he wanted to fire Betty and was successful on getting Betty to quit on her own.

"Wow, as usual every story has two sides. I did not know you could be so mean Mr. Fitzpatrick. I thought all the ladies like you but now I find out you really just want to fire women working for you."

Even though Michelle is kidding, he knows there is a lot of 'truth in jest.' Jack responds, "Michelle you know I am a nice guy and I do not randomly fire people." Turning on the charm, "When I am in Reno, I will make sure I am on my best behavior."

Luckily for Jack, Michelle starts flirting back, "Does being on your best behavior mean you are not going to take me out drinking and gambling again as you promised?"

He smiles to himself, "Being on my best behavior definitely means I will be taking you out."

"So what exactly do you have planned when you take me out?"

He pulls into his driveway, right behind Colette. Colette is now walking over to Jack's car so he needs to stop flirting and wrap up the call. Just as Colette walks up to the car he says, "That is a surprise for right now. Hey, I need to get going, I will give you a call tomorrow."

Michelle pouts, "Okay." She paused before saying, "Hey, I am serious about not telling anyone at CM what Betty told me."

"No worries."

Colette comes over to the car, "Were you talking to your girlfriend?"

Jack laughs, "No worries honey, I was just talking to Billy about tonight's NBA basketball games." Changing the subject, "What can I make you for dinner tonight?"

Colette, Harrison, and Jack have a quiet evening at home, just what he needs. The Spurs and the Lakers are playing an 8p.m. pacific game, so he will not get a chance to see the game. He internally debates staying up for some of the game but with all the stress in his life, needs his sleep. Plus he needs to get in early tomorrow and start investigating Betty's claim of account irregularities at CM.

29
The FBI Calls

"Just the minute the FBI begins making recommendations on what should be done with its information, it becomes a Gestapo."
J. Edgar Hoover

Thursday morning, getting ready for his morning run, Jack turns on ESPN to get the score of the Lakers and Spurs basketball game. He is waiting to run until he gets the score from last night's game. Scrolling across the bottom of the screen are the game scores. Up next Basketball, *"BOOM,"* he won with the Spurs winning by fifteen points. He bounces out the door for his run.

A run that typically takes about forty minutes only takes thirty-eight minutes, because he is so excited about the Spurs winning. Jack showers and is off to the office before Colette or Harrison are even awake.

Jack is not surprised to see his voicemail light blinking, assuming another message from Bunar at three a.m. 'Fitzy nice win last night. I was hoping to send Stevey to your office again today but it looks like it will have to wait until tomorrow.' Bunar is referencing today's game between the Hawks and the Knicks. Even though he is from Georgia, he decided to bet against the Hawks and go with the Knicks. He is happy Stevey will not be visiting him today. *When does Bunar sleep, the guy is leaving me voicemails at three a.m.* He laughs realizing being a bookie is not a nine to five job. *It is probably more like a five p.m. to nine a.m. job.*

With a one day reprieve from Bunar and his goon, Jack focuses on winning the Reno Regional and Memorial deals. He is also going to do some snooping on CM's accounting. He starts by looking on-line. Because he is a VP at CM he has full access to CM's sales CRM software and limited access to CM's accounting software.

CRM stands for Customer Relationship Software and includes everything from call logs for sales people, generating quotes, to logging client support calls. CM's CRM software and accounting software are integrated. Once a new clients sign with CM, all of their information goes to the accounting software.

Where to look? Betty covered the states of Nevada, Oregon, Utah, and Idaho, so it is where he starts. CM has one client, Memorial, in Nevada, four in Oregon, three in Utah and one in Idaho. Running a quick report in the CRM software, he gets the list of CM clients in the four states. The list matches Jack's knowledge of the territory. He then runs a report on the accounting software and against the list matches.

To reduce time, he runs a report of all US clients in the CRM software then a similar report in accounting software. The total number of clients matches, so if CM is cooking the books, they are not adding fake clients.

He is thinking about stopping right now after just running four reports. He was trying to get Betty to quit, so she could very easily be making up the story about accounting errors at CM. Even though Jack did not like Betty, he did think she was an ethical person, so thinks, *Where else can I look?*

Going back to the CRM software, runs a report of all clients in Betty's territory and all the CM products they own. He then runs a report on the accounting system. To his surprise the accounting system states the clients own more products than the CRM system. Jack zeros in on Memorial because he has been working the account knowing which products they own. The accounting system says Memorial owns CM's physician portal which is not true. He tries to find out how much CM paid for the Physician Portal, hoping the number is zero, but unfortunately does not have that level of access.

Jack is debating contacting his boss, Kevin, to see if he can get access to the accounting system, when he is startled by the phone ringing. Looking at the caller-ID, the call is from Boston. *Maybe the call is from Bunar but his caller-ID is 'Unknown'. I shouldn't answer the phone but it is a ringing phone,* "Good morning, Jack Fitzpatrick."

Relieved, when he hears the voice is not Bunar's but gets scared when he hears, "Mr. Fitzpatrick, my name is Tim Stephenson with the FBI. Do you a few minutes?"

What have I done wrong? Jack stumbles out, "Ah, of course, how I can ah help you. Ah, what is wrong? Oh my God is someone hurt? Is my wife and son okay?"

Agent Stephenson responds, "Mr. Fitzpatrick, this call is regarding a Mr. Justin Bunar."

Jack is glad to hear this is not about his family, and simply answers, "Okay."

"Can I ask you a few questions about Mr. Justin Bunar?"

Jack has never personally been in trouble with the law but he has watched enough TV to ask, "Should I get an attorney?"

"Mr. Fitzpatrick, at this time you are not under investigation and therefore you do not need an attorney."

Jack responds honestly, "I have never spoken to the FBI, and I am nervous."

In a FBI-like manner, "If you have not done anything wrong you do not have anything to worry about and again, you are not under investigation, at this time."

"Okay, I will answer some questions but I am going to leave my option open to stop answering questions and get an attorney."

"Your choice Mr. Fitzpatrick, but in my years in law enforcement, innocent people do not need attorneys this early in a case."

Jack gets a little aggressive and asks, "So are you saying innocent people do not need attorneys?"

"Mr. Fitzpatrick, if you would like me to come to your office or house and flash my FBI badge, I am happy to do that. I am simply doing some follow up on a case, and out of courtesy, I am calling you versus coming to you."

When Stephenson says 'flash my badge', Jack starts getting a little paranoid. *How do I even know if this guy is with the FBI? Is this a friend of Billy pulling a prank on me.* "Just in case someone is playing a joke on me, can I call you back at your office via the main number?"

"Of course, I am Senior RICO Agent Tim Stephenson and you can reach me at my office at 617-742-5533."

Jack hangs up and calls Stephenson right back. "Are you now ready to answer a couple of questions?"

Taking a deep breath, "Yes."

"Do you know a Mr. Justin Bunar?"

Goes with a one word answer, "Yes."

"How do you know Mr. Bunar?"

Jack cannot believe it took him this long to figure out why the FBI is calling. They either want him or Bunar for gambling. If what Agent Stephenson said is true, and he is not in trouble, then Bunar must be. He has not had time to think about this conversation and instead of answering the questions, he asks, "Can you tell me why you are contacting me about Bunar?"

"Yes, Bunar is part of a confidential investigation and I show here you had lunch with him this week."

"Can you tell me why you are investigating Bunar?"

"Not at this time. Depending what information you share with me, I will tell you about our investigation." Stephenson asks again, "How do you know Bunar?"

Jack tells a partial truth, "He is a friend of a friend."

"Are you referring to William Nestler?"

Jack is numb. He cannot believe this FBI Agent knows so much about him. This call appears to be more than a simple follow up. At the same time, he does not want to piss of the FBI saying, "Yes."

"How long have you known Mr. Nestler?"

Jack has never been in law enforcement but he knows the power of questions from his sales experience. In sales, you can lead prospects where you want them to go by asking questions. You also ask simple questions in the beginning to get the back and forth, and before they know it they are answering more sophisticated questions. He is watching himself but he keeps answering the questions, "About three years."

"How long have you known Mr. Bunar?"

"About two years."

"Do you know what Mr. Bunar does for work?"

Answering confidently, "He runs McCraken's." Obviously Bunar is a bookie too but for all Jack knows the FBI could be calling about sanitary issues at the restaurant.

Wrong, "Have you ever gambled with Mr. Bunar?" There it is. After all the simple questions, there is the trap question. *Does Agent Stephenson have evidence I am betting with Bunar or is he simply fishing? If I say 'No' does Agent Stephenson go away or does he just turn up the heat. There is no way I am saying 'Yes' without an attorney. Also, Agent Stephenson did not ask me 'Are you betting twenty grand a game with Bunar?' He asked me have you ever gambled with Bunar which could mean anything. I am trapped. In the movies the safest thing is to ask for an attorney. At least I know Chip.*

"Are you still there Mr. Fitzpatrick?"

Jack is actually thinking about hanging up but is smart enough to know that will create more problems than it will solve. He should have told Agent Stephenson he was busy or said he is not going to answer questions before the first question was asked, "Yes, I was just thinking about your question. Before I answer, can you give me more details on your investigation of Bunar?"

"Please answer my question I will give you more information on our investigation."

Jack's hands are shaking. If Agent Stephenson has half a brain he will know he is betting with Bunar. Maybe he had better get an attorney. "Agent Stephenson, thank you for your time this morning but I need to head to another meeting."

Agent Stephenson asks a more direct question, "So Mr. Fitzpatrick, you are not going to answer my question on whether or not you are placing illegal wagers with Mr. Bunar?"

"I have a lot on my plate, and, if possible, I do not want to get involved with the FBI."

"That is your choice but next time I will not be as accommodating as I am today. You have my contact information if you want to share more information on Bunar in the future. Good day."

Jack's hands are still shaking as he hangs up the phone. Does he call Billy or Chip or even Bunar to tell him about his exchange with the FBI? Wondering if Bunar got arrested today, would this mean he doesn't have to pay until Bunar gets out of jail? Even if Bunar is in jail, he will want his money. He also knows Bunar slashed his tire for being a hundred short, imagine what he would do if Bunar found out he was helping the FBI. He sits on the information with the hope the FBI does not call him back.

Hope is not a good strategy. There is even a sales book called, 'Hope Is Not a Strategy, 6 Keys to Winning the Complex Sale' by Rick Page. In sales if you are relying on hope you are going to lose the sale. He needs another plan besides hoping the FBI does not call him back.

Jack calls Chip Savard to see if he is available for lunch today. Chip is not available but will meet him on Friday as long as they can have lunch near his office in Bourne. For now the FBI strategy will be lunch with Chip on Friday, and to not saying anything to anyone else.

The phone rings again. Jack is expecting it to be the FBI calling back but sees it is Kim Savard. She asks if he has time to review Reno Regional before their meeting next week. Looking forward to doing some real sales work, Jack tells her to get Larry and they can review Reno Regional and Memorial together, because both deals are in Nevada, and both are competing against Betty and MacroHealth.

30

Miller Heiman

"The general who wins the battle makes many calculations in his temple before the battle is fought. The general who loses makes but few calculations beforehand." Sun Tzu

Kim and Larry come into his office ready to review Reno Regional and Memorial. Jack has set up two flip charts, one for each account. He follows the strategic selling method by Miller Heiman or officially, 'Strategic Selling: The Unique Sales System Proven Successful by America's Best Companies' by Robert B. Miller, Stephen E. Heiman, and Tad Tuleja. The first thing he does is have Kim and Larry outline who the players are at their respective prospects.

The first person to determine is the 'Decision Maker'. Simply put this is the person who signs the contract. Very often in selling, the sales person never gets to meet the true decision maker. For example the CEO may have to sign the agreement, but his or her people will do all the leg work and the CEO will sign at the end, or at larger organizations the decision maker, the person who signs the agreement, may be in a different state or country. So they first determine who is the 'Decision Maker' and if CM does not have access to the decision maker it is a 'red flag'. If you do not have access to the 'Decision Maker' you need to find out who are the influencers. In today's complex business environment, 'Decision Makers' do not make unilateral decisions. They typically try going for a consensus before making a decision. At the same time if you have a choice of having the 'Decision Maker' or the 'Decision Influencer', you want the 'Decision Maker'. One thing Jack likes about Strategic Selling is it makes selling more objective and helps you find your strengths and weaknesses in the account. At Reno Regional, Cheryl Scharff, the CFO, is the decision maker and she will sign the agreement. The 'Decision Influencers' will be on the selection committee and CM is meeting them next week. At Memorial, they do not know who will sign the agreement, a red flag. Howard Black, the CIO at Memorial, is an influencer on the decision maker, but he will not sign the contract. Another red flag at Memorial is they do not who the 'Decision Influencers' are in addition to Howard Black.

The next person they work on is the 'User Buyer'. The 'User Buyer' will use or manage the product. At Reno Regional the user buyers are Peter Galetta,

Michelle Parks, and the nurses and doctors who they have not met. The doctors and nurses at Reno Regional get a 'red flag'. At Memorial, Howard Black is a user buyer plus the nurses and doctors they have not met, another red flag for Memorial.

Next are the 'Technical Buyers' or 'Gate Keepers'. Technical buyers have the ability to say 'No' but they do not have the ability to say yes. For example if a hospital will only work with Microsoft products, then a technical buyer has the ability to tell you 'No' because you do not use Microsoft. At the same time if you do use 'Microsoft' they cannot say 'Yes'. RFP's (Request for Proposals) are typically used by 'Technical Buyers' to weed out vendors. At both Memorial and Reno Regional, CM has gotten through the technical buyers. At this stage of the deal, all three agree they have gotten through the technical buyers.

Next is finding your 'Coach'. A 'Coach' is someone at the prospects who wants to see you win and gives you information he or she is not giving to your competition. The ultimate 'Coach' is the 'Decision Maker' because this means they want you to win and they are making the decision. It is also good to develop multiple coaches. This way you can get information from multiple sources and you have multiple people wanting you to win. At Reno Regional, CM's 'Coach' is Michelle Parks. The good news is they have a 'Coach', the bad news is they are concerned about how much influence Michelle will have on the selection committee. Kim is not 100% sure Michelle wants them to win. Because Kim is friends with Jack's wife, he does not tell Kim nor Larry about his relationship with Michelle. Jack kept his promise to Michelle and did not tell Kim and Larry about Betty saying CM has a possible accounting fraud. They agree they need to develop another 'Coach' at Reno. At Memorial their 'Coach' is Howard Black. Another red flag for Memorial is Jack doesn't know if Howard wants CM to win.

Sometimes Jack reviews who is a 'Sniper' at the account, someone who wants to see CM lose. For the sake of time, they skip this one.

Kim and Jack, with Larry's input, agree during next week's on-site presentation they need to enhance their relationships with Peter Galetta and Cheryl Scharff, and they need to find out who are the key doctors and nurses and build relationships with them. Jack tells Kim he will call both Peter and Cheryl today to try and build those relationships.

Jack and Larry, with Kim's input, agree they are at risk at Memorial. CM is putting all their eggs in one basket, called Howard Black. Typically, you are excited to have a strong relationship with the CIO but there are too many red flags at Memorial. Jack is playing golf with Howard and one of Memorial's doctors and needs to get a lot of information on where Memorial is with their decision on selecting a physician portal vendor. Kim and Larry know he usually does a good job of building relationships with 'Decision Makers' and 'Decision Influencers' but he does not do a good job of building multiple relationships with prospects. They see this with Howard Black at Memorial and push Jack to do a better job at Memorial, and not fall into his comfort zone of building only one strong relationship.

Now that they have determined who the players are, they try to guesstimate who the players would vote for today. In every case from Michelle Parks to Howard Black, they do not know which way the committee members would vote. This is another huge red flag because if you do not know someone is voting with you, you should assume they are voting against you.

Jack can see Kim and Larry are getting depressed during this sales strategy session because they are uncovering a lot of red flags and they are learning they are in second place at both opportunities. "Hey guys this is the really good stuff. Would you rather think we are in first when we are in second or would you rather know we are in second? I personally would rather know we are in second because we have time to do something about it. Let's work on what is important to the individual players and how we can get them to see the advantages of going with CM Solutions."

The three of them next attempt to outline what is important to each person. They decide to start with the Chief Information Officer / CIO position because they can do Peter Galetta with Reno Region and Howard Black with Memorial at the same time.

From a macro-level the CIO is responsible for managing the hospital's computer system and the CIO's customers are the hospital employees and physicians. So the CIO wants a successful project. The next step is to determine what is a successful project: Is it the project is on time, the project is on budget, or the project meets expectations? The ultimate goal is all three but there is usually one driver between the three. Typically the end users do not care about the budget because it comes out of the CIO's budget. They will typically care about the go-live date, if it disrupts their workflow or they delay at the last minute, and the quality of the product or service.

The timeline usually has some form of external pressure. Is the current system going away with a specific date so a hospital has to be live by? Has someone told the board or CEO the system will be live by a specific date? Is the CIO's or other manager bonuses based on going live by a specific date?

The budget is defined by the organization's financial stability and corporate culture towards spending. In Jack's experience if the timeline and quality of the project are important, organizations will spend more on projects. Sales people like to think price and budget are top priorities, but statistics show there are other issues more important than budget. *Who wants to be in charge of a project under budget but does not work?*

With business issues covered, the next questions are personal; how does this project affect the CIO financially, his career, or how he is perceived internally or externally? How can the CIO win by selecting CM and have a successful project? Is there something in the CIO's compensation plan that is tied to this project? If the project is successful, does the CIO have the opportunity to be promoted? Does the CIO want to see his name in lights, such as getting written up in trade journals, put on press releases, speaking at conferences? The biggest personal risk is if the project proves unsuccessful, and they get fired. There can be other losses. How does an unsuccessful project affect the CIO politically? Will he get less budget for future projects?

Jack, Larry, and Kim discuss the dynamics of personal wins and losses for each position. What they are consistently finding is they do not have enough information. Because both organizations are getting close to making a decision, and time is not on their side, they start formulating a strategy as to how to proceed.

Because they are second in both accounts, they decide to focus on how they are different from MacroHealth. One thing that is different at the two opportunities is that at Memorial they are the incumbent, and should win if there is a tie. At Reno Regional they are a new vendor; with a tie they might not win. So the goal at Memorial is to get into a tie for first and at Reno Regional the goal is to win outright because a tie may mean they lose.

Another of Jack's many sales theories is the "Purple Cow Strategy" from Seth Godin's book 'Purple Cow: Transform Your Business by Being Remarkable'. In a nutshell, Seth was driving through the French countryside enjoying the beautiful cows. After a couple of hours Seth realized all of the cows looked the same. After a few more hours Seth was hoping to see a purple cow. As a marketer Seth realized if you are not one of the first one or two cows your only chance to stand out is to be different, i.e. a 'Purple Cow'. The 'Purple Cow' strategy is risky because you are not mainstream.

There is also a group of people of who believe in the 'Non-Purple Cow Strategy'. This strategy is to be the best brown cow you can be and you will stand out. Jack only believes in this strategy if you are the market leader.

So the question is what can CM do to standout at Memorial and Reno? They decide to focus on the doctors and push CM's own doctor, Dr. Carson Alvarez. Dr. Alvarez can be a pain in the ass but they decide he is their best choice. Jack calls Dr. Alvarez to see if he can come to their meeting. As expected Dr. Alvarez is not available but he can meet with them tomorrow at eleven. Jack books the meeting and stresses Dr. Alvarez has to make the meeting because they travel on Monday and present first thing Tuesday morning.

Jack wraps up, saying, "Let's continue our planning tomorrow at eleven with Dr. Alvarez." Feeling pretty good he won twenty grand last night, and if he wins again he will only owe Bunar seven grand plus the five grand he owes Chip. If he wins he is not worried about the FBI because he will stop betting with Bunar. He calls Michelle.

31

Jack Calls Michelle

"In order for the light to shine so brightly, the darkness must be present." Danny DeVito

Getting Michelle on the first ring, they have some small talk until Michelle asks, "Have you had a chance to look at any accounting problems at CM?"

Jack tells a small lie, "Yes and I have not found anything", because he just started looking there is no need to tell Michelle about what he found because he does not want to screw up the deal. "Have you heard anything more from our ex-employee, Betty?" Stressing Betty is no longer with CM.

Michelle whispers, "As a matter of fact Betty called me this morning", she pauses.

"You cannot hold out on me now."

"I am worried I am telling you too much. You may have to buy me dinner in addition to taking me gambling"

"No worries, I am taking you out Tuesday night."

"Come on. You are taking me and twenty Reno Regional employees out too." Michelle pauses, "I am looking for something a little more………" Jack is afraid Michelle is going to say 'Romantic' but she says "Fancy".

"I can try to fly out earlier on Monday. How about dinner Monday evening?" This would work out great for Jack because he can get and give information for Tuesday's demo.

"Deal."

"I will get you more information on Monday. You can pick any place in Reno and dinner is on me. Now about Betty."

Whispering, "Well she called me to get my feedback on yesterday's meeting. I told her the meeting went well but based on our conversation yesterday I told her I thought she was grandstanding on the accounting problems at CM, and if she did not have proof she should not bring it up again." Jack smiles to himself. "Well it was like I shot her dog. Betty gets all upset and says she is not a liar and she would not bring it up if it was not true. I was getting a little heated too, so I asked her straight out 'Do you have proof?' Betty said yes. So I stayed on her, 'Well when are you going to show me?' Now Betty gets all quiet and says, 'If I show you will you vote for MacroHealth?' I must be learning something from you Fitzy, because I said, 'This is a loaded question and you know it. You show me and if it really is a big deal, I will vote for you. If not, I will vote for who is the best clinical solution for Reno Regional.' Betty does not saying anything for minute, so I stay on her and say 'Are you going to show me or not?' Betty reluctantly says 'Yes'."

Now it is his turn to be quiet. Thinking either Betty is a great bluffer or she really has some dirt on CM.

"Fitzy you there?"

"Yes, I am blown away. I thought Betty was just making this up. Either she really has something on CM or she is stupid. If she sends you bullshit she is in trouble, if she sends you nothing you caught her in a lie, so I figure she must have something. Are you going to send to Cheryl what you get?" What he really wanted to ask, *'Are you going to send it to me?'*

"Betty said she would call me on Monday."

"Well it looks like we may have an even more interesting dinner on Monday night." They discuss logistics for next week, including dinner Monday night.

After the call, Jack pulls up the accounting system and re-runs the reports on Memorial to see about the products that supposedly have been purchased. This time he prints versus looking on his computer screen. Waiting for the reports to print, Kevin Blair unexpectedly comes into the office.

He is about to tell Kevin what he finds on Memorial when Kevin tries to casually say, "Jack, we have been having some problems with our accounting software, so if you find anything out of place please let me know."

Jack knows something is off because Kevin usually calls him 'Fitzy', and because he was just in the accounting software this morning. Jack gets a little paranoid and decides to not say anything about Memorial saying, "Sure, what is up?" He tries not to stare at his printer right next to Kevin, as it is printing the Memorial report.

"Accounting is going through a software upgrade and they asked me to let them know if my team finds any irregularities."

Jack pushes him, "Why are they asking us? Can't they find and correct the problems themselves?"

Kevin keeps trying to act casual but Jack senses an intensity, "They just want to make sure there are no problems."

Jack does not push any further especially when proof of Kevin lying is only inches away from him, "If I find anything I will let you know."

Jack gets up to get the accounting reports from the printer when Kevin turns around, "Don't get up, I will get these off the printer for you."

Jack holds his breath as Kevin hands him the papers without looking at them. When Kevin leaves, he is sweating. Jack starts going through the reports and quickly identifies CM has billed Memorial over twelve million in phantom invoices.

When Jack goes back to his computer to look at Memorial closer in the accounting system, to his surprise the twelve million is gone. Either Kevin was telling the truth about the problems with the accounting software or Kevin knows he is looking at Memorial and someone just cleaned up the Memorial account. Either way, Kevin must have known he was in the Memorial account.

Jack is not a certified public accountant (CPA) but he does know you cannot just make twelve million disappear. He takes his report and goes to the copier to make multiple copies. He puts one in his desk and the others in his briefcase to bring home.

After hiding the copies, he takes the originals to Kevin's office to tell him he did find some problems. The door is closed. Jack knocks as he walks in. CM's CFO, Dennis Hintz, is in with Kevin. The three of them exchange uncomfortable hellos.

Kevin curtly demands, "What do you want?"

Jack nervously answers, "When you came by office a few minutes ago, you asked if I found any problems with the accounting software and yes I found one." To cover his tracks Jack continues with, "I am getting ready for the meeting at Memorial and I ran the list of what Memorial owns from the accounting system." He tries to lighten the mood by making fun of the mistake, "And to my surprise it looks like Memorial already owns our Physician Portal and they paid a cool twelve million."

No one laughs at his joke. With a straight face Dennis the CFO says, "Have you found anything else?"

"Nope but if I find anything else should I bring it to you or Kevin?"

"You can bring it to Kevin. Have you made any copies of this report?"

"Nope but I do want to know what Memorial has purchased, so I can be prepared for next week."

"I will work on this now with Kevin and it should be fixed by the time you get back to your desk."

Jack just wants to get out of Kevin's office, knowing they are lying because the report is already fixed. Looking at his watch, "No rush, I will try to run it again tomorrow. I got to go. Talk to you guys later."

Back in his office, closes the door to write down his options:

- *Forget this whole account thing happened*
- *Try to dig deeper to see if he can find more accounting problems*
- *Call Michelle and tell her what he found*
- *Go to Kevin and come clean on what Betty is telling Reno Regional*
- *Go to Dennis Hintz and ask him for more details on the accounting problem*
- *Call Betty directly to get more information on what she found*

He reviews the list an options. Quickly crosses out doing nothing because he has enough evidence between the Memorial accounting report, Betty's accusations, and Kevin and Dennis acting suspicious. Keeping the option of digging deeper, he crosses out telling Michelle. He wants to win the Reno Regional deal and does not see any way of telling Michelle because it will put the deal at risk. He can always tell her later if he gets more concrete evidence. He crosses out going to Kevin or Dennis, because both of those guys were acting weird today and, if they are up to something, all Jack is doing is putting his career at risk and limiting his access to additional information.

He circles calling Betty. When Betty quit, Jack figured he would never talk to her again. Now he is thinking about calling her to ask for more details on her accusations. What would he say, 'Hey Betty this is your old boss you hated. I know you are at a competitor, we are competing on a twenty-eight million dollar deal, and I just want you to tell me everything you are telling the hospital, especially the part about our accounting problems.' He laughs to himself but does not totally discredit the idea of calling Betty. He focuses on digging deeper.

- ~~*Forget this whole account thing happened*~~
- *Try to dig deeper to see if he can find more accounting problems*
- ~~*Call Michelle and tell her what he found*~~
- ~~*Go to Kevin and come clean on what Betty is telling Reno Regional*~~
- ~~*Go to Dennis Hintz and ask him for more details on the accounting problem*~~
- *Call Betty directly to get more information on what she found*

Jack knows some of the people in accounting, and *if there is a conspiracy who is in on it?* There is no way CM could cook the books and have everyone in the know without getting caught. Plus he figures accounting people do not know the deals nor the clients, just the paper they push. If Dennis or Kevin told them to book a fake deal, they would never know. What about the audits?

Jack decides to go down to accounting to see if he can get access to the Memorial files. When he gets to accounting, Dennis's office is empty and he hopes Dennis is still meeting with Kevin.

Before walking into the accounting, he takes a slow deep breadth to steady his nerves, *Now is as good as anytime.* If he gets caught, he will simply say he was getting a hard copy before the Memorial meetings. Jack is allowed to have access to the contracts but as a VP, he is not supposed to make copies. Walking in the accounting office he tries to find someone he recognizes. CM has added so many new employees in the last three years he has been with the company, it takes him a minute to finally see someone he recognizes, Maureen O'Shea. They started at

CM at the same time and both went through the same two week orientation class. Plus with both having Irish names, they keep in touch.

The easy part is getting Maureen to get the file. The hard part is getting copies and having Maureen not tell Dennis. He makes some small talk with Maureen then asks, "The reason I came down is to get a copy of the Memorial contract and all their add-ons."

"No problem, let me get it for you."

When Maureen comes back with the contract, "Ah, I am going to be a while. Would it be easier for you to make a copy for me?"

"You are not supposed to make copies. How about you just read it in here? Take all the time you need."

This avenue is not working, "Actually, I need to get to another meeting. Can you make a copy?"

"I am not supposed to, but if it will help you. It will take me about ten minutes to make a copy. Also, because I am making you a copy you need to sign the log book with today's date, your name, and the contract number." Maureen opens up the contract signature book and hands it to Jack.

"No problem," he grabs the signature book, sitting down. Maureen turns around and heads in the filing room to make copies. He acts like he is filling out his information but he is not writing anything. He shuts the book and waits, betting Maureen will not open the book.

Scanning the long hallway which leads to accounting, he sees Dennis Hintz heading to accounting, he is trapped. If he leaves he will run into Dennis and will have to explain why he is in accounting. Jack is looking around the waiting room but there is no escape. He looks out towards Dennis, and it appears Dennis does not see him. He could pretend he's reading a magazine in the hopes Dennis passes him. *Stupid idea.* Jack is working on his story about getting prepared for the Memorial meeting, when he remembers there is a bathroom in the accounting office. He quickly gets up and speed walks to the restroom. Jack closes the door, putting his ear up against it. He does not hear anything. He chuckles when he realizes the thick door is not designed to let noise in, but it is designed to keep bathroom noise from getting out. Looking at his Tag watch, he decides to wait two full minutes before opening the door. After two minutes which seem like two hours, he cracks the door and peeks out. He can see Dennis is not in the accounting waiting area but he also cannot see if Dennis's door is closed. Panicking he waits one more minute. He needs to time his departure before Maureen comes back asking for him.

Lucky for Jack, just as he opens the bathroom door, Dennis closes his door. All Jack sees is Dennis's closed door. He waits in the hallway outside of accounting because he can see if Dennis is about to come out of his office and can watch for Maureen.

He is pacing the hallway when Maureen comes out of the filing room with a copy of the contract. "Thank You," then sprints to his office.

Back in his office, he reviews the Memorial contract. Going through the contract, he is surprised and disappointed because everything looks fine. There is nothing on Memorial buying a phantom 'Physician Portal' from CM. Jack leans back in his chair. He jumps when there is a knock on his door, covering up the Memorial contract before he says, "Come in".

Maureen O'Shea, with her cute freckles and short orange hair, is standing in Jack's office. Jack's mind starts racing, figuring he is caught even though he did not find anything, "Maureen what can I do for you?"

"The reason I came up to your office is when I was putting back the Memorial contract, I noticed in the back of the file cabinet there was another folder, 'Memorial'. I figured you would want this one too, so I made copies of those too."

"Thanks", as he is debating whether to tell her to put the file back where she found it versus back in the Memorial file. It would call too much attention to the situation so he says nothing.

As soon as Maureen closes his office door, he opens the second Memorial file. Immediately, he sees the phantom twelve million dollar order from Memorial for a 'Physician Portal' with an obviously forged signature on the contract.

'Boom'. There is the evidence CM is cooking their books. Now the question is what to do with the smoking gun. Jack goes to the copier and makes more

copies. He puts these copies with his other printouts from the CRM and accounting software.

What to do next? He starts writing another list of options

- *Get more evidence*
- *Get another job like Betty*
- *Become a whistle blower and tell the SEC*
- *Tell Michelle at Reno Regional*
- *Tell Howard at Memorial*
- *Tell his wife*
- *Call Betty at MacroHealth*
- *Tell their CEO what he found*
- *Tell his boss what he found*

He doesn't rush into a decision and decides not to tell anyone what he has found. Plus he needs to get home to watch the Hawks versus the Knicks on TV. If the Knicks win he will only owe Bunar a manageable seven grand. He does not consider what will happen if he loses and owes Bunar another twenty grand plus the 10% vig for a total of forty-nine thousand.

Shaking his head thinks, *How did I get myself in this situation?* Putting the evidence in his briefcase, he heads home.

32

Knicks Game

"The next best thing to gambling, and winning; is gambling, and losing." Jimmy the Greek

On the car ride home, he gets a call from Billy Nestler to see if he wants to meet later at the 'Charlie Horse' to see the Hawks-Knicks game tonight. "Great, I could use a bucket of Sam Adams. I will meet you there at eight." Jack should get the okay from Colette first, but he figures with his and CM's finances crashing down around him he can use a few beers.

At home, Colette and Harrison are playing in the back yard. He knows if he tells Colette he is going to 'Charlie Horse' tonight it will start a fight. So he needs Colette to agree to the decision. He wishes he could simply say *'I am going out tonight'* but three years of marriage has taught him those statements, *Go over like a lead balloon.* Colette is a great person but she just does not like being told something. With the right timing, she is usually very supportive.

Jack joins Colette and Harrison in the backyard. Colette asks how his day went at the office. He talks about his day but he does not say anything about the accounting fraud. He is focused on getting her okay on going out tonight.

Because Jack is from Georgia, he plays the hometown card to get the okay on seeing the Hawks-Knicks game with Billy. "Hey, after Harrison goes to bed, are you okay with me meeting Billy to see my home town Atlanta Hawks play the Knicks at the Charlie Horse?"

With the look on her face, "Come on, you are traveling ALL next week."

He is prepared, "I do not have to, but it has been a busy week at work and I would like to blow off a little steam."

With a sly smile, "You can blow off a little steam with me."

Smiling back, "How about both, I will blow off some steam at the Charlie Horse then I will come home and blow off some steam with you?"

Smacking his arm, "That is not what I meant and you know it. I meant you can hang out with me at the house and watch the basketball game."

He begs, "Come on, I will put Harry to bed and I will be back by ten-thirty."

"With all the weird things going with you, I do not know why, but okay."

He gives Colette a big hug, "You are the best. Let's get a babysitter for tomorrow night."

"Great idea. You can take me to the place in South Boston?"

He is not planning on taking Colette to McCracken's ever, but says, "Great idea, do you want me to call the babysitter?"

"I will and I can tell you are not planning on taking me to South Boston."

He forgets how well she knows him, "Honey, it is a bad section of town. It is one of those places packed for lunch but empty for dinner because most people will only go there during the day when the sun is out." Jack continues, "Is there somewhere else you would like to go on Saturday night?"

"I will get the baby sitter. You pick the restaurant." He plays with Harrison before putting him to bed and going over to the Charlie Horse.

The Charlie Horse is packed because it is 'Thirsty Thursday'. Billy is already at the bar. One nice thing about the 'Charlie Horse' having so many TVs is you can see five TV's with five different games from any seat. They even have TVs in the men's room.

Jack and Billy order Sam Adams Summer Ales. They are both avoiding the Bunar topic because Billy knows Jack has twenty grand riding on the game. He doesn't tell Billy about the FBI calling him. Jack does not want to get Billy in the middle and does not want Billy to tell Bunar the FBI has contacted him. After two beers, Billy says, "So Fitzy, what is your plan on paying Bunar if the Knicks lose tonight?"

Jack laughs, "I am surprised it took you so long to ask. My only plan is very simple, I plan on winning." After saying it, he realized how sad and true the statement is. *What if I do lose?* The biggest variable on losing is if Bunar wants any money tomorrow. Based on Bunar calling him every night after the game, if he loses Bunar will be calling looking for his money. The bigger question is how much would Bunar want? *Would he want another five grand? Would he want the whole forty-nine grand?*

"Holy shit, you really do not have a plan if you lose."

The beers are starting to affect him, and Jack is loosening up. In his best Ed McMahon to Johnny Carson imitation voice, "You are correct sir!"

Billy gets serious, "Well the plan better not be me calling Bunar to see if he will take more bets from you?"

"You never know." Jack gets positive, "No worries man, the Knicks will win and my problems will go away."

They settle in to drinking beers and watching the basketball game. The first half is a good with the Atlanta Hawks up 2 points at half time. The third quarter is back and forth and at the end of the third quarter the Hawks are still up two points. The Knicks start off the fourth quarter by hitting a three pointer on the first shot to put them up by one. Jack jumps off his bar stool, "Boom", high-fiving Billy.

The Knicks are home and Jack has to give up three points, so he not only needs the Knicks to win, he needs them to win by more than three points. Five minutes into the fourth quarter the Knicks build a six point lead. Just when it looks like the Knicks are going to blow out the Hawks, the Hawks make a run and tie up the game. The game goes back and forth with neither team getting up by more than three points. With less than forty seconds to go the game is tied and the Hawks have the ball. In the NBA each team has twenty four seconds to shoot after they get the basketball. The Knicks will get the ball back whether or not the Hawks score. The Hawks run the clock down to about 15 seconds and run a play and they score on a pick and roll play to put the Hawks up by two points. The whole bar yells when the Hawks score. The Knicks have 12 seconds to score and they call a time out.

During the commercial he says to Billy, "I need the Knicks to tie the game up to go into overtime, because if they win by one, I lose. If the Knicks go to overtime they will have a chance to win by more than three points."

Billy states, "Gambling makes watching games more exciting, but it does make you root for weird things, like in football when you hope your guy misses a field goal to not beat the spread."

Jack very seriously responds, "No shit, now let's root for the Knicks to put this game into overtime, so I can win my bet."

The game comes back on the TV and the Knicks inbound the ball with 12 seconds left. With five seconds left in the game, the Knicks run a screen to give their guy a three point shot. Just before the buzzer goes off the guy on the Knicks launches a three pointer and it goes in. The bar goes crazy as the Knicks win a great game. Jack is simply stunned. How could he bet against his home team Hawks and what is he going to do with Bunar?

Billy asks, "Are you okay?"

"I have been a lot better." Looking at his watch, it is just after eleven. Jack should be getting home but, "You got time for one more beer?"

"I really should be getting home, but I got one more beer in me. Order me another one while I hit the head." Billy heads off to the restroom.

Billy has left his cell phone on the bar. Instantly, Jack realizes he can get Bunar's cell phone number, so he can negotiate with Bunar directly versus through Billy. Picking up the phone it takes him a second to figure it out. He hits the menu to get the phone book. He scrolls through the A's to get to the B's looking for Bunar. "Shit", Bunar is not in there. He looks over the bar towards the direction of the restroom to see if Billy is coming back. Jack tries to shake off the alcohol fog and says out loud "Think, Billy has to have Bunar's phone number in his cell phone. I have seen Billy call him from the phone." He forgets Bunar is his last name and Billy's phone sorts by first name.

What is his first name? Goes back to the A's scrolling down one name at time. *Who knew Billy had so many friends?* Feeling like there is a thousand names in his address book. He is through D's while looking to see if Billy is coming back from the restroom. He gets to the J's and there it is Justin Bunar. He does not have a pen and looks for the bartender, but he is on the other side of the bar with another customer. He sees Billy coming out of the bathroom. When he asked Billy for the number earlier in the week, Billy was adamant about not giving him the number, so he is not about to ask him. Jack cannot write the number down, so he tries to memorize it. Saying to himself over and over, "617-555-0025, 617-555-0025, 617-555-0025."

As soon as, Billy sits down Jack gets up, "I have not ordered the beers yet. Can you order the beers while I go to the little boys' room?"

Walking to the bathroom, he grabs his cell phone to type in the number because he doesn't have a pen. First he types in 617-555-0052, he hits 'send' then immediately he hits 'end'. This way the number will be in the phone but he did not call the person. Going into the bathroom, he takes out the phone to look at the number. The number does not look right but he is not sure why. Closing his eyes, he says the number again to himself, and this time says, "617-555-0025." He types in 617-555-0025 repeating the process of 'send' 'end'. With the alcohol affect he is not sure which number is right, but he is confident one of them is correct.

As soon as he sits down at the bar, Billy asks, "So how are you going to pay Bunar?"

"In all honesty, I have no idea. What do you think Bunar will do?"

"I don't know. I try not to talk too much to him about his gambling business. I do know he will want to get paid sooner rather than later."

They are both quiet for a minute. "I don't have the money."

"Not good. You need to get the money. What about refinancing your house?"

"With all the money we have been spending, my house is maxed out. Do you think you can get me an extension?"

"We have been through this twice before and each time I helped a little but you still had to come up with some cash."

They are quiet again, when Jack blurts out, "Colette has some money I can probably get to."

"Fitzy, I am your friend and I do not want to say I was right but you are in deep shit and you need to get out. If getting the money from Colette will get you out, get it."

"I am going to Reno, Nevada next week and there is a chance I could win fifty grand to pay off Bunar."

Billy does not laugh, "You are not going to gamble yourself out of this problem. You are going to face the fact you lost, and you now need to work your way out of the problem. I can't believe I let you get yourself get into this situation in the first place."

Jack is no mood for a speech and leaves, saying, "I got myself into this problem. I will get myself out of this problem. I will talk to you tomorrow."

While driving home, he debates calling Bunar. He is not sure what he will say, plus he does not know which number in his cell phone is correct. Instead he calls his office voicemail to see if Bunar has left him a message. Jack is happy to hear 'You have no new messages.'

Jack may have a way to pay off Bunar.

By the time he gets home it is midnight. He tries to sneak into the house but when he gets into the bedroom Colette is up watching television. Jack is not ready for a Colette confrontation, so he smiles saying, "I am surprised you are up", he gives her a kiss on the cheek.

"Jack, I thought you were going to be home by ten?"

"I was, but the game took longer than I thought. I figured you would be asleep, so I did not want to call and wake you up."

"Jack you have not been the same person lately. You are staying out late, coming home in the middle of the day, working late, and not spending much time with Harrison and I."

"You are right honey. I have a lot going at work and it is spilling over to you and Harrison."

"I am not talking so much about work but about staying out late with Billy. Should I be concerned about all the time you are spending with him?"

Knowing Bunar is the problem and not Billy, "No worries honey. I will cut back on my time with Billy." Jack starts rubbing Colette's back, "You still have enough energy to help me blow off a little more steam?"

Colette smiles, "You are a lucky man Mr. Fitzpatrick because I do."

33
Friday at the office

"The business of America is business."
President Calvin Coolidge

Jack oversleeps. He has a big meeting Friday morning and hurries to get ready. Just before he leaves the house he looks in the closet to find the box where he keeps all their financial information. In the box is an account in Colette's name. He grabs the last statement and a box of unopened checks for the account and sprints out of the house without saying goodbye.

During the drive to the office, he checks his voicemail. He is confident there will be a message from Bunar, he just does not know how much money. "You have five new messages." Looking at this watch, *It isn't even nine a.m.*

First new message at 2:47 a.m., 'Fitzy, this is Bunar and it is time for you to pay up. I will be sending Stevey over to your office today at four to get the whole forty-nine grand you owe me. You know what will happen if you do not have the cash.' Jack deletes the message.

Second new message at 7:07 a.m., 'Jack this is Dennis in Accounting. When you get in please give me a call at ext. 252.' Unbelievably, he is no longer thinking of Bunar, he is now thinking about the Memorial contract he has in his briefcase. Jack deletes the message.

Third new message at 7:50 a.m., 'Fitzy, this is Billy. Thanks for coming out last night and I am sorry about the speech. Give me a call when you get a chance this morning.' Jack deletes the message.

Fourth new message at 8:23 a.m., 'Fitzy, this is Larry and I want to remind you we have the internal meeting with Dr. Alvarez at eleven this morning.' Jack deletes the message.

Fifth new message at 8:49 a.m., 'Fitzy, this Kevin and I want to make sure you are all set for our meetings in Reno next week. Please stop by my office when you get a chance.' Jack deletes the message. He hears, 'You have twenty-seven old messages, press one to listen.' He hangs up.

He is more focused on Dennis Hintz's voicemail versus the one from Bunar because Dennis never calls him. He wonders if Dennis found out he made a copy of the Memorial agreement. He is trying to figure out what he is going to say to Dennis. He sprints up to his office and closes the door. First he checks his e-mail. He has over 30 new e-mails. Even with CM's e-mail spam server the majority of the e-mails are junk and the rest can wait. Next, he checks his schedule, he has an extremely busy business day and needs to run personal errands. The Carson Alvarez meeting is at eleven, then his lunch to pay back his loan to Chip Savard, and the two o'clock meeting with the Reno Regional presentation team. He sends Chip an e-mail to see if they can meet half-way in Middleboro at Peirce's Chicken House at twelve-thirty.

Time to make the Dennis call. He takes a deep breath and fortunately gets Dennis's voicemail.

The next problem is Bunar and his goon, Stevey. Jack looks at his cell phone and the sent calls from last night. He writes down both of the numbers he tried to get off Billy's cell phone last night. He is not ready to talk to Bunar but he wants to find out which number is correct. He first hits *67 to block his caller ID. With the first number, he gets 'This number is no longer in service'. On the second number, 617-555-0025, it rings about five times before Jack hears a gruff, 'This is Rhonda, leave a message." Jack hangs up and obviously does not leave a message. *I know one of those two numbers is correct but I must have had more beers than I thought. Now to call Billy to see if he can help head off Stevey from coming to my office.*

Jack gets Billy on the first ring, "Billy it is me Fitzy, no worries about the speech last night. I deserved it. The reason for my call is your friend Bunar. The bastard left me a message this morning saying he is sending Stevey today to get all his money. I need you to call him and make the number as small as possible and to see if he takes checks."

"As I said last night, I will call him but no promises. How much money can you come up with today?"

"If he can take a check, I can get him ten grand today. If he needs cash it will take me until Monday and I will get him twenty grand."

"No promises but I will give him a call."

"Out of curiosity, is Bunar's girlfriend's name Rhonda."

Billy immediately responds, "How did you get Bunar's phone number?"

He could go with playing dumb but comes clean, "I got it off your cell phone last night. I called the number this morning and I when I heard you reached Rhonda, I thought I had the wrong number, but I thought maybe Bunar uses someone else's phone."

Billy shoots right back, "Bunar can see you called the number."

"No worries, I hit *67 before calling to block his Caller ID."

Billy sternly scolds him, "Throw the number away and do NOT call Bunar's cell phone number. There are a lot of people who would like to have the number, both the good guys and the bad guys. You would put yourself at risk if Bunar knew you had the number. He would send Stevey for a special visit and get another cell phone number. There is no Rhonda and the bill goes to someone who is not even on Bunar's payroll."

"Calm down, I will not call Bunar but I need you to call Bunar to see if he will take a check."

"I am disappointed you put our friendship at risk. I know you do not want another speech but look at yourself. I am still your friend and I will call Bunar but throw the number away."

"Okay, give me a call right after you talk to Bunar."

He hangs up and the heads down to Kevin's office.

Jack knocks on the door and walks in without waiting for a response. Dennis is in with Kevin. Kevin flips over the paperwork on his desk. Jack notices this but takes the high road, "Lucky for me, I just left you a voicemail Dennis, so now I can kill two birds with one stone. What is up guys?"

Neither one responds. Jack now expects to get kicked out of Kevin's office. Dennis and Kevin look at each other. Kevin responds, "Fitzy, just give us a second to finish up." Neither one says anything. They simply put the paper work into a folder on Kevin's desk.

Jack does not sit down. He uncomfortably stands as Dennis and Kevin pack up the paper work without talking. Kevin turns on the charm, "Fitzy, I want you to review your sales forecast and make sure you are all set for next week. Dennis just wants to make sure you are ready with the status on the Memorial deal."

Dennis weakly smiles, "Jack, do you have any questions on the Memorial account?"

"Nope, I am all set."

Kevin reiterates, "Fitzy, you are satisfied the accounting is in order for Memorial?"

"Yes."

Kevin sternly stares at the CFO, "So then Dennis, are we all set?" Dennis slowly nods his head up down to signal yes, without speaking to Kevin.

Kevin asks Dennis to leave so he and Jack can review the Memorial and Reno Regional accounts. Jack is surprised Kevin bullied Dennis in the meeting. He assumed Dennis as the CFO was the leader on the accounting fraud but now he is not sure.

Kevin starts asking Jack about the accounts. He is upfront that he believes they are losing both deals, stressing the presentations are huge this week. He invites Kevin to their Reno Regional internal pre-presentation meeting at two this afternoon. After twenty minutes of reviewing both deals, Kevin says "We need both of these deals this month."

Jack starts to feel Kevin is in on the accounting fraud. He refocuses, "Agreed", even though he knows the odds are against them. He heads back to his office.

When Jack gets in his office, he shuts the door, and the very first thing he does is reach into this briefcase and takes out the documents he took from home this morning. When Colette's dad passed away, his insurance policy left Colette over one hundred grand. They have used some of the money for the down-payment on their house, and they dip into it every now and then for stuff. There is $53,784.93 in the account. The account is in Colette's name but she never looks at the account because he handles all of their finances. He never thought he would steal from this account. Their plan is to use this for Harrison, and any future kids for their college education. It was also a little bit of a safety blanket if they needed cash. Lastly, emotionally, Colette likes to talk about how her dad helped them pay for their house and now is helping pay for the kid's college education.

Jack takes a deep breath and in his best Colette handwriting he writes a check to Chip Savard for $5,000. He stares at the check before putting it in his pocket. His plan is to pay the $5,000 right back with his commission checks hopefully from both the Reno Regional or Memorial deals.

Jack prepares for his eleven o'clock meeting with Dr. Carson Alvarez. Because Carson is a stickler, he needs to be prepared. Jack reviews the products he knows Memorial is using. He reviews his notes on their 'Purple Cow' strategy. He invites Kim Savard into his office to get her feedback before the meeting.

Kim walks in. "Hey, you didn't tell me you are having lunch with my husband."

Now he wonders if Chip told his wife about the five grand he borrowed or him asking about the FBI. Jack is putting Chip on the spot by borrowing five grand and asking Chip not to tell his wife.

"Yea we are meeting halfway in Middleboro. I am excited about the basketball game Sunday night and I figured we could strategize for the game. Also, with all the work on Reno Regional and Memorial, I can use a lunch with Chip. Do you have any messages for your hubby?"

"Nope." By Kim's casual manner, Jack figures Chip has not told his wife about the loan.

"Let's get to work and win this deal." They walk over to Carson's office together. Kim tells him she is a little nervous and she can be intimidated by Dr. Alvarez. He tells a story about his uncle, who was a janitor at a hospital where the doctor's wanted to be called, Dr. Smith verses their first name, his uncle would proudly tell them, 'Okay Dr. Smith but you have to call me Mr. Fitzpatrick.' Kim laughs, "I guess I will be 'Mrs. Savard' during this meeting."

Larry meets them in front of Carson's office. After the pleasantries, they get to business. When they play golf, Jack needs Carson to influence Memorial's doctor. They work on their 'Purple Cow' strategy for Memorial. The options:

Purple Cow:

- *Get their doctors names in article on technology*
- *Make Memorial a show site*
- *Make them a development partner*
- *Stress how they are a small company focused on Patient Safety*

Brown Cow:

- *Stress the ease of implementation because they are the incumbent vendor*
- *Stress the price advantages of CM*
- *Decision Support for doctors*
- *Ease of use for Nurses*

After they have the list, the three of them go back through the list:

- *Get doctors published in articles*
    - *Hard to actually do but easy to say. We should find a doctor with a big ego who likes technology and have CM's PR firm get his name in a couple of articles*
- *Make Memorial a show site*
    - *This is a possibility but it is a lot of work for Memorial to host site visits. Jack does not believe Howard Black will want to be a show site but Carson can ask Dr. Heins when they meet*
- *Make them a development partner*
    - *This is also a possibility and is less work than being a show site. Jack will ask Howard Black and Carson will ask Dr. Heins*
- *Stress how they are a small company focused on Patient Safety*
    - *In reality what healthcare company is going to say they are not focused on Patient Safety. Even though CM believes they are more focused on Patient Safety this is not different enough, so it is not a 'Purple Cow' strategy*
- *Stress the ease of implementation because they are the incumbent vendor*
    - *This is good too because MacroHealth does not have any applications at Memorial, so this is different*
- *Stress the price advantages of CM*
    - *Anyone can sell price, so they agree this is not a differentiator*
- *Decision Support for doctors*
    - *Like 'Patient Safety' MacroHealth says they are doing this too*
- *Ease of use for Nurses*

- *Carson, a doctor is not going to care if the product is easy for nurses.*

So they agree there is not one 'Purple Cow' strategy jumping out at them, so they decide to combine show site and development site and go with a two prong 'Brown Cow' strategy.

Looking at his watch, it is noon. Jack is going to be late for his lunch with Chip. He winks at Kim and tells Carson he is late for a lunch meeting sprinting out of Carson's office. On his way out he reminds Carson of the two p.m. meeting to review Memorial.

Jack calls Chip on his cell phone and tells him he will be about ten minutes late. Peirce's Chicken House is a hole in the wall right off the highway that has all you can eat chicken on Sundays. On Sunday nights you cannot get even get close to the place. Colette's mom loves to go there on Sundays, even with the long waits. Jack chose Pierce's because it is between his and Chip's offices and there usually is not a wait for lunch.

Parking in the dirt parking lot, he walks from the bright sunlight into the very dark Peirce's. Because there are only a couple of small windows to the outside world it takes a minute for his eyes to adjust to the lack of light. There is a faint smell of stale beer, most likely left over from last night. Jack sees Chip sitting at a table in the corner. *How appropriate to have a corner table in a seedy restaurant to go over my gambling problems.*

Jack and Chip shake hands and have small talk mostly about their Sunday night basketball team. Jack takes out of his wallet the check for five grand, "Here is a check for the five grand. I really appreciate you helping me out of a bind. Did you tell Kim about the money?"

"No way. This will put both of us at risk, me for loaning you five grand and you because she works for you." Chip sees it is signed by Colette. "Fitzy, this does not look like a woman's hand writing. If I had to guess, I would guess you wrote this check, which even a non-attorney knows is illegal."

Jack winks and smiles, "No worries, it is Colette's handwriting, just please do not ask her about the check the next time you see her."

"It is illegal for me to cash a check I know is a forgery."

"I did not tell you it is a forgery, so please go ahead and cash the check." Jack transitions to the FBI, "This check is the least of my problems. The reason I invited you here is I got a call from the FBI this week."

"Holy shit, what have you gotten yourself into?"

Jack tells Chip the whole story about Bunar, from the bets, to the slashed tire, to the early morning phone messages at the office, to the FBI calls and the $49,000 he owes. Chip does not a say a word. Chip's cell phone rang twice and each time Chip immediately muted the ringer.

Jack closes with, "The reason I came to you and no one else is the FBI scares me and you are the only attorney I know."

"Fitzy, I am a corporate attorney not a defense attorney, but I obviously know something about the law however not enough to help you. We have a couple of guys in my firm who are defense attorneys and familiar with racketeering law."

"So what do you recommend?"

"I recommend you get yourself a real defense attorney."

"Come on. I am up to my ass in debt and I got a bookie wanting his money. The last thing I need financially is lawyer bills."

"Fitzy, the last thing you need is to go to jail for illegal gambling."

"With all the internet gambling, why would the FBI care about my gambling?"

Chips talks quickly, "Because they are really after Bunar and they will use you to get to Bunar. Your next question should be why are they going after Bunar? What else does Bunar do besides taking illegal bets?" Jack shrugs his shoulders. Chip keeps talking, "Plus the State of Massachusetts wants to put in casinos like the ones in Connecticut and if they cannot control illegal gambling, how are they going to control legal gambling. The State is making a big push to take down the bookies in Boston and around the state."

"So again what do you recommend, besides me hiring a defense attorney and all his fees?"

"If you are not going to hire an attorney yourself, which I strongly recommend, I will talk to one of the guys at my firm. In the meantime do not call the FBI and do not call nor go near Bunar. If the FBI has something, they would have charged you. The FBI is obviously watching Bunar."

"Thanks man, you are a life saver this week. Can all of this fall under attorney client privileges? i.e., not telling your wife?"

"I am not sure why you want Kim to divorce me, but if she finds I have kept all of this from her, I am in wicked deep shit."

Jack looks at his watch and it is just after one-thirty. "No worries, I have not told Colette and I am definitely not going to tell Kim nor anyone at CM. Let me know what your lawyer friend says and I will stay away from Bunar and the FBI. Again, thanks for your help. I need to get back to the office."

Pushing open the heavy wood to head outside,, he is blinded by the sunlight after leaving the cave-like atmosphere of Pierce's Chicken House. His first call is to Kim to tell her his lunch with Chip ran over and to have her start the Reno Regional Pre-Presentation meeting without him because he will be fifteen minutes late. He then calls Billy to see if he spoke with Bunar. Stevey is supposed to come by the office at four today and he does not have any cash. Billy answers on the first ring, "Fitzy, I got some good news. Bunar was pissed but he will take $30,000 in cash on Monday. As usual, he is going to send Stevey over to your office on Monday afternoon."

Jack is about to say okay when he remembers he is flying to Reno on Monday. "Can I hand deliver the cash to Bunar on Monday around eleven at McCracken's? Be sure to tell Bunar I do not have time for lunch. Last time he was mad I did not stay for lunch."

"I do not see why Bunar would mind. Also, one other thing, after Bunar said he would take the thirty grand on Monday he said, 'I should teach Fitzy a lesson about delaying payment with me. The guy is always pushing back on paying me.' I immediately asked 'Are you going to hurt him?' Bunar laughed and said, 'I am not going to hurt him, and I probably will not do anything.'"

"So I am glad he is not going to hurt me and I hope he does not do anything."

"Pay him the thirty grand on Monday and the other nineteen grand as soon as you can and your problems will go away."

Laughing, "I wish it was easy for me to come up with fifty grand." Jack does not want to take the whole fifty grand from Colette but it looks like his only option.

Jack is not sure of the banking laws but he is pretty sure they will not just give you thirty grand in cash. He deposits $9,900 in his checking account, another $9,900 in his savings account, and withdraws $9,900 directly from Colette's account. Jack does not have time to make deposits on his checking and savings account now. He will have to run out right after the internal Reno Regional meeting.

Jack pulls into the CM parking lot at just after two and runs to the CM conference room where the Reno Regional meeting is being held. When he gets there the room is full, but they have not started the meeting. Kim is timidly trying to get everyone organized. When Kevin sees Jack, he claps, "Fitzy, we really appreciate you making your own meeting, especially for a deal that is so important to me."

Jack fires back, "So Kevin, did you tell everyone the good news that you will be going to the meeting. When I learned you were going, I figured you could run this meeting."

Because they are in front of other people in the company, Jack and Kevin watch how much they tease/push each other. Kevin keeps pushing, "This meeting is important for you and for CM, which is why I am going." Kevin gets in one more barb, "Fitzy, you are wasting valuable CM resources by having them sitting here waiting for your meeting to start."

"On that introduction, let's get rolling."

The first thing Jack does is get a roll-call of who is at the meeting, who is going to Reno Regional, and who is going to Reno but is not at the meeting.

Jack gets into the logistics. The two system engineers are flying out on Sunday to set up the room and the equipment on Monday. Because the presentation is so important, CM is sending all of their own equipment from servers to PCs to flat screens to projectors. The systems engineers confirm the equipment went out yesterday to make sure it would be there first thing Sunday morning.

The next step is to review the agenda and who is presenting what. They review the scripted demo. Jack first thanks the team for putting together the script in such short time. To fire up the team he says, "Betty tried to push us under the bus by not sending you the scripted demo. She totally underestimates you guys. With your hard work we are going to kick her ass." He wants to spend some time on the scripted demo because he is afraid it is set up to MacroHealth's strengths. The team talks about where they are strong in the scripted demo and where they are weak. They strategize on how to handle the weaknesses.

They discuss pushing the parts where they are weak to the end of the demo in the hopes they run out of time. They can even extend the parts where they are strong to increase the odds of not having enough time. Jack reminds them if Reno Regional makes them stay on schedule they will have to finish where they are weak and that is no way to end a scripted demo with the prospect remembering where CM is weak.

Jack reminds the team, "The audience will not remember most of what you said. They will remember how they felt."

The group agrees they will focus on where they are strong because they have a lot of strengths and minimize the weaknesses. The discussion is who will lead the presentation. The choices are Kim, Jack, or Kevin. Because Kim has never been on-site she is quickly dismissed as an option. The next options are Kevin as the executive vice president or Jack the regional vice president. The advantages of Kevin are he is a seasoned sales person on CM's senior management team. The weakness for Kevin is he is not as familiar with the account as Jack. The advantages for Jack are he knows the account having been on-site. They decide to have Jack lead the presentation with Kevin chiming in when appropriate.

The next discussion is how they are different from MacroHealth or the 'Purple Cow' strategy. Like earlier in the day, Kim gets up and starts writing on the board focusing on the CIO and doctor. At Reno Regional, CM believes the CFO first and then nursing will be the decision makers, so CM goes with:

- *Low Risk Implementation for CFO*
- *Smaller Company where Reno Regional can have an influence on the company*
- *Ease of use for the Nurses*

Jack closes with, "I am really excited about this deal. We are in second place but we can move to the front with a great presentation next week. And as always, do not correct anyone during the presentation. If someone says we make green cheese, keep your mouth shut and do not say anything. The reason is they will remember if someone gets corrected. They will most likely not remember we make green cheese. If needed, we can strategically follow up after the meeting to correct our error."

Looking at his watch, it is almost four o'clock. He is walking out when Kevin congratulates him on a successful meeting. Kevin asks Jack if can set up a meeting for him with Memorial while he is in Reno. He would invite Kevin to join them to play golf but they both agree five people are too many for a foursome. Kevin asks him if can set up a meeting with Memorial's CEO.

Then Kevin asks Jack if he wants to get together for a beer. He needs to get to the bank before having dinner with his wife tonight. He tells Kevin they can get a drink when they are in Reno.

Jack goes into his office and forges three more checks made out to him for $9,990. He heads out to withdraw on one check and deposit the two other checks before the banks close, so he can withdraw the money on Monday morning.

Jack's hands are sweating as he grabs the wheel. He strategically withdraws cash from Colette's account first before depositing the other checks. Chip has most likely not deposited his check. If he waits until Monday, the teller could see all of the withdrawals and question him. He looks at the check, double checking his forgery before going into the bank. It is not perfect but it is not too bad. He decides to go through the drive-thru in case there any problems so he can just drive away. It wouldn't take the bank more than two seconds to figure it out who it was but at least driving away is an option.

Jack puts the check in the pneumatic tube and sends it up and over to the bank. Over the scratchy intercom, 'Mr. Fitzpatrick this withdrawal will not fit in the tube system. You will need to come into the bank.' *Shit, what if this is a trap? But I have no choice, I need the cash*. Inside the bank, the teller is an attractive young woman in her early twenties, "That is a lot of money. You must of known we just increased our maximum withdrawal without prior notice from five thousand to one dollar under ten thousand."

Jack smiles and whispers, "We are doing an under the table construction job." He is not sure why he just told her.

She whispers back, "Be careful this is a lot of money. I have to use four different envelopes to put the cash in."

"Thank you," Jack puts the ten grand in an old gym bag in his trunk.

A new problem, what if either one of the next two banks has a policy of $5,000 for the maximum daily withdrawal. Next stop is his savings bank, which has a $10,000 maximum too and they say the money will be cleared by Monday morning. Jack and Colette's joint checking bank has a $5,000 maximum and can withdraw the cash on Monday morning. He deposits the $9,900. Now he will be $5,000 short for Bunar and hopefully Bunar will take a check. Chuckles to himself, *just another problem I will have to figure out by the time I meet Bunar on Monday.*

When Jack is done it is almost five o'clock. He is deciding if he should go home or go back to the office and try to get some more work done. Because he is leaving first thing Monday morning, he goes into the office. Back in the office his first call is to Howard Black, three hours behind in the pacific time zone, to see if can set up a meeting for Kevin Blair. Jack tells Howard one of CM's senior managers is in Reno next week and available to meet with Memorial's CEO. Howard teases him because Kevin's real reason for coming to Reno is to see Reno Regional. Jack reminds Howard that Kevin could easily have flown out a day later versus seeing Memorial. Howard states, "I cannot promise anything but I will try to set up the meeting."

Jack checks his e-mail. He is going through his e-mail when his phone rings, from the caller ID he can tell Colette is calling from home, "Honey, how are you doing?"

Colette is fuming, "My tire is flat and our car has been keyed. Also, I am pretty sure the tire was slashed."

"Back up, what is going on?"

"I was going to run some errands before our date tonight, when I noticed my car had a flat tire. I figured no big deal. I simply ran over a nail or something, but I took a closer look at the tire I could see a cut in the side and there are key marks up and down one side of the car."

Jack interrupts, "When I get home I will change the tire and check it out. Are you sure it is slashed?"

"Yes and I am pissed. We live in a great neighborhood. I cannot believe some high school punk would slash my tire and key the car in the middle of the day."

Suddenly, Jack understands Bunar slashed, or most likely his goon Stevey, slashed the tire, *Son of a bitch.*

"What was that?"

"Nothing, go on."

Colette keeps rambling about the tire. Jack recognizes this is another message. One asking for an extra day, and the second is he better pay the thirty grand on Monday. He is just glad Colette thinks it was a neighborhood kid. Half listening Colette asks his, "Should I call the police?"

"What? No way, what are the police going to do?"

"I do not know but they may have an idea who did it. Maybe there is a rash of these in the neighborhood? The police should know."

Jack does not want Colette calling the police. "I know it is hard but let's just forgot about it. It is just some high school prank."

Colette goes on another tirade about high school punks. Jack tries to change the subject by asking, "Did you get the baby sitter lined up tonight?"

"Yes, I got Madison across the street, but I am not sure if I want to leave Harrison and the baby sitter home tonight with a tire slasher running around the neighborhood."

"They will be fine, plus Madison's parents live right across the street. I will get out of the office here in the next hour and we will be out the door for dinner by seven. We can take my car tonight and I will fix the tire tomorrow morning."

He can only imagine what Colette would think if she knew Bunar and his goon slashed the tire.

Jack gets back to printing out information for his meetings next week in Reno. Looking at his watch, he is not even close to being done so he will have to come into the office over the weekend. Jack makes one call to Kim Savard's cell phone. He leaves a voicemail, "Kim this is Jack. I need you to handle all the logistics at Reno Regional on Monday. Please go to Reno Regional as soon as you land on Monday. I will have my cell phone all weekend, so please call me if you have any questions. Have a great weekend."

Jack sprints home to Colette. Even with living so close to the office, he will still be late. He makes two more calls on his ride home. The first is to Colette to tell her he will be late. The second is to Michelle to confirm their dinner on Monday night. Jack is happy to get Michelle's voicemail because he really did not want to talk to her.

When Jack pulls in the driveway he sees the flat tire. Looking at the tire and the keyed car, *Obviously Bunar*.

34

Dinner with Colette

"Love is an irresistible desire to be irresistibly desired." Robert Frost

By the time Jack and Colette leave the house it is after seven-thirty. They decide to go to dinner at Stars on Hingham Harbor, a beautiful restaurant, not too expensive and not too far away. It is a little chilly so Jack has Colette bring her jacket so they can eat outside on the patio overlooking the picturesque harbor.

Jack and Colette have a great dinner. They talk about Harrison, Colette's volunteer activities, and the neighbors. He is glad they are not talking about the slashed tire and he is avoiding talking about work. Being pro-active, he tells Colette he is planning on playing golf in the morning, basketball Sunday night, and in between all this, he needs to go into the office for a few hours to get work done before he flies to Reno. Colette pouts a little but they decide to do something as a family on Saturday afternoon.

Jack's cell phone rings and it is Kim Savard. Colette asks if it is the babysitter but Jack tells her the call is from Kim. He is not planning on answering the phone, when Colette says go ahead and answer it. Kim quickly explains she just got the message and she wants to make sure they are all set for the meetings next week.

Colette only hears Jack's half of the conversation. "Right, I will not be going to the hospital on Monday. I am planning on getting to the hospital around six a.m. on Tuesday."

Jack wraps up the call with Kim. "Why are you flying out early on Monday if you are not going to the hospital on Monday. Can't you fly out late on Monday?"

This is a slippery slope because he has to drop off the cash for Bunar and is having dinner with Michelle. He goes with a partial truth, "I am having Dinner with Reno Regional Monday night, and as you know it is not easy to get to Reno from Boston."

"No, I do not know how hard it is to get to Reno because I have never been."

"Come on, you know I have to catch a connecting flight and Reno is on the other side of the country." *This nice dinner is taking a turn for the worse, I need to get off this subject and soon,* "Let's not worry about next week and enjoy tonight."

"You better not be going early just to gamble."

He laughs out loud, "I promise I am not going out early to gamble. If I could fly out later I would."

"While we are on the subject of gambling, how much are you planning on losing when you are in Nevada?"

"As you know I never plan on losing. Plus, I just won on my last trip." Jack was going to say the amount but he cannot remember how much he told Colette he won.

"Seeing as you won last time you are due to lose, how about if you do not gamble at all."

"Come on, how about just a little bit of gambling."

"Then let me pick the number. How about fifty dollars?"

Laughing, "Honey you have been very funny this evening."

"Okay one hundred dollars. You have been all over me about watching what I am spending."

Unless Jack starts winning right off the bat like the last time, he will definitely spend, or as he likes to say invest, more in gambling. "I will do my best." He switches the conversation to Harrison, so they can enjoy the rest of their evening. After dinner they decide to walk around Hingham. It is a very romantic evening with the moon shining on the harbor and the boats in the harbor. They walk down one of the many docks holding hands and enjoying the boats. There are so many boats, from sailboats to fishing boats to party boats to yachts. They joke about buying a boat one day. Finally, they decide it is time to walk back to the car, so they can get home and relieve the baby sitter as it is getting late.

On the way back to the car, they pass a standalone ATM and Colette says, "Hold on, I need to get some money." Their balance will be over $10,000 in their joint checking account if the check has cleared.

"Wait, this one is not our bank, I will get you money after golf in the morning."

"Golfing is why I want to use this one. When you are playing, I want to go run some errands."

"Let's stop at our bank on our way home, so we do not have the ATM fee."

"Jack, I know we are watching our money but when do you care about a two dollar ATM fee, Mr. Las Vegas." Colette continues to walk over the ATM machine. Jack starts to panic.

Do I tell her I just got a big commission check. No way. He always tells Colette when he gets a big check. As they are walking to the ATM, he takes out his ATM card to their joint account and says with an English accent, "How much money do want Madame?"

"Fifty Dollars, sir." Colette is having a great time so she does not question his behavior.

Jack gets the fifty dollars out of the ATM. He quickly looks at the balance, $11,027.05, he crumbles up the receipt and throws it away.

"Hey, what is our balance?" She starts walking towards the trash bin to grab the receipt.

Jack does not break stride and starts walking towards the car. At the same time he is trying to very quick subtract $9,900 from the balance. He says, "About $1,200. I get paid next Friday so we should be covered." He slowly turns around to see if Colette is going through the trash. He is relieved, when he sees her walking towards him.

They get home to find the baby sitter watching TV with Harrison asleep in his room. Jack walks the baby sitter home. Then he and Colette finish up a romantic evening in the bedroom. Falling asleep, Jack grins because he also need a romantic evening with Colette, plus he gets to play golf tomorrow.

35

Sunday at the office

"Computers are useless. They can only give you answers." Pablo Picasso

On Sunday morning Jack does some chores, feeling guilty about going out of town again tomorrow and playing basketball tonight. He is slowly trying to get caught up on his never-ending 'Honey Do List'. He takes Harrison with him to Home Depot and then lunch at McDonald's. He wants to spend some one on one time with Harrison and to give Colette a little break.

After mowing the yard and fixing a broken door upstairs, Jack heads into the office. He needs to get ready for next week by printing out contracts, proposals, handouts, sign-up sheets, make marketing CDs, etc. for both Memorial and Reno Regional. While printing, he thinks about the accounting irregularities at Memorial. He wonders how widespread the fraud is and if there are any other clients besides Memorial. He sneaks into Kevin's office.

Kevin keeps his office unlocked. Jack looks around and there is no one in the office. Kevin's office is right down the hall from his office. Even with no one around, Jack casually walks down the hallway and slips into Kevin's office. He is not surprised to find Kevin's desk and file cabinet are locked. "No wonder he does not lock his door."

He boots up Kevin's computer. At CM not only do they have user name and passwords for security, they also have security by PC. So not only can CM tell if he logs in as Kevin in his office, CM can also block what a user sees on their office PC. Jack knows this because as a VP he has access to some sales report he can only read at his desk.

Jack knows Kevin's password. About six months ago, Kevin was on the road traveling and needed some information in CM's account software. Kevin had him go into his office and log in as him. Jack wrote down Kevin's password for future reference. The password is 'Belize6'. Kevin likes to Scuba dive and went on a trip to Belize a couple of years ago. He types in kblair for the user name and 'Belize6' for the password. The computer responds 'Incorrect Password, Please Enter Again'.

"Shit, what would he change the password to after he gave it to me?" CM has employees change their password every three months, so Jack tries 'Belize7'. The computer says, 'Incorrect Password, you have one more attempt before the computer shuts down.' He now has a decision to make because if he is wrong again, not only will he be unable to log in but this will be on the user administration error log for CM information services department.

Jack is about to head back to his office and not risk alerting Kevin someone tried to log into his computer. Doing the math, if the password was Belize6 six months ago, then the current password is either Belize8 or Belize9. He is trying to think exactly when they had the conversation but he cannot remember so he takes a risk and goes with 'Belize9'. He hits enter, and waits for the response. The screen goes black. He catches his breath then the screen comes back blue as he logs in as Kevin.

Now online, the next decision is where to go and what to look for. Jack brings up both the accounting and CRM software. He runs some reports but they all look normal to him. In reality, he found Memorial accidently.

Jack closes down both applications because this is like looking for a needle in a haystack when you are not sure what the needle looks like. He starts searching for documents on Kevin's computer. He searches on deals, contracts, accounting, revenue, bookings, and even Memorial. All the searches come up empty. He laughs and tries fraud, illegal and corrupt. These also lead nowhere. He is about to give up when he searches by date. He searches all files by typing *.* in the search box, which brings up every single file on Kevin's PC. He sorts the list by date. Hoping if Kevin has a file of the illegal transaction on his PC, he has done it recently. All the files look normal when he sees an excel spreadsheet titled, 'short'.

Jack double clicks on the spreadsheet. Across the top of the spreadsheet are the following columns Client Mnemonic, Product, Date, Amount, State and a bunch of other fields. Scrolling down the client mnemonics, there is MEMN for Memorial Nevada and across is the phantom patient portal deal. He then brings back up the accounting software. He sees KENG for Kennesaw Medical Center in Georgia. Because Jack went to school in Kennesaw, he keeps tabs on this client though they are not in his territory. The spreadsheet shows KENG has recently purchased a pharmacy and radiology system. He knows they only have CM's financial software. He checks the accounting software and it also says they have

Pharmacy and Radiology. He brings up the CRM system which confirms they only own CM's financial software.

Scrolling down to the bottom of the spreadsheets, he sees the total is over $40M. It definitely looks like CM has illegally booked a bunch of deals to make their numbers for Wall Street. Printing out the long spreadsheet, he luckily looks out Kevin's window to see Kevin walking into the building. Shutting down Kevin's computer, there is no way he is going to get out of Kevin's office before the printer stops. Jack's only hope is Kevin stops somewhere else before coming up to his office. He gets all the applications closed and hits the shut off button. He peeks out Kevin's door as he is coming down the hallway. Looking around, the only place to hide is in the closet. Jack starts towards the closet when he realizes the printout is on the printer on the other side of the office. He sprints to the printer, grabs the spreadsheet, and sprints in to the closet.

Just as Kevin is walking in his office, Jack shuts himself in the coat closet and the door clicks shut. He waits as he hears Kevin say to himself, "I thought I shut the lights off."

36

Kevin in the office

"Knowledge of the world is only to be acquired in the world, and not in a closet."
Lord Chesterfield

Kevin thinks, *'I guess the cleaning people left the lights on when they vacuumed over the weekend.'* Kevin turns on his computer and calls Jack's office on speaker phone, "Fitzy this is Kevin, it is Sunday and I see your car in the parking lot but you are not in your office. Give me a call, so we can talk about next week." Kevin then calls Jack's cell phone.

Suddenly Jack's phone is ringing in the closet. He shuts it off after half a ring.

Kevin thought he heard a phone but it stopped. When Kevin gets Jack's cell phone voicemail, "Fitzy it is Kevin again, where the hell are you?"

Kevin says to himself, "This is kind of weird." Kevin gets up and closes his door. Kevin checks his voicemail on speaker phone, he has one new voicemail from Dennis Hintz. "Kevin this is Dennis, I am getting really concerned about the numbers, please give me a call over the weekend on my cell phone."

"Hey Dennis this is Kevin, what the hell are you doing?" Kevin does not wait for a response. "I was doing okay until I got your voicemail. What the hell are you concerned about?"

With Dennis on speaker phone, Jack can hear him timidly respond, "I am getting really concerned about these numbers. Jack Fitzpatrick found the accounting changes. As we fake more sales, more people are going to find out. I was thinking we need to come clean and announce we have some accounting irregularities and to take a onetime charge against this quarter's numbers."

"You are shitting me right."

"Well, no."

Kevin asks a rhetorical question, "Do you remember our meeting last June?"

Even though Kevin wasn't looking a response, Dennis mocks him, "Yes I remember, when you were two million short in sales and you asked me to book forged contracts."

Kevin is pissed and shouts, "That's right and we are BOTH now forty million short, so BOTH of us are in this together."

To get off the past, Dennis timidly said, "When do you think they will sign?" Kevin committed to them signing last July. Dennis and Kevin put together a sophisticated plan to cover up their numbers for a month. The problem has been that Kevin is continually short on his sales numbers and Dennis keeps having to create false accounting records.

They are cooking the books by Kevin and Dennis forging fake contracts. Dennis would put the deal in sixty day receivables until Kevin signs the actual deal. As they got more aggressive, Kevin kept forging more deals, so Dennis has to get creative with managing receivables and until the client would pay their real bills he would credit part of the payments towards the phantom deals. The only negative for the stock market is longer receivables but it is not affecting the stock price because the market has been looking for top line sales and bottom line profits. With time and more fake deals, they now have over forty million in fake deals and Dennis is having trouble managing the accounts.

Dennis answers Kevin's rhetorical conversation. "I cannot keep up with it, we need to come clean."

Kevin stops Dennis, "You know who gets fired when we announce accounting problems?" Kevin does not wait for a response. "Right, you get fired first. They fire me next because I am not making enough sales. Then the feds step in and all of us, including you, could go to jail. And worst of all our stock goes in the toilet and all your shares and options go right down the toilet. So are you still sure you want to announce the account problems?"

"Well, if we don't do something soon we are going to get caught and we will still go to jail. If we come clean now, we may only get fired and not have to go to jail."

Kevin gets friendlier, "I am working hard on wining deals, so we don't have to get fired nor go to fail. We are only off by a manageable forty million. I am going to Reno this week and both deals are worth a total of forty million. We get these two deals and we are off the hook."

"Kevin, it is not that simple and you know it."

"You were able to put forty million in phantom deals in our financial numbers, I always assumed you had a plan to put the forty million back."

"I do, but it is just not that simple. How about we announce a forty million write-off?"

"For a CFO, you need help on the stock market. There is no way we can have a non-forecasted write off and not have the stock go in the toilet. I will get you an additional forty million in deals this month; you need to figure out how to work those into our sales numbers so we do not get caught."

"What about Fitzy?"

"What about Fitzy? He is all set. We gave him a great explanation and he bought it. He is not that bright, plus he believes everything I tell him. If someone else finds out, we will handle them too."

"What if you do not close the additional forty million in deals?"

"I will get both of the deals and the forty million. If we do not, you need to keep the charade up until I book enough deals to make up the short-fall in accounting. Remember, you were just granted another 100,000 in options, so stay focused on keeping the numbers working for the stock market. You and I are making a lot of money in the market and we just need to keep our eye on the ball. I need to get going. I have got a bunch of work to do before I fly out to Reno on Monday. Have a great weekend, and I do not want to have any more calls like this."

Kevin goes to work on research for both accounts and the hospitals in the Reno area. Kevin wants to understand the financial make-up of both hospitals. He wants to know what departments are making money and which departments are losing money. He also wants to understand the competitive nature of Reno and what services the hospitals promote, because he needs the deals even more than Fitzy.

37

In Kevin's Closet

"I like to listen. I have learned a great deal from listening carefully. Most people never listen."
Ernest Hemingway

In Kevin's closet he hears the whole conversation, even about him not being that smart. Jack has more proof of CM's fraud, the Memorial forgery, the hard copy of the phantom deals in his hands and the conversation he just heard. *Now what to do? First get out of the closet.* He is getting more uncomfortable and needs to come up with a reason why he is not in his office.

Jack cannot see his Tag watch, so he very quietly kneels down on all fours and puts his wrist at the bottom of the door. He can see it is five-thirty. He has to leave by six-thirty to make his basketball game. With everything going on, he is worried about not making his basketball game. He is also wondering when Kevin is going to head home. Jack is even more uncomfortable down on all fours so he quietly stands back up. As he is standing up he knocks off a coat hanger. He tries to catch the coat hanger but not before it hits the door. He freezes and listens to see if he can hear Kevin standing up and coming over to the closet. All he hears is Kevin typing at the keyboard. He is sweating from the lack of air in the closet and the pressure of hiding.

Jack is not sure how much time has passed since he knelt down to check his watch. He is tempted to try again but does not want to risk making another noise. Hearing Kevin getting up from behind his desk, he tenses waiting to see if Kevin opens the closet door. He hears a door open and, for a split second, *Shit*, Kevin is coming into the closet. He is relieved when he hears Kevin leaving his office. He waits a minute then cracks open the closet door. There is no one in the office. He sprints to the office door peeking outside. No one is in the hallway, so Jack casually walks towards his office.

Five steps from his office Jack hears, "Fitzy." He turns around to see Kevin walking down the hallway towards him. His first thought is Kevin saw him coming out of this office. Kevin is smiling, so he assumes he did not get caught sneaking out of Kevin's office. Now he needs an excuse where he has been. He spent an hour in the closet and never came up with the excuse. Maybe he will get lucky and Kevin will not ask him where he has been.

Nope, he is not that lucky, when Kevin's first question is, "Fitzy, where the hell have you been? I stopped by your office and I even called your cell phone but I could not find you."

Jack is holding the list of accounts CM and Kevin illegally booked in his hand. *Think Think Think,* the best he can come up with is, "I was hungry and I went down to get a candy bar from the vending machine and I got stuck reading Friday's newspaper." Jack quickly changes the subject by asking a question. "Are you ready for our Reno trip next week?"

"Fitzy, I do not need you to remind me how important both of these deals are to you, CM, and me."

No shit, you need both of these deals to get you out of the hole you have been illegally digging, but he says, "Both of them are going to be dog fights."

"Let's go to your office for a few minutes and strategize on the deals. Hey what is the paper in your hand?"

Jack pauses, "Nothing." Kevin stares at the paper as they walk to Jack's office together. When Jack gets to his office, *I need to get rid of this paper,* he folds up the pages and throw them in his waste basket. The waste paper basket is near his door and right behind where Kevin is standing. Kevin ignores the garbage and drills him on both Reno Regional and Memorial.

They review both deals individually. Following Miller-Heiman sales strategy, Kevin hammers him on their pitch to the decision makers, coaches, user buyers, gatekeepers, and snipers. Kevin gives his feedback and his goals to get to the decision makers at both hospitals. Looking at this watch, it is quarter of seven. "Hey, I do not mean to push you out the door but I got a basketball game at seven in Canton and I need to get going."

"Okay, but you know you are going to be late. Are you playing with the gigantic guy you introduced me to last week?"

Jack is taken back, "Ah Nope, I decided not to play on the big guy's team. And Yes, I know I am going to be late."

"Let's get going and I will walk you out."

Jack stares at the crumpled up papers in the wastepaper basket. He is really running late and is not going to grab them in front of Kevin. Jack wonders if the house-cleaning staff comes in on Sunday nights to pick up the trash. He will stop back at the office on his way home from basketball.

Getting in his car, he calls Chip Savard to let him know he will be late for the game. "Great, you not playing means I will finally get a chance to shoot the rock." Jack laughs, then calls Colette to update her on his schedule. Colette asks him if he can come right home after basketball versus going out for beers. "Great idea, I only have to make one stop back at the office before heading home."

"Jack Fitzpatrick 'One Stop' better not be a code word for having beers with your buddies. You have been at the office all afternoon. What were you doing at the office?"

Jack fakes a laugh, "No worries honey, I am not going out for beers afterwards and I only have a couple of quick things to get done at the office before heading home." He obviously does not tell her he spent an hour in Kevin's closet.

It is quarter past seven by the time Jack parks the car and gets into the gym. His team is down ten points and Chip immediately tells him, "Thanks for showing up. Now get your ass in the game."

"Sorry man, but I need at least five minutes to stretch out. I am not as young as I used to be. If I get hurt I won't be much help to anyone."

"Make it quick and be careful Mrs. Fitzpatrick. Don't hurt yourself stretching out." Jack gives Chip the finger.

With his team already down 15 points, Jack enters the game. He misses every shot he takes and at half time, the team is down 18 points.

Chip tries to pump up the team. "Come on guys, we are better, we just need to play better. And you Fitzy, how about you practice your jump shot for the second half." As they get ready to start the second half Chip whispers, "Fitzy, use some of your gambling and FBI energy to light these guys up."

Jack is livid but winks. "I am going to drop thirty points on these guys in the second half." Immediately he is in the zone. As soon as he touches the ball he fires up a three pointer, all net. Jack is all over the court. His team ends up winning by ten points. After the game, "Fitzy, you were fired up the whole second half. The first beer is on me."

Jack is pumped. The game is just what he needed. He would really love a beer, but he promised Colette he would come home and he needs to get the list out of his wastebasket at the office, "Sorry man but I will be out of town all next week with your wife, and I need to stop by the office."

"One beer, it will take just fifteen minutes. We can talk about the steal and three pointer you made during the game."

"No dice but I will take a rain check."

"Well, Kim said she was going to stop by the office tonight, so should I start getting concerned you are spending tonight and all next with my wife."

Jack grabs his sweaty shirt, "Unless your wife has a thing for sweaty smelly basketball players you should be okay."

Chip laughs and grabs his sweaty shirt "I actually hope she does. Well I am going to get a beer with the rest of the team. If you see my wife, tell her I will be home by eleven."

"Deal." Driving into the parking lot he sees Kim's car. *Nothing is ever easy.* He has to walk by Kim's cube on the way to his office. Kim has a stack of hand-outs on the floor around her desk.

She is startled. "Fitzy you scared me, I thought you would go out for beers with Chip after the game."

"I would of liked to, but I needed to get one quick thing done at the office for our meetings tomorrow."

"Hey, did you guys win?"

"Yup and your husband played great. You, Colette, and Harrison need to come to one of our games."

"Really, I did not know wives were allowed in the gym?"

Laughing, "I will talk to Colette about it and we can all go out for dinner after." Jack asks, "Are you all set for this week?"

"I am nervous that I am forgetting something but I should be all set."

"You will do great. Use your nervousness to make sure you have covered all your bases. With Kevin coming to the presentation, this will give you a chance to shine."

"Thanks Fitzy, but you and I both know Kevin will do all the talking."

"True, but you will get some one-on-one time with Kevin. He will be impressed with all of the prep work you have done."

He goes into his office and grabs the papers out of the trash, makes two more copies, knowing he is building a strong case against CM. By the time he gets home and takes a shower it is almost midnight. He has a nice conversation with Colette about the upcoming week before he goes to bed. Drifting off to sleep he imagines tomorrow's meeting with Bunar, and pushing back on the SOB for slashing his wife's tires.

38

Banks and Bunar

"A bank is a place that will lend you money if you can prove you don't need it." Bob Hope

Jack gets up early on Monday to run. During the jog, he mentally reviews his strategy and puts his plan for Bunar, *today is going to be a very long day and you need to be on your A game.* Seeing as he is five thousand short and is heading out of town, he simply is going to offer Bunar a check made out to 'Cash' for the five thousand. Bunar can figure out how to cash the check.

Even after paying Bunar thirty thousand today, he will still owe Bunar nineteen thousand but is thinking about betting the usual three games with Bunar for twenty thousand a game. Billy recommends paying off his debts and to stop betting. *Screw Billy,* he goes back to thinking about betting twenty grand per game. If he could win all three games he would win sixty grand minus the nineteen he owes Bunar, he could put the thirty-five grand back in Colette's account and still be six thousand up, finishing up his run, he decides to go with the three bets at twenty grand a piece.

Jack showers, packs, says good bye to Colette and Harrison, then drives to the banks. First stop is his joint checking account with Colette to see if they will give him ten grand versus the five grand daily withdrawal policy. The bank says he can only withdraw five grand today and can come back tomorrow to get the additional five grand. At the second bank and has no problems getting the ten grand. He puts all of the money in a gym bag in his trunk and drives to McCracken's to meet with Bunar.

It is almost eleven when Jack gets to McCracken's. His flight is at one and with access to the Ted Williams tunnel in South Boston, he is only ten minutes from Logan International Airport. This early in the day, there is a spot right in front of McCracken's. *Being right out in front of McCracken's, hopefully Stevey will not slash my tire again.*

After his eyes adjust to the lack of light, he sees there are only three people in the bar. Bunar at his usual table with Stevey and the sexy dark haired bartender behind the bar cleaning up. Nodding to the bartender, he walks back to Bunar's table. Surprisingly, he is not nervous, but is angry, because every time he has short paid, Bunar does something to him. He is relying on Bunar to take the five grand check. If not, Jack has to push back hard, so he knows his family will be safe.

"Fitzy, I am glad you made it. I was afraid I was going to have to send Stevey back to Bridgewater for another visit."

Thinking about the slashed tire. "Let's get this over with." He slides the gym bag over to Bunar. "There is twenty five grand in the bag and as a bonus you can keep the bag."

Bunar makes a note in his iPhone shaking his head. "Fitzy, Fitzy, Fitzy why do you consistently short pay me?"

Jack interrupts, "Bunar, I got a check right here for five grand. Just let me know who I can make it out to, or I can leave it blank, or I can make it out to cash."

Bunar shakes his head again, "Fitzy, Fitzy, Fitzy, does Stevey look like a damn bank teller?" Jack does not move or say anything. Bunar answers for him, "No he does not." Stevey lets out a big laugh and Jack still does not move. Bunar stops smiling, "Because we are not a bank, I only take cash."

Jack firmly pushes back, "That is not my problem. I have the five grand right here in a check." Stevey backs his chair up.

Bunar puts his hand on Stevey's forearm, "That is your problem. I told you thirty grand cash today and because you cannot follow simple directions it is your problem."

"Looks like we both have a problem. So what do you propose?"

"You bring me ten grand in cash, tomorrow."

For obvious reasons, Jack has not told Bunar he is going out of town. Because he wants Bunar to take another sixty grand in bets, even though he is furious, he puts on the sales charm, "Bunar, in the past two weeks, I have paid you over thirty grand in cash. Based on the amount of money I am paying, I figured you would be asking me to make more bets versus asking for more money."

Bunar purposely pauses with a nasty stare, then breaks the silence with a smirk. "So do you want to make some more bets?"

Jack believes Bunar just walked into his trap on taking more bets. He does not want to move too quickly plus he needs to make sure Stevey does not come to his office or house while he is out of town. Jack asks, "What about the five grand?"

"You are not that smart Fitzy. I know you want to make more bets. You think you are smarter than the dockworker who is betting one hundred a game versus ten thousand a game? All you guys are the same, win or lose you just want to bet until it hurts. So, how much and how many games?"

Jack continues to press, "Before we get into more bets, seeing as you are not going to accept my check, what do you want do about the five grand besides me paying you ten grand tomorrow?"

Bunar does not answer and asks a question. "Before I can answer your question, I need to know how much and how many games you want to bet?"

Jack compliments Bunar. "You would make a great salesman. Instead of answering my question you ask another question. Looks like we have a situation where neither guy wants to go first. Well seeing you are the one holding all the cards, I will tell you what I want to bet, but it is contingent on what you want to do with the five grand. I want to bet twenty grand a game on three games."

Bunar asks another question, "So you want to make your usual bet for twenty grand?"

"Yes, based on how you want to handle the five grand?"

Bunar keeps asking the questions, "So how do you recommend I handle the five grand you owe me?" Bunar looks at his iPhone, "Even with you just paying me twenty-five G's, in reality you still owe me twenty-four grand."

"Easy, if I were you, I would take the twenty-five grand in cash, float me the other twenty four grand another week and take the sixty K in bets."

Bunar laughs, "You are persuasive, Fitzy."

Jack can no longer hold back on Bunar slashing Colette's tire, "While I am being persuasive, if you decide to take my recommendation, I also do not need any more messages. I know you slashed my wife's tire on Friday."

Bunar gets serious again, "I do not know what you are talking about," then he pauses, for what seems like an eternity, before continuing, "and I will send you messages when you need them."

Because he is going out of town and believing Bunar wants the bets. He replies, "If you want my sixty grand in bets, I need you to promise no more visits from Stevey."

Stevey growls, "I will visit you any time I want, Fitzy."

Jack says to Bunar, "Please, have your lap dog sit down."

Stevey pushes the table into Jack's gut. Jack looks at Bunar, not saying anything. He is holding the table back with his two hands, waiting for Bunar to intervene. Bunar says nothing. Stevey stands up and walks over to Jack's side of the table, "What did you say, Fitzy?"

Jack likes to talk smack on the basketball court and every now and then someone wants to fight him, but he always has his team around him. He has no one with him and made an error thinking Bunar would calm Stevey down. Stevey would easily kick his ass. Jack smiles, "I said Stevey please sit down but if you want to stand up you are more than welcome to stand up."

In a dumb voice, "What if I want to sit on you?"

Jack keeps fake smiling, "You can sit anywhere you want, but I would prefer if you did not sit on me."

Stevey looks at Bunar, "Boss, can I hit him?"

"Not just yet, but why don't you have a seat next to Fitzy, just in case he says something stupid again."

Jack is irate. He was just physically bullied by Stevey and mentally bullied by Bunar, "That's it. My bets are off, I will figure out a way to get you your ten grand by tomorrow evening."

"Fitzy, why do you have to ruin our great conversation by leaving?"

"Because this is bullshit, I have paid over thirty grand to you and you are treating me like dog shit."

Bunar stays cool, "Jack, when you short pay me, whether it is five grand or fifty bucks, you are going to suffer the consequences for your actions."

Now Jack stand ups. "Fine, you will get your ten grand tomorrow."

"Fitzy, please sit down, and we can talk about your sixty grand in bets."

Jack is shaking he is so mad. *Come on man, pull it together, this is just like a tough contract negotiation and you need to keep your cool.* Jack keeps standing. A Stevey visit while he is out of town is a deal killer. "Before I make any more bets. I need your word, no more visits from Stevey." Slowly calming down, he gets his swagger back, winks at Stevey, "No Offense."

"I promise Stevey will not visit your family while you are out of town this week."

Jack turns white. *How does Bunar know I am going out of town?* He tries to hide his surprise but blurts out, "How do you know I am going out of town this week?"

Bunar had talked to Billy yesterday but he keeps this information to himself. "When someone owes me fifty grand, I know if they are going out of town."

"It is only forty-nine grand and how did you know?"

Bunar changes the subject by asking another question, "Now, Stevey is not going to Bridgewater this week. How about those bets?"

Jack may be a million dollar sales person but he does not have the street smarts and experience of Bunar. Bunar is right. After making sure Stevey does not visit Colette, he really does want to make the bets. The NBA playoffs are now in the third round. Jack makes the bets and takes the Celtics versus the Hawks on Tuesday, the Lakers versus Utah Jazz on Wednesday, and the Chicago Bulls versus Orlando Magic on Thursday.

"Now that we have successfully concluded our business, please sit down and have some lunch."

"As you know I have to head to Reno. I will take a rain check."

Jack starts walking out when Bunar slaps the table, "You owe me two lunches and don't lose all my money in Reno."

Jack takes a long deep breath as he gets in his car to go to the airport, *If I can just win these three bets all of my problems will go away.* He is not a half-mile from McCracken's when his cell phone rings, "Mr. Fitzpatrick, this is Agent Tim Stephenson with the FBI, and I am curious why you left your duffle bag inside of McCracken's?"

Before he drives off the road, Jack pulls off to the side. The FBI is watching McCracken's and Bunar, "Agent Stephenson, how are you doing?" Jack adds a little humor, "I am surprised you did not come in and join us for lunch." Gathering himself as he is thinking about what Chip said, do not to talk to this guy, but Jack is still foaming by the way Bunar treated him a few minutes ago.

"I was kind of busy. I was very surprised to see you, and from my view you could of either dropped off a bag of cash or a bag of drugs. For your sake, I hope it was money."

"You forgot about option three. I was dropping off my laundry."

"The last time I checked, Bunar was not running a dry cleaner."

"My understanding is McCracken's is looking to add another revenue stream to its restaurant by adding dry cleaning."

Agent Stephenson ignores Jack's attempt at humor. "I will come down to your office this afternoon to get together."

At least the FBI does not know I am flying out today. Changing his mind, it is probably good idea for the FBI to know he is out of town, "I would love to meet you today, but I am on my way to Logan to catch a flight."

"Great I am going that way."

Shit, "I have a 2p.m. flight and last time I checked, if you do not have a ticket, you cannot get into the gate. We can talk when I get back."

"When do you get back?"

"I get back on Friday. Have a great day." Jack hangs ups to end the conversation.

Jack gets to the airport and to his gate with no problem. He is on the cell phone with Colette when a geekish looking guy in an ill-fitting suit and glasses with no luggage sits down next to him, scratching his bald spot. Jack nods to him and continues talking. The guy keeps staring at him. He says goodbye to Colette and aggressively says to the guy, "Can I help you?"

The guy says, "As a matter of fact you can. I am Agent Tim Stephenson, and it is a pleasure to meet you in person."

"No shit." Listening to Stephenson on the phone, Jack figured he would look like James Bond, not Elmer Fudd.

"How did you find out my flight and get to my gate?"

Agent Stephenson smirks. "Jack you think after 9/11 it takes the FBI more than one minute to find any passenger on any flight in the United States of America or the whole world?"

Nodding, "Makes sense." Taking Chip's advice, "I simply had lunch at McCracken's."

Agent Stephenson gets a little closer. "Jack I think you are underestimating Justin Bunar. He is not a nice person. In addition to being a bookie, he is running drugs. His muscle, Stevey O'Rourke, has a rap sheet as long as your arm and is a suspect in a murder slash missing person's case. Just because Bunar is a friend of William Nestler does not mean he won't hurt you or your family. He has already slashed the tires of you and your wife's cars."

"How do you know about Colette's tire?" Jack assumes the FBI saw Stevey slash his tire watching McCracken's but not his house in Bridgewater.

"We know." Just like with Bunar, Jack knows Tim is not going to tell him.

"Again, I was just having lunch, but if what you said is true, you give me even more reasons to stay away from Bunar and the risks of just talking to you."

"Jack you are missing the point. I want to get Bunar. If you do not help me get him, I will get you first, then get him next."

"Should I get an attorney?"

"Up to you, but I would think about helping me first."

"Hypothetically speaking, what do you want me to do?"

"It is simple. We just need Bunar on tape either taking your bets or you paying a debt. Getting him to admit to slashing your wife's tires would be a big bonus." Stephenson hands Jack a device that looks like a stick of gum. "All you need to do is carry this in your pocket, and turn it on the next time you have lunch at McCracken's."

Jack is twirling the stick of gum in his hand, when Stephenson grabs it and presses one of the buttons. He hears their conversation clear as day. He shows how it works. The device is all digital and does not make any noises and it can hold up to 12 hours of conversations. The device can also be voice activated, so you can leave it somewhere and pick it up later. Jack tries handing the device back saying, "Keep it.", but Stephenson doesn't take it. Jack tries again to hand it back to him.

Stephenson stays the course, "Keep it. You can play with it. Your call if you want to bring it into McCracken's." Jack tries a third time. "I am not taking it back."

Jack puts it in his pocket, "I am not going to use it," pauses, "So Agent Stephenson, are you saying if I record a conversation with Bunar you are not going to prosecute me?"

"Jack, can I see the stick?" He hands it back to him. Stephenson replays the question, deletes it, and hands back the recorder. "First, I am impressed you figured out so quickly how to use the device. Second, I like that you are trying to protect yourself. A good sign. Third, I am disappointed you think I am stupid."

With a big smile. "It was worth a try. They are calling my flight. You have a good day and you can put in your report I simply had lunch at McCracken's. You should go there. The burgers are great."

Jack is walking on the airplane when his cell phone rings. Looking at the caller ID, Jack angrily answers, "Billy you cannot tell Bunar my travel schedule."

"What do you mean?"

"I mean I saw Bunar today and he knows I am going out of town."

"What is the big deal?"

Jack, fresh off his conversation with Agent Stephenson, "The big deal? I am out of town and who knows what Bunar and his lunatic Stevey would do to Colette or Harrison. Do you know his buddy Stevey is up on a murder charge and Bunar is also a drug dealer?"

"Calm down. Bunar would not hurt your family, he is not a drug dealer but I am not surprised about Stevey. Who told you all of this?"

Jack does not want to tell Billy about the FBI for fear he might tell Bunar. Whispering, "I owe the guy twenty-four grand, and I just bet another sixty grand. I called a friend of a friend who knows a Boston police officer who ran a check on Bunar and Stevey. I am getting deep into Bunar. I want to know who I am into."

"Bunar is no saint. He knows the guys dealing the drugs but he is not a dealer, I can promise you. I don't think Stevey is a murderer but I am not as confident on him as I am about Bunar dealing drugs. Instead of doing background checks on Bunar and betting even more, I thought you were getting out of this. I will call Bunar to see if I can cancel the bets, and I will make sure he keeps Stevey away from your family."

"Do not call him. I want to make the bets and Bunar promised not to send Stevey to Bridgewater. I got to go. I am on the plane but in the future, do NOT tell Bunar about my travel schedule."

Jack is now wondering if Agent Stephenson is misleading him or if Billy is blinded by his friendship with Bunar. Even with Bunar slashing his tire, he likes Bunar, but needs to makes sure he does not get caught up in Bunar's web.

39

Dinner with Michelle

"I just put my feet in the air and move them around."
Fred Astaire

Jack lands in Reno at six-thirty. When he gets off the plane a man in a grey suit asks are, "Are you Jack Fitzpatrick?"

Jack is startled, "Yes, I am."

"Can you please come with me?"

"Who are you?"

"Agent Keith Brown with the Reno FBI."

"Am I under arrest?"

"No, not at this time."

"Then I am not going with you. If you have some questions for me please ask them now. I just left an Agent Stephenson with the FBI in Boston." It hits Jack. This is just for Agent Stephenson to show his power and reach. *This is all for naught because I already know the FBI's reach is far and deep.*

"This will just take a few minutes. Please come outside with me I have a car waiting. Do you have any luggage you need to get?"

"I already have my luggage and I really do not want to go for a ride with you."

"Mr. Fitzpatrick I am trying to make this easy on you. I could make a scene at your hotel."

"Okay, if you drive me to my hotel?"

"Okay".

"Do you need to know the name of my hotel?" Agent Brown shakes his head 'no'. Jack should have assumed the FBI would know where he was staying. On the car ride to the hotel, Agent Brown asks him some basic questions and stresses the importance of cooperating with the FBI in Boston. The FBI drops him off in front of his hotel. Agent Brown is extremely polite and Jack is becoming more seasoned because he is not as rattled by the Reno FBI. He is surprised Stephenson is putting this much effort into himself and Bunar. *There may be something bigger going on with Bunar?*

When Jack gets to his hotel, his first call is to Colette to talk to her before she goes to bed. He then calls Michelle to confirm he will be at the restaurant at seven-thirty. He has just enough time to check in, change, and make it to dinner.

Jack meets Michelle in the Atlantis Hotel and Casino at their Sushi Bar on the Sky Terrace. He walks into the restaurant and immediately notices the beautiful view of the city and the mountains. He looks around for Michelle but does not see her. He puts in their name for a table near a window and orders a Kirin beer at the bar. Before he even has his beer, he gets a tap on the shoulder hearing, "Hi stranger. How long have you been waiting?"

Michelle looks beautiful. She is wearing her auburn hair down and a casual black dress. Jack takes in her beauty in, before responding, "I just got here. You picked a great place. I have asked for a table by the window. Do you want a drink while we wait for our table?"

"Yes." They have a very comfortable conversation. He is amazed this is only the second time they have met and they have clicked. After a nice dinner and conversation, Jack figures Michelle will want to hit the casino, but instead she asks, "Fitzy, do you know how to Ballroom dance?"

Jack is surprised by the question but he answers with the truth, "As a matter of fact, I do." He took lessons with Colette before they were married.

"One of the reasons I choose The Atlantis Hotel is they have a Ballroom with a Big Band playing tonight. I was betting you would know how to dance."

He knows he is standing on the line with his wife and is very close to stepping over the line with a prospect, but he is having so much fun he goes dancing. *What will a little dancing hurt?* Michelle must sense Jack concerns. "Fitzy, all I want to do is dance. I love dancing, and I have not had a chance to dance since I have moved to Reno." The two of them head to the Ballroom. Michelle grabs Jack by the arm. "This will be fun, then we will go gambling."

The Ballroom is set up like a 1940's Ballroom. Jack jokes, "Just as I expected. All 'Blue Hairs', I bet the average age is seventy five."

"Don't ruin this for me, Mr. Funny Pants. Let's dance."

They have a great time dancing. Jack and Colette have not danced since they had Harrison. He is enjoying dancing with Michelle but he is actually thinking about Colette and needing to take Colette dancing when he gets back. Colette and Jack learned the Waltz, Tango, Foxtrot, and Quickstep.

Michelle and Jack are slow dancing when Michelle whispers, "Thank you. I know I am putting you in awkward position but I am having so much fun I cannot resist."

"The last thing I would call dancing with you is awkward."

Michelle gets even closer, "Very sweet of you."

Jack leans back to make a little more space. "This is the least I can do for you."

They dance the rest of the song without speaking. When the song is over there is a pause before they let go. Michelle smiles, "Thank you for taking me dancing. It has been a lot fun."

"Do you want to keep dancing, or head downstairs play some craps, or do you want to call it a night since we start at seven tomorrow morning?"

"If it is okay with you, let's get another drink before we decide."

As they sit down, Jack is sweating, "This is a lot of fun. Look at me. I am sweating just trying to keep up with you. I will be right back." He gets up and goes to the men's room. Splashing cold water on his face, thinks, *what are you doing? You are either teasing a prospect or you are cheating on your wife. Fitzy you are looking at a lose-lose situation.* He goes back to the table to talk business, "Are you all set for tomorrow?"

They have a conversation about setting up for the demos, who will be at the meetings from Reno Regional, what Michelle thinks are their chances of winning, on MacroHealth, etc. Jack asks if Betty has brought up the accounting issues again. Michelle says no but does not know if Betty has communicated with Cheryl directly. After about 20 minutes and another drink, Michelle stands up. "Enough business let's dance some more. There is another section of the casino with music for our generation." Michelle and Jack grab their drinks walking to the 'Center Stage Bar'. They keep dancing until almost one in the morning. He can see Michelle is having a great time but he needs to be at the hospital at six-thirty. "I really need to get some sleep before our presentation tomorrow."

Michelle is feeling the effects of the alcohol and having a great time. She whispers to Jack, "I know you are a happily married man and part of this is just because I am a prospect but…," she pauses and looks around, "I was thinking we could be like President Clinton and Monica Lewinsky."

There it is, Michelle's offer to cross the line. Jack has a big, quick, and complicated decision. His big head, *Come on man, you love your wife, and your son.* His little head, *She is a beautiful and available woman.* His strategic sales head, *If this goes south I could lose the deal.* His tactical sales, *If I take her up on her offer there is no way she can vote against me.* His manhood, *She would look great naked.* He finally goes with his marriage and Colette, *How do I let her down easily?*

Michelle senses this is not an easy decision for Jack. She retreats, "Fitzy, I know you are a good guy, and I have never been with a married man, but I guess I am having so much fun tonight, I wanted to put a cherry on top. Not only that, I have not been dancing since I moved to Reno. I have also not been with a man in a while."

"You are beautiful. You just need to get out more often. I am really tempted but I just can't." Jack does not want their evening to end this way, especially with still needing her vote. "I really do need to get some rest and so do you. You promised me gambling, how about after the dinner tomorrow night, you and I sneak off and do some gambling?"

Michelle blushes, "Fitzy, why do you have to be married?"

He gives her a hug, "Let's get a cab together and we can drop you off first."

In the cab, they uncomfortably hold hands, not saying anything until the cab pulls in front of Michelle's apartment. "Fitzy, I had a lot of fun and I am sorry about the Lewinsky comment."

He laughs, "That is the biggest compliment I have gotten this Century."

She smiles back. "Thanks again, and I will take you up on your gambling offer tomorrow night."

Checking his voicemail on the cab ride back to the hotel, he has ten new messages from the CM employees in Reno. They have been calling him about dinner, asking where he is, and telling him to meet in the lobby at six-fifteen in the morning so they all can head over to the hospital together. Jack will need to come up with some excuses about getting in late because he does not want Kim to know about his one-on-one dinner with Michelle. He strategically calls Kim's voicemail at the office to tell her he will meet them in the lobby in the morning.

40
The Demos

"For every sale you miss because you're too enthusiastic, you will miss a hundred because you're not enthusiastic enough." Zig Ziglar

Jack calls Colette at six a.m. local, nine a.m. her time. He is a little groggy after all the beers with Michelle and only getting about three hours sleep. Colette is ornery. He wants to get off the phone as soon as possible.

Colette is complaining how Jack is gone all week, and she needs help around the house with Harrison. He really does need to get going, telling her, he will call her this afternoon when he gets a chance and that he loves her. Colette simply hangs up without saying anything. *Maybe, I should have taken Michelle up on her Lewinsky offer.*

Jack gets down to the lobby around 6:20 a.m. and there are four people waiting for him. Kevin Blair gets right on him, "Fitzy, glad to see you are going to join us. I made the executive decision to send Kim and other members of the team over to the hospital while we waited for your royal highness."

"Thanks, now let's go. Today is a big deal towards making CM twenty-eight million richer." Jack fiddles with the digital recording device in his pocket. He is going to record Kevin's presentation this morning.

They get to the hospital at quarter of seven. The room is empty except for CM personnel and Michelle. Jack gets nervous, *I am in deep trouble if I okayed ten people from CM to fly out for a presentation where no one shows up.* Michelle and Jack see each other. Michelle blushes and Jack is a little embarrassed about last night. He knows last night is one of the many risks of combining business with alcohol. He is prepared for this, going over to Michelle where no one can hear him, "Thank you for last night. I had a great time."

"I am sorry."

"For what, complimenting me?" He winks, "On my dancing." Jack switches to business and the empty room. "Michelle is anyone going to show up this morning?"

"Everyone is typically fifteen minutes late for meetings at Reno, especially the doctors."

Laughing as Kim is coming over, Jack formally introduces Kim to Michelle. He is confident Michelle will not bring up their relationship. Kevin comes over and winks at him as he is introduced to Michelle. Slowly the room begins to fill up, and at exactly seven a.m. Cheryl Scharff, Reno's CFO, walks in and comes right over to Jack. He introduces Kevin to her. Cheryl recommends they wait a few more minutes to give time for more people to come to the meeting.

Jack looks at today's agenda:

Location: **Medical Center Auditorium**
Vendor: **CM Solutions**
Topic: **Clinical Information Demonstrations**
Date: **Tuesday, June 17th**

Attendees:
Reno Regional Clinical Information System Steering Committee

- 7:00am to 7:30am Reno Regional Overview
- 7:30am to 8:00am: Vendor Company Overview
- 8:00am to 10:00am: Vendor Scripted Demo
- 10:00am to 10:30am Break
- 10:30am to 12:00pm: Vendor Scripted Demo (cont.)
- 12:00pm to 1:30pm: Lunch
- 1:30 pm to 2:30pm: Physician and Nursing Information System Demo
- 2:30 pm to 3:00pm: Laboratory Information System demo
- 3:00 pm to 3:30pm: Break
- 3:30 pm to 4:00 pm: Radiology Information Systems demo
- 4:00pm to 4:30 pm: Pharmacy Information System demo
- 4:30 pm to 5:00pm: Wrap up/ Questions and Answers

Just as Michelle predicted, at quarter past seven there are about thirty people in the room and more are still coming in. Cheryl gets the meeting started.

Cheryl gives a thirty-minute overview on Reno Regional. She talks about why they are doing the project and how it is part of their strategic plan. Jack, Kevin, and Dr. Alvarez ask strategic questions. By the time Cheryl has finished it is quarter of eight and Jack's turn.

As part of the purple cow strategy of being different, they are going to minimize their focus on CM and maximize their focus on Reno Regional. Jack starts out, "Thank you for your time this morning and over the next two days. To stay on schedule, I will make our company overview quick, so we can get going on your demo and stay on your schedule." He takes five minutes to talk about how they want to partner with Reno Regional on developing software that will increase patient safety. He turns it over to Kevin for five minutes and hits the record button on his digital recorder as Kevin talks about the company and how the stock has tripled over the past five years and that the stock market believes in CM and gives them the ability to raise capital to enhance their solutions. This leaves Dr. Alvarez five minutes to talk about how their software will make the doctors more productive.

Jack is feeling good with their introduction. It was short and mostly focused on them. He watches the audience and they are very attentive. When it comes to questions, they ask basic questions, like how many employees, how long in business, how many physicians on staff, etc. He notices the attendees are checking off a list as they are asking questions. This means they have a scorecard. When they take a break, he is going to ask Michelle for copy of the scorecard. When they wrap up the CM introduction it is 8:05 a.m. and they are back on schedule.

Kim Savard takes over to start the scripted demo. Kim and the CM team go through a patient coming to the emergency department (ER), getting registered as an inpatient, how the orders and results from the ER come across to the inpatient, to surgery and back to ICU, etc. They go through how physicians can order pharmacy, radiology, and laboratory orders, how nurses can document the patient visit and access the information, and the medication administration process. The whole time Dr. Alvarez interjects where CM can save them time and increase patient safety.

At a few minutes after ten, Michelle interrupts and calls for the thirty minute break. Kevin goes over to Cheryl to see how they are doing. Dr. Alvarez goes over to Dr. Harold Mainer with Reno Regional who has been asking a lot of questions. Jack goes up to Michelle. "How do you think it is going?"

"You guys are doing great. You are blowing the doctors away."

Jack whispers, "Can you get me a copy of your score card?"

Michelle pauses before saying, "Cheryl specifically asked we do not share the score cards with the vendors."

Smiling, "I will not share it with anyone"

"If you get caught, you did not get it from me. I could get fired."

"No worries."

Michelle goes into the auditorium and comes backs with a folded piece of paper. Jack pops into the auditorium and taps Dr. Alvarez on the shoulder in the middle of a conversation. Dr. Alvarez gives him a look of 'Why are you interrupting when I am talking to other doctors', but Jack ignores the look, "I hate to interrupt Dr. Alvarez but I need a minute before we start the demo."

"Two minutes, Fitzy."

He impatiently waits. As soon as Dr. Alvarez is done, Jack pulls him into the lobby. He finds a corner with his back against the wall so he can see anyone coming. Dr. Alvarez sees the scoring card, "How did you get this? I tried to give Dr. Mainer the secret doctor hand shake. He still wouldn't give me a copy."

Jack winks, "Because I am good at what I do. Now hurry up and remember as much as you can for the next ninety minutes. Then we will review again at lunch and with the whole team after the presentations."

Michelle calls everyone back into the meeting. When the scripted demo starts after the break, CM focuses on the patient billing and reporting. CM gives a script of their ancillary applications of Pharmacy, Radiology, and Laboratory. CM brings in box lunches so everyone can eat and CM can mingle with Reno Regional. Jack is tempted to sit with Michelle because he is comfortable with her but he really should sit with Cheryl. He has learned the hard way, it is not who you like but who is making the decisions. Cheryl thanks him for the lunch and says she is impressed with CM, especially Dr. Alvarez. Cheryl asks, "If we go with you guys will we ever see him again?"

"I will personally guarantee he will come out during the implementation and for your go-live."

"Will you put it in the contract?"

Jack laughs, "If I put it in your contract, will you cancel your meetings with MacroHealth next week?"

Now it is Cheryl turn to laugh, "You are smooth but will you put it in the contract."

Jack gets serious, "I don't think our attorney will allow it, but I will send you an e-mail and cc Dr. Alvarez. We are very excited to work with Reno Regional and I know Dr. Alvarez is excited too."

"So about those references?"

Jack had been staying clear of Memorial by talking about CM clients in California and Seattle. There is no way around the Memorial reference, so he asks Cheryl if she knows the Memorial CFO. Cheryl cautiously, "I do know Brian Lietten. He said he is not familiar with CM."

Jack notices Cheryl does not mention that Memorial is looking at CM and MacroHealth. Kevin is meeting with Brian on Friday, so Jack is going to try and get some information on Brian. "My boss, Kevin Blair, is meeting with Brian later in the week. Do you have any advice for me to give to Kevin?"

"Be careful because Brian really likes MacroHealth. He used to work at a hospital using MacroHealth."

Jack smiles to himself, not because Brian likes MacroHealth, but because Cheryl just gave him insider information, which usually means she likes CM and him. In turn, he gives Cheryl some insider information she probably already knows, "Thank you. Memorial is also going through a selection for an enterprise vendor, and we are the finalist with MacroHealth."

"I know, Betty told me. He is so positive on MacroHealth, I was not surprised when Betty told me."

More good news, Cheryl is telling me about Betty. "I have never met Brian, so hopefully he will be open minded about our solutions plus we already have three applications installed at Memorial"

"Good luck, and you better promise I get a better deal than Memorial."

"Obviously you will have to buy what they don't have, but you will get a better deal on the other applications." Jack feels like a used car salesman but he really does not have a choice. Switching the conversation to personal, he asks her, How long she has lived in Reno? Does she have kids? How long has she has worked at Reno? Cheryl is really starting to open up, unlike their first meeting.

After lunch the afternoon demos continue to go great. During the second break Kim, Jack, and Kevin talk about who will do the wrap up of the meeting after Q and A. Jack offers it to Kim first. Kim is nervous and asks him if he can do it. Jack pushes her to do it and Kevin agrees on Kim.

At the end of Q and A, Kim thanks the audience for their time and reminds them of the highlights of the presentation and why they should choose CM. Kevin tells Jack, Kim is doing a great job. Just before Kim wraps up Jack interrupts, "I would like to invite everyone and their significant others to dinner tonight at Sierra Vista right on Lake Tahoe at seven. All I need you to do is to tell Kim Savard or Michelle Parks how many will be attending before the end of business today, so I can make sure we have enough seats."

As always, Kevin has to have the last word. "I know we will be here tomorrow and you will be working with Jack and Kim, and feel free to contact me anytime. As CM's executive vice president, I am excited to have the opportunity to work with you. I am going to leave a stack of business cards up front. I hope to see all of you at dinner."

41

Prospect Dinner

"I cook with wine, sometimes I even add it to the food." W. C. Fields

When the CM team gets back to the hotel, they have a meeting in one of the bars. Jack passes around his only copy of the scorecard, and they talk about where they were strong and where they were weak and how they can improve tomorrow. They also discuss who they should focus on at the dinner and what the message needs to be. They have a half hour before they need to head to Lake Tahoe for the dinner.

Jack steps in the bar to have a beer and get an update on the Celtics Hawks NBA game. The game starts at 6:00 p.m. local. If the Celtics win, he will only owe Bunar $4k. He needs to get rolling, so he heads up to his hotel room to change and call Colette.

It is nine-thirty eastern when he calls Colette. Colette is fuming, he has not called once since this morning. He apologizes and tries to explain he was tied up in the meetings, but she is not buying it. They have a very strained conversation before hanging up so he can get to the dinner.

Including the ten people from CM, there are forty people at the dinner. The good news for CM is Cheryl and Reno's CIO Peter Galetta show up at the dinner with their significant others. Dr. Alvarez is a wine connoisseur, so Jack knows the bill will be over five grand. The CM team strategically sits next to the Reno employees. Kevin sits near Cheryl, Jack sits near Peter, Kim sits near Michelle, and Dr. Alvarez sits next to Dr. Mainer. He would rather sit with Michelle and is a little nervous about Kim talking with Michelle, but this is the right peer-to-peer sales decision.

Jack is consistently downloading the score from the basketball game to his cell phone. At the start of dinner the Hawks are up three points. He is trying not to be obvious while constantly refreshing the scores, holding the phone just under the table. He is struggling holding a conversation with Peter and his wife, while focused on the game score. At half time, the Celtics are down five points.

Other than Jack's focus on the game, the group is having a great dinner, and the wine is flowing. Peter finally asks Jack why he keeps checking his cell phone. He explains the Celtics are playing the Hawks, and he lives in Boston but grew up in Atlanta. Obviously he does not tell them about the twenty grand wager.

It is ten when the group starts to break up. The game is over and the Hawks have won by five points. Jack puts on a fake smile, after losing another twenty grand to Bunar. He is now into Bunar for forty six grand. The Reno employees thank CM for the dinner and joke about being late for their seven a.m. meeting tomorrow morning. He eyes Michelle. They have not talked all dinner. Michelle gives him the let's get out of here look. Jack now needs a plan to escape without the CM employees. He is tired and thinking about canceling on tonight. *But, man does Michelle look great and I did not gamble last night.*

Michelle walks over. "Stranger you ready to get out of here?"

Jack looks around, "You bet, but I need an exit strategy."

"Easy enough. Tell them I am giving you a ride back so I can give you the inside story."

"And I was worried about my escape plan when you had the answer the whole time. What about you?"

"The only ones I need to worry about are Cheryl and Peter, and they have already left."

Jack walks over to Kevin and tells him Michelle is driving him back to the hotel. Kevin smiles, "You dirty dog congratulations."

His skin crawls when Kevin insinuates he is a cheater. "It is not what you think."

"I may have been born at night but it was not last night. Make sure you wear protection."

Jack is heated and steps closer to Kevin. "It is not what you think. You should be thanking me for getting the inside scoop on your twenty-eight million dollar deal."

"You want me to thank you for taking one for the team with a beautiful woman?"

Jack knows he is not going to win this conversation, "It is not what you think. I will see you at six-fifteen in the lobby tomorrow morning."

"I want details and pictures if possible."

Jack walks away. He wants to talk to Kim before leaving to let her know, so it doesn't appear he is sneaking off. Kim says, "Watch yourself, she has a crush on you."

"No worries. You know and I would not do anything to hurt Colette."

"I know, but just be careful."

As they drive back to Reno, Michelle grins, "You ready to win some money tonight?"

"No question, we need to pick a casino but not at my hotel. I do not want us to run into any CM employees."

"For good luck I think we need to go to Fitzgerald's or better known as Fitzy's. I think it would be appropriate for Fitzy to win at Fitzy's."

Jack turns the conversation to business, wanting to find out what the other committee members are saying about CM. Michelle states, "You guys were definitely in second place before today, but you blew them away. The doctors were really impressed with Dr. Alvarez. I may be seeing a lot more of you Fitzy."

Jack drills her on specifics and looks for negatives so they can address them tomorrow. The only real red flag is their financial applications. Cheryl is concerned CM is too focused on the clinicals and is not deep enough in the financial side of their business.

By the time Jack and Michelle get to the Casino it is nearing midnight. He does not like to jump right into craps. The game is so fast, you can lose five hundred before you even know what hits you so he wants to play blackjack first. He has played at the Fitzgerald Casino before and has a credit line. He takes out five hundred dollars against the line and gives Michelle one hundred. She pushes the money away but he insists, "Let's split your winnings."

He has the gambling itch and is comfortable with Michelle, so he starts out with $50 a hand. In about twenty minutes the five hundred is gone.

With the gambling itch needing attention, he wants to gamble alone, fake smiling, "Not the same magic as last time. I am getting tired and we have another early morning."

Michelle snuggles up close, "I brought a hundred and seeing as I lost yours let's use mine on the craps table?"

Jack needs to scratch his gambling itch. He takes out an additional thousand against his line at the craps table. After another twenty minutes all the money including Michelle's one hundred is gone.

He is doing a good job of hiding his disappointment in losing because Michelle grabs Jack around the waist. "I am going to put you on the spot one more time. Obviously we are unlucky on the table but do you want to get lucky? We could get a room here at Fitzy's."

Michelle looks great but he is totally focused on making up his losses, "Michelle, I really like your persistence, and I hope you can respect my decision. I love hanging out with you, but that is it."

Michelle gives fake frown, "Thanks for hanging out with me even though I keep putting pressure on you. I like hanging around you too, and when I get some drinks in me, I think about taking our hanging around to the next level, please don't hate me."

He laughs, "No worries. Hate you? You are great and I take all of your interests as a big compliment."

Last night he said no for his wife. Tonight he is saying no because he wants to get back to gambling. "I will walk you back to your car and will take a cab back to my hotel." Michelle offers to give him a ride home but he refuses.

Instead of heading to the taxi stand, goes back to the blackjack table. He does not gamble back at his hotel for fear of running into CM employees. He sits down at the blackjack table and gets another thousand dollars on his credit line.

It is almost 2:00am, he is wired with gambling energy. When Jack first started coming to Nevada he was surprised that he felt awake early in the morning when gambling. He thought it was the adrenaline from gambling, but the casinos also pump in oxygen to keep you awake and gambling.

He is doing okay on the blackjack table. Around three a.m., counting the fifteen hundred he lost early in the night, he is about even. He steps up his betting to $250 per hand and is playing three hands simultaneously.

He gets hot and is up a quick two grand. It is after 3:30am. He starts betting $500 per hand. He is not going to sleep pushing his luck while winning. At four in the morning, he's up five grand after paying off his twenty five hundred dollar marker. *Its five a.m., I can play until 5:30am, go back to his hotel, take a quick shower and get ready for today's meetings.* For the last half hour Jack goes to five hundred per hand on all three hands. In five minutes all the money he is up is gone. He now has to decide if he goes back to the hotel or go back to his marker. Already down twenty grand on the Celtics loss, He takes his full marker of $5,000. In another ten minutes, at one thousand dollars a hand, the five grand is gone.

Jack asks for a bigger credit line. The pit boss says they cannot do it until after eight a.m. when their credit office is open. Hanging his head, he reluctantly takes a cab back to his hotel.

On the hotel ride back his cell phone beeps letting him know he has a message. The first message is from an unknown number at 12:15 a.m., hearing the now familiar voice of Bunar, 'Fitzy please do not lose all your money in Reno. You now owe me forty six grand and I want my money when you return to Boston.' *Man he gets excited when I lose. I wonder how many calls he makes a night or are they just to me and his high-rollers?*

He gets into his hotel just before six a.m., and lies down for a quick second.

42

Day 2 Demos

"There are no secrets to success. It is the result of preparation, hard work, and learning from failure." Colin Powell

At six-thirty, Kim calls Jack's cell phone. He is in a dead sleep when the cell phone wakes him up. He sleepily says he is running late and will take a cab to the hospital. Kim asks, "Are you alone?"

He gives her his familiar laugh, "No worries. Michelle was home by one a.m. I will take a cab to the hospital and if I am not there by seven start without me."

For a split second, he considers not taking a shower but he has the stink of gambling all night. He takes the quickest shower of his life. He calls Colette during the cab ride to the hospital. He tries doing a quick check in and will call her later. "Nope, you said that yesterday and I did not hear from you until ten o'clock at night. What did you do last night?" Before she gives him a chance to answer, she asks, "Did you gamble last night? How much did you drink?"

He is exhausted and doesn't have the patience for this call, "I have got to go. I am going to be late. I will call you later today."

"I take not answering as yes, and a lot to both. Besides gambling, what are you doing out there? You have not once asked me about Harrison."

"I am sorry honey, but I really need to go."

"You better call me soon or I may not be around when you get back."

"I promise I will call you later today."

By the time Jack gets to the hospital auditorium, the meeting has already started. He stands in the back and grabs an agenda from the back of the room.

Reno Regional Day 2 Clinical Information Demonstrations

Attendees: Departmental Teams

- 7:00am to 8:00am Physician Outreach
- 8:00am to 9:00am Physician Computerized Order Entry
- 9:00am to 10:00am Admitting and Financials
- 10:00am to 10:30am Break
- 10:30am to 12:00pm Nursing Information Systems
- 12:00pm to 1:00pm Lunch
- 1:00pm to 2:00pm Laboratory Information System
- 2:00pm to 3:00pm Radiology
- 3:00pm to 4:00pm Pharmacy
- 4:00pm to 5:00pm Wrap up / Question and Answer

Dr. Alvarez is speaking about how physicians can use the solutions both in their offices and remotely anywhere over the web. Jack looks around the auditorium and sees Michelle, Kim, and Kevin. Reluctantly, he does not see Cheryl but does pick Peter Galetta out of the crowd. Even though he just walked in the auditorium he gets a sense the presentation is going well based on the attendees paying attention and they are asking questions.

Jack reluctantly bites the bullet and sits down next to Kevin. Kevin whispers, "I am disappointed you are late. You better have gotten laid last night."

"Sorry I am late and sorry to disappoint you. Nothing happened last night." Kevin is his boss, so he does a little sucking up. He tells Kevin about Michelle's positive update. Kevin laughs, "Fitzy, I assume she was positive when you were banging her."

Jack is getting more frustrated but hides his emotions, "Let it go Kevin. Nothing happened."

At the same time, Michelle looks back and waves to Jack.

Kevin smirks, "Sure nothing happened. Is she a moaner?"

"Let it go. Nothing happened."

"You are consistent. Let's talk at the break."

You bastard, I am going to get you.

Dr. Alvarez is speaking and Jack has seen his presentation a dozen times, also Jack does not need to say anything until this afternoon. Jack's mind starts drifting as he dreams about winning both of his next two bets with Bunar and falls asleep. Kevin elbows him and whispers as loud as he can, "Pull it together. This is a big deal we both need. You falling asleep does not show your commitment to this deal."

Jack is embarrassed. He prides himself on 'Ringing the Bell'. 'Ringing the Bell' means you can party hard at night but the next morning you 'Ring the Bell' by being on time and productive. For the first time in his life, he did not 'Ring the Bell' by meeting his team in the lobby this morning. Now to make it worse, he just drifted off to sleep in front of his boss. He is angry at himself, "Sorry Kevin, I will pick it up." Trying justifying falling asleep and restating that he didn't cheat on his wife, "After Michelle went home, I stayed up gambling."

"Fitzy, you better pull it together and ASAP. I need your 'A' game to win this deal." He simply nods and gets up to get a coffee. He focuses hard for the rest of Dr. Alvarez's presentation.

At the break, Michelle comes over to thank him for last night and to kid him about being late. Jack then thanks Kim for calling him and for starting the meeting without him. Hopefully, Kevin was the only one who saw him fall asleep.

Still struggling to stay awake, he sneaks down to the cafeteria to get another coffee. He goes into the parking lot to call Colette. He needs to suck up to Colette too, telling her how much he misses her and Harrison, and cannot wait to get home. The conversation goes okay.

Back in the auditorium, with the caffeine assistance from another coffee, he stays awake for the rest of the presentations. At the end of Q and A, he gives his closing five minutes and begs for the business, "We are very excited to have the opportunity to work with Reno Regional Medical Center. We really want your business. We brought our top team for this presentation, including Kevin our Executive Vice President, and Dr. Alvarez our Chief Physician Officer." He uses Dr. Alvarez vs. Carson because he wants to highlight that CM brought a doctor. Next he assumes the sale, "We are really looking forward working with Reno Regional and being a development partner, leveraging your clinical and business expertise to enhance our product offering." Being a complex sale, Reno Regional cannot sign a contract at the end of his presentation, so he goes for a trial close.

Trial closes are asking simple questions looking for agreement or disagreement in your offering. "Is there anything you wanted to see this week you did not see?" The crowd says nope, which means CM has it all. "Did you like what you have seen over the past two days?" The crowd nods, which means they are saying yes they like CM. To make sure there are no open questions, "Is there anything else?" There are no questions. He simply closes with, "Thank you and feel free to contact any of us at any time."

The team heads back to the hotel. Some of them are taking red-eyes back to Boston. Others are flying out in the morning. Carson and Jack are staying to play golf tomorrow with Memorial and Kevin is staying to meet Memorial's CFO, Brian Lietten.

In the hotel lobby, Kevin asks Jack and Carson out to dinner. Jack is exhausted. "Sorry man, I am exhausted and I need to get some rest before golf tomorrow."

Kevin gets on him in front of Carson. "You are very lucky the two days of presentations went great because if they did not you would be taking a lot of heat. Fitzy you are the youngest VP at CM and you are showing a lot of immaturity this week. You stay out late with a prospect, which is very risky. Then you are late and, worst of all, you fall asleep."

Carson interrupts and laughs. "Fitzy, you fell asleep today?"

Kevin glares at Carson. "During your presentation." Then Kevin looks at Jack, "Now because you are tired, Carson and I are going to miss the opportunity to debrief Reno Regional and plan for our Memorial meetings."

Jack knows Kevin is right, but he is not going to take it lying down. "One of the reasons we kicked ass this week is the prep work I personally did on this account. I have built a non-sexual relationship with one of the key members of the selection committee, and the relationship is helping us get access to inside information. I am embarrassed about falling asleep." Jack turns to Carson. "Please keep this between us. I really need to get some sleep. How about we meet for breakfast in the morning?"

Kevin smirks. "Your call but this is another mistake."

Jack tells Carson and Kevin to enjoy their dinner. He will meet them at seven in the morning for breakfast. Up in his hotel room, makes a brief call to Colette, then falls fast asleep before six in the evening. He does not even have the energy to stay up and watch the Lakers vs. the Jazz, with his twenty grand riding on the results.

Jack is sound asleep when his cell phone goes off at midnight local time, three a.m. eastern. *Shit, why didn't you turn off your damn phone.* The caller ID, 'ID Unknown', it must be Bunar and the Lakers must of lost. He is not in the mood. Exhausted he does not answer the phone and tries to fall back asleep, thinking he owes Bunar sixty-eight thousand.

Thinking about the game and Bunar, he cannot sleep. Jack turns on the ESPN News, and quickly learns the great news. The Lakers won. He checks his voicemail, "Fitzy, congratulations on the Lakers win. Even a blind squirrel gets a nut every now and then. Seriously, congratulations, and you need to start answering your phone."

With the good news, Jack falls right back to sleep.

43

Golf with Howard Black

"I like trying to win. That's what golf is all about."
Jack Nicklaus

Jack gets up at five a.m. with a spring in his step. Great night sleep, playing golf today, and the Lakers beat the Jazz. He watches the highlights of the Lakers and Jazz game on ESPN. When the announcer on TV says, "The Lakers win". *Now if I can only win tonight,* he will only be down $6k, after factoring in the 10% vig he has to pay on Tuesday's loss. Between winning and getting over ten hours sleep, he is jazzed. He heads down to the hotel gym to get in a workout.

After the workout, he writes thank you e-mails to all attendees. He figures they will be impressed with getting a thank you e-mail the morning after the demos.

At seven, he heads down to have breakfast with Carson and Kevin. The conversation starts out casual and Jack learns after dinner they played blackjack then went to a strip joint. Nobody brings up falling asleep yesterday. They strategize on Memorial. Jack gained a lot of valuable in-sight from Cheryl Scharff when she said Memorial's CFO, Brian Lietten, once worked at a hospital using MacroHealth. Now it appears Kevin's meeting with Brian is more important than the golf outing. Jack was blindsided with MacroHealth being in the deal and starts surmising Howard Black was blindsided too, but he did not want to confess it to him.

They talk about what is important to a CFO and how Kevin can position CM versus MacroHealth. They settle on emphasizing CM is less risky and costly, because CM already has applications installed at Memorial. Jack commits to getting more info on Brian during golf with Howard. They need to decide how much influence Memorial's doctor, Tony Heins, has on Brian. They hope Carson can influence Tony and, in turn, Tony can influence Brian.

One sales strategy is to ask the same question to multiple people to see if you get the same answers. Very often you get different answers. As a sales person, you have to decide who has the power, who is telling the truth, and who has the influence. All three of them have to-do lists for the day. On their list is getting all three out to dinner tonight.

Jack and Carson head over to the golf course to meet with Howard and Tony. Kevin goes up to his hotel room because his meeting is not until eleven. At the golf course, Jack does the introductions with him and Howard sharing a golf cart. Tony and Carson share the second golf cart. Jack cannot resist gambling during golf, so he recommends a friendly wager with the team, the low score wins the hole. They will only play for $2 a hole. For Jack these little stakes are to just have fun. They decide to split teams with Jack and Howard versus Carson and Tony. If it was CM versus Memorial, Jack would make sure the client wins. He will try to get a sense of whether it is important for Howard or Tony to win. He will sway the results in a non-obvious way if possible.

On the 10th hole Jack's cell phone rings, it is Colette. He sends the call into voicemail, figuring he can only get in trouble with Colette when talking to her on the golf course after being on the road for three days. To his surprise Colette calls right back. They have a signal where if Colette calls right back he always needs to answer.

Before he can even say hello, Colette tells him. "I locked the damn keys in the car and I am stranded in downtown Boston with Harrison. I decided to do some shopping today and of course there was no parking, so I am parked in a bad part of town. I am lucky my cell phone was in my pocket and I did not lock Harrison in the car."

"Are you okay?"

"Yes, but I need help and you are on the other side of the country and you do not want triple A."

This is one of the big downsides of traveling. Knowing he can't help her, he offers advice, "Have you called your mother?"

"Yes, and I called three of my friends. I cannot get a hold of anyone. I need your help."

He gets the exact location. "I will get a locksmith to come right over. I will call you back in five minutes."

He quickly hits his golf ball and tells the other guys to keep playing, then calls Billy Nestler. "Billy I need a huge favor and I need it quick."

"I am in the middle of something. What's up?"

He explains the situation and asks Billy if he can call a locksmith to help Colette. He gives Billy Colette's location and her cell phone number.

Billy will take care of it right away but can't resist a comment. "I am glad I can rescue your wife while you are playing golf on the other side of the country." Jack laughs, thanks Billy, then calls Colette with an update. Colette is nervous but she will wait by the car.

Jack does not tell anyone what has happened to Colette and keeps playing golf. He will call back in twenty minutes if he does not hear from her.

44

Colette and the Car

"The safety and happiness of society are the objects at which all political institutions aim, and to which all such institutions must be sacrificed" James Madison

Colette is standing the by the car when a group of four teenage street kids come walking down the street. It is broad daylight but Colette is nervous. She looks around for support from other people, but no one is around. The side street is empty. She picks up Harrison as the four shabbily dressed teenagers get closer on the deserted Boston street. Colette can tell the kids are trouble, but, because it is the middle of the day, she hopes they will just walk right by her. Colette contemplates walking down the street in front of them, but where will she go with Harrison. She could call Jack or the police but is she just being overly cautious?

The teenagers sense her nervousness which provides the opportunity for harassment. The four of them encircle Colette and Harrison. Colette grabs her phone and threatens to call the police when the apparent gang leader says, "Lady, put the phone down."

Colette obeys the command, "Please do not hurt my son."

The leader slowly looks around. They are on a side road, all alone. "What do you want to exchange for us letting you go?"

All Colette wants to do is protect her son, "Take whatever you want. Just let us go." Colette sees a car coming down the street and hopes the gang will run.

The leader is very cool. He keeps looking around, seeing the car too. "Look casual and the car will drive right by." Just as the leader said, the car the drives right by. He refocuses on Colette, "Lady, how much cash you got, and I need the keys to your car."

Colette only has her credit cards and no cash. She is shaking and she cannot give them what they want. She stutters, "I – I – I l-l-locked the k-keys in the car." She starts sobbing.

As she is sobbing another car comes down the street. The leader gives the gang a look to act cool. This time the car stops next to them.

The person gets out of the car, "Lady are you okay?"

Sobbing, Colette says nothing.

The person says to leader of the gang, "Woody, you and your boys get out of here."

Woody says, "Where is Stevey?"

The person walks through the group and stands right between Woody and Colette. He does not answer the question, "I need you and your friends to leave this nice lady alone."

There is tension in the air as Woody decides his next move and asks again, "Where is Stevey?"

The person does not answer him and just stares at him. If she wasn't holding Harrison, Colette thinks that she would faint.

Woody takes a step closer to the stranger, so they are nose to nose and then he smiles widely asking, "Without Stevey you afraid to even speak?"

The stranger doesn't answer but head-butts Woody so quickly, that Colette only sees Woody falling to ground. The stranger then picks him back up just as quickly. A dazed Woody says to his boys, "Let's get out of here."

As soon as the teenagers leave, while still holding Harrison, Colette hugs the man. Sobbing she says, "Thank you, Thank you, Thank you, Thank you."

"You are fine. Don't worry they are just some local kids. They would not of hurt you."

Colette wipes the tears from her eyes, "Who are you?"

"Just a concerned citizen."

With a weak smile she replies, "Thank you, concerned citizen. Can I get your name and address so I can send you something?"

He laughs, "Not necessary. I am just glad I could help you."

"Do you mind waiting with me until the locksmith shows up?"

He gives her a big smile. "I am man of many talents." He opens the trunk of his car gets out a slim jim. He walks over to the passenger side door and puts the slim jim between the window and the rubber. Two seconds later the door is unlocked.

"Wow," she claps her hands.

Colette gets her stuff out of the car. The two of them have a nice five minute conversation about nothing as Colette calms down. He says, "I need to go."

"Thank you again, and are you sure I cannot send you something?"

He just smiles and drives off.

45

Golf Continues and dinner

"One lesson you better learn if you want to be in politics is that you never go out on a golf course and beat the President." Lyndon B. Johnson

Colette calls Jack from her car and tells him everything. He is blown away. Colette keeps going on about the guy who rescued her. Jack is on his blue tooth head set and keeps playing golf while listening to his wife.

He calls Billy to tell him the story and to cancel the locksmith. Billy laughs, "Who do you think the guy was?"

"I have no idea, I am just glad he showed up."

"It is Bunar."

"Shit, that guy is following my wife!"

Billy keeps laughing, "Following? I asked him to help her out. He must not have told her who he was."

"Wow, that SOB helped my wife." Jack's attitude goes from fear to thankfulness. He asks again to call Bunar and thank him personally but Billy refuses. Billy will send his thanks to Bunar. He tries to refocus and play some golf. He is very relieved Colette and Harrison are okay, but is dumbfounded about Bunar. *Back to business.*

During golf he learns from Howard that Brian is running the show at Memorial and dropped this project and MacroHealth into his lap. Howard even apologizes for being so abrupt at their last meeting. "The decision is being rammed down my throat, so I decided to ram it down your throat. If I had it my way we would stick with CM, but now it looks like a long shot." This confirms Jack's thoughts that Brian is making the decision and wants MacroHealth.

"Thanks for being upfront. My boss is meeting with Brian today. He can be pretty persuasive. Plus, with us already having three applications installed, we can do your project cheaper and quicker than MacroHealth.

Tony and Howard are good guys, and the four of them have a great time. At the end, Howard and Jack owe Tony and Carson $8 bucks a piece. After paying up, the four of them agree to dinner that evening. After they leave, Jack and Carson stay at the golf bar and review what they learned.

They learn Memorial's CFO is cleaning house at Memorial and it looks like MacroHealth will be his decision. It appears Dr. Heins will have more influence over Brian than Howard. They agree to head back to the hotel to get an update on Kevin's meeting before dinner and hope Brian agrees to dinner.

Kevin is at the hotel, and the three of them have a drink at the bar. The first thing Jack does is get an update on the Chicago Bull versus the Orlando Magic basketball game. The game started at 8p.m. eastern, which is 5p.m. local. The game is in the first quarter and the Bulls are up five points, a good omen for Jack.

Kevin updates them on his meeting with Brian. Kevin learns Brian worked at Sacramento Medical Center before coming to Memorial. Brian is tasked with cleaning up Memorial's balance sheet and one of things he wants to do is put in a new hospital information system to help him manage their financials. Memorial has a bunch of disparate software applications and wants to put them all on the same platform. Kevin smirks, "As usual it's down to us and MacroHealth. He really likes MacroHealth, but I was able to get in some points and I offered to pay for Brian to fly out to Boston to meet the CM's management team and developers. I need you two to bring your 'A Game' to dinner tonight. We need to win both of these deals but it will take a lot of work." Kevin turns toward Jack, "Do you think there is any way we can get Reno Regional or Memorial to sign this quarter?"

Jack knows Kevin is cooking the books, and needs these deals, "No way, there are only seven business days left until the end of June. Reno Regional has MacroHealth coming next week. They want to do site visits, and we have not even sent them a contract. Even if we are selected, I think we will be lucky if they sign by the end of September. On Memorial, I just found the deal this month but if any deal has a chance for this quarter it is Memorial. We already have a contract in place, so we do not have to do the legal negotiations and it appears Brian can make unilateral decisions."

Kevin straightens up, "I am going to put the full court press on Memorial. When are you guys flying out?" Both of them say they are flying out first thing in the morning. "I may need you guys to stay Friday. If we can get additional meetings with Memorial." Jack hopes they can fly out early Friday morning so he can get back to see Colette after her traumatic day. He does not say anything to them about Colette and Bunar.

The three of them head out to dinner. Jack gets another basketball update and the Bulls are now up seven points in the second quarter.

They meet Brian, Tony, and Howard at the Steak House in downtown Reno. They are having a nice, casual dinner, when Kevin turns the conversation to business by asking the group, and specifically Brian, "Is there anything I can do to have us come to agreement this month, so we can start your project early next month?"

Brian gets very serious, "No, we need to go through a thorough due diligence process, and it will take time."

Kevin is not giving up easily. "I know you want to get all your applications on the same platform sooner rather than later. Obviously, the longer it takes you to select a vendor, the longer it will take you to get up and running on the same platform. Additionally, we have three major applications already installed. If you choose another vendor you will have to re-install those applications, which takes time. Also, think about the time and money you will save by picking a vendor now versus going through demos and site visits."

Brian warms up a little. "You make a good argument, but it does me no good to rapidly install applications which may not be a good fit for Memorial."

Kevin keeps up the heat. "What information do you need on CM? I can fly you and your team out to Boston next week to meet with us. I can set up a site visit next week."

"Kevin, I appreciate your enthusiasm, but it is just impossible to sign a contract so quickly."

Brian walked into his own objection, and Kevin pushes, "Brian, we already have a contract in place, all we need to do is add an addendum to your current agreement."

Brian keeps pushing back. "I do want to fast track this decision but the end of this month is just too soon. End of September is more realistic."

Kevin does not let go. "As you know we are a public company, and as a public company the stock market cares about our quarterly numbers. We are going to make our quarterly numbers, however your agreement can put us over the top. I can really make it worth your while financially."

Brian strategically says, "I am not making any commitments, but what is the number?" If Brian gets a heavily discounted number out of CM now, he can use the number against MacroHealth during future price negotiations.

Kevin knows Brian is smart. "I cannot give you a number tonight but I can get you a number tomorrow." Next Kevin is looking for a commitment from Brian. "It will take my team time to put the numbers together and I will have to push out some other projects. I am willing to do this but if there is no chance you will sign this month, I do not want to disrupt our internal processes?"

"Howard and Tony are you willing to stick out your neck with me if we make a rush decision?"

Jack, Carson, Howard, and Tony have all been on the sidelines watching this sparring session by two seasoned senior executives. Now they are being pulled into the ring. Tony goes first. "Brian, I like what I have seen so far but I was expecting to see a full dog and pony show by both vendors."

Brian asks the same question to Howard. Jack watches Howard closely knowing Howard is in the CM camp, "I really enjoy working with CM as a vendor and we are satisfied with the applications they have installed. I have been planning on using the next two months to put together my team for the project. I could go with the decision but I still need time to put together my implementation team."

Brian says to Kevin, "You heard both responses, your call if you want to put together a proposal."

"This is a very tough call. Are you available in the morning to have a meeting? One of the advantages of being on the West Coast is the time difference. If we meet at nine your time which is noon eastern, it should give me enough time to have my team on the east coast put together your pricing."

"I will meet with you, but no guarantees."

Kevin goes for an assumptive close. "Great, sorry about interrupting our dinner but I am so excited about working with you and helping you achieve your goals."

Brian winks, "Mr. Blair you are good."

Jack keeps checking the score on his cell phone. The Bulls are up eight points in the third quarter and thirteen points in the fourth. The six of them mix business and pleasure during the rest of the dinner. Memorial asks pointed questions about CM, and CM brags about their clients and solutions. Jack is trying to not be suspicious, especially while he is in Kevin's doghouse, but when he checks the score, the Bulls have won and he is now only down six grand. Jack says out loud, "Boom, now that is what I am talking about!"

Kevin stares at him. "Fitzy anything you want to share with the rest of the group."

"I was just checking my e-mail via my phone and I got an e-mail alert the Bulls beat the Magic by 15 points, and I am a Bulls fan too." They all laugh, and Brian asks if he can see Jack's combo phone / e-mail / pda.

As Jack hands Brian the phone, he smiles knowing he is now into Bunar for only six grand. Winning two out of three is huge this week. Now he just needs a minor plan for the last six grand.

They wrap up a successful dinner. Kevin casually asks, "I do not want to offend anyone, but I understand Reno has some interesting adult entertainment."

Jack is shocked Kevin would ask Memorial to go to a strip joint because it is a very risky question. He figures Kevin must want to spend more time with Brian and it was worth the risk, but Jack only sees a downside.

Brian is definitely the leader because both Howard and Tony wait for Brian to respond. Brian stoically, "I have to get an early start tomorrow to make room for your meeting."

Kevin is disappointed not only because Brian said no, but also because he could have offended Brian. Kevin also does not want to take Howard and Tony, so he does not ask them. Kevin just keeps talking to Brian. "I hope I did not offend you and I am looking forward to meeting you in the morning." Kevin turns to Jack. "Fitzy, you and I need to go back to the hotel and start working on Memorial's proposal."

All of them leave the restaurant. In the cab ride home, the three of them review the dinner. Kevin states, "I came on really hard. I think we have a ten percent chance they sign this month but it is worth the risk. Fitzy, I need you to get online and submit the proposal to our pricing team this evening. In the notes section, write I okay moving this proposal to the front of the queue and we need it by eleven eastern tomorrow morning. I will send some e-mails to Dennis Hintz to make sure the proposal is ready in the morning." Kevin asks Carson, "Your call if you want to stay or fly out in the morning?" Carson reluctantly agrees to stay.

When they get back to the hotel, Jack gets on-line for two hours inputting the details of the proposal. By the time he goes to bed, it is two in the morning.

46
Brian Cancels Meeting

"Anger is never without a reason, but seldom with a good one" Benjamin Franklin

Jack gets up and calls Colette. He will be home later than expected due to the turn of events at Memorial. Surprisingly, Colette takes the news okay.

Still in his hotel room packing and getting ready for their nine a.m. meeting, his cell phone rings. It is Kevin, without saying hello, "Come to my room right now. I have already called Carson."

"I am just finishing packing. I will be there in ten minutes."

Kevin yells, "Stop packing and come to my room right now, asshole."

WOW, Jack stops packing. By the time he gets to Kevin's room, Carson is already there. Kevin yells, "Brian, that SOB, cancelled our meeting. He called me this morning and said there is no way they will sign a deal by the end of the month. I said, 'My team is putting together the pricing at the eleventh hour and we would still like to meet with you.' That asshole said," Kevin changes to whiney voice, "'He has a full morning agenda and does not have the time'"

Jack tries to calm Kevin down. "You said last night this was a one in ten chance."

"That was based on having this meeting with that SOB now we have a zero in ten chance. We are going to stalk the bastard and go to his office this morning until he will see us."

Jack pushes back. "Kevin, you are not going to win the deal by bashing into his office. And worse, you could potentially lose the deal for all of us. I personally am not going to his office."

"You shut your mouth, and you will do what I tell you. I need this deal. You need this deal. CM's stock price needs this deal. What are we going to do to win the deal in the next seven business days? Fitzy, you call Howard, and Carson, you call Tony."

Jack wants to win this deal too but Kevin is out of control. "What are we going to say? 'Your boss is too busy to meet with us but will you sign this twelve million deal for him? I am bringing the contracts right over.'"

Kevin does not laugh, he stays on Jack. "I invited you in here to come up with good ideas, not stupid ones."

"Maybe you shouldn't have invited Brian to a titty bar."

"I took a risk so I could get even more information out of him at a strip joint over a few more beers. That is done, so do not bring it up again. Let's stay focused on getting in to see Brian."

"You pushed hard to get the deal this month. They cannot do it this month, but hopefully our aggressive push will get them to sign next month, which is still a very short sales cycle."

"Another stupid idea. You do not get it Fitzy, I want ideas on how to win the deal this month, not excuses. So what are you going to say when you call Howard?"

"I am not calling Howard, and if I do it will be to give him an update. You need to calm down before you lose this deal. Let's head to the airport, and we can call them on Monday."

Kevin yells, "Get the hell out of my room assholes!" Kevin looks at Carson, who has not said a word, "Goes for you too."

Jack and Carson go into the hallway. Carson speaks for the first time. "Wow, I did not know Kevin had such a temper. I am glad we are out of there."

"Me too. Kevin can really turn on the charm but he can also get pissed. I am not sure if you know this but one of Kevin's favorite sayings, is 'If you can fake sincerity, you got it made.'"

"I always thought Kevin was a good guy. He has been good to me."

"Let's see how he is when we are back in Boston next week. All I know is he better not go to Memorial today and screw up our sale. Once he calms down he will be fine. How about you and I meet in the lobby then head to the airport together?"

"What about Kevin?"

"He is a big boy he can figure a way back to Beantown. If you want, you can call him and tell him we are going to the airport, but I am not calling him."

Carson smiles, "No thanks."

Jack and Carson get in the cab when Jack says to Carson, "I need to run one quick errand." Jack has the cab take them to the Fitzgerald Casino so he can pay his five grand marker. He does not want the bill coming to his house. Carson waits in the cab and it takes fifteen long minutes to write the check and pay off his marker. Luckily, or probably more unluckily, he had the extra five thousand in their joint checking account because Bunar didn't take the check.

Carson asks, "Why did you have to go to casino?"

"Ah, I left something, ah my jacket there the other night, and I went to 'lost and found' to check on it. No luck." Luckily for him, Carson buys his white lie.

Both of them are able to get an early flight to Boston. Jack strategically picks his seat so he is not sitting near Carson on the plane, so he can review and work on his CM fraud. He needs to get some work done on the plane, not wanting Carson to bother him. He is also able to get an empty seat next to him so he can have some room to work. Jack asks the airline customer service agent. "If there is a Kevin Blair on their flight?"

She says she cannot answer the question. He turns on the charm but again she says, "I am sorry but I cannot share his information." Jack gives her the 'pretty please' look and she looks around. Without saying anything, she shakes her head 'no'. He winks and says thank you.

Jack still looks for Kevin on the plane but the airline lady was right. Kevin is not on the plane. After take-off, Jack starts copying, editing, and backing up the audio conversations with Kevin on his laptop. The FBI listening device is really cool and easy to use, and when he gets home tonight he is going to look up these devices on the web to see how expensive they are and if a regular citizen can buy them or if they are just for the government.

Not sure if he has enough evidence on CM, he again debates calling Betty to see if she has more information on CM's accounting problems, and if she looked into reporting the company. Jack is deep in thought when Carson taps him on the shoulder. "What are you working on?"

Jack has the paperwork on the accounting fraud in front of him and has the audio software up on his laptop, which he labeled, 'Kevin Lying'. He slams his laptop shut, "Ah just doing ah catch up work from our trip."

Carson is a smart guy. "I did not know 'catch up' is labeled, 'Kevin Lying'."

Jack is silent for which feels like an hour before he says, "I am just pissed about the verbal beating you and I took today."

"What are you up to?"

"Nothing. Just blowing off some steam."

Carson advises, "You be careful."

"I will be fine by the time I see Kevin on Monday."

Jack puts the accounting stuff away and shuts down the audio software. He does real CM work by answering e-mails and sending thank you e-mails to Howard Black and Tony Heins for golf and Brian Lietten for dinner. With the end of the quarter right around the corner, he updates his sales forecast for June and Q2. With Kevin and Dennis cooking the books and Memorial most likely not signing this month, Kevin will be on him first thing Monday morning.

One nice thing about Memorial canceling the meeting is Jack is able to get home on Friday versus Saturday. Colette has the kitchen light on when he pulls into his driveway. He gets tense because the last time he came home late from a trip Colette was awake they got into a big fight.

As he walks into the kitchen, sure enough Colette is sitting at the table reading a magazine. Jack is braced for a fight when she gives him a big hug. "I am so glad your meeting was cancelled today, and you were able to come home sooner."

Jack is confused and jokes, "Excuse me miss but have you seen my wife. She is really pretty like you, but she does not get excited when I come home at midnight."

"Stop it. I have made dinner plans just for you and I tomorrow, and I was afraid if you were flying back tomorrow I would have to cancel our plans."

"What is the special occasion? We already celebrated my birthday last week."

Colette smirks, "Can a wife ask her husband out on a date?"

Jack smiles, "Yes but what is the occasion?"

"No occasion."

"You are hiding something. What did you buy while I was out of town this week?"

Colette frowns. "I did not buy anything. Now stop it. We are going out to dinner tomorrow night."

Jack sees this as an opportunity for this evening, even with it being so late. "How about we go upstairs and have a little fun before we go to bed? And before you answer, I have some good news too. I am not going to play golf tomorrow." He had left Billy a message earlier today saying he is out for golf. Tired from the trip, plus he really wants to research listening devices and even better, he gets the added benefit of scoring points with his wife by not playing golf.

"It is late but I think I might be able to accommodate your request." Jack and Colette go upstairs holding hands.

47

Bugs, Bets, Babies

"Do not bite at the bait of pleasure, till you know there is no hook beneath it." Thomas Jefferson

As expected, on Saturday morning The Fitzpatrick's phone rings. Jack wakes up from a sound sleep and hangs up the phone without answering, knowing it is Billy and the boys from the golf course. They call right back, "Come-on guys. You are going to wake up my kid and just to make you feel better, you did succeed on waking me up."

Everyone is asleep when Jack heads down stairs to get a cup of coffee. The first thing he does is boot up his computer and start looking at listening devices on the web. He is amazed there are so many out there, and, to his surprise, you can buy them at Radio Shack. They are marked as recording devices for learning, but it is very obvious what they can be used for. He also finds you can easily buy technology to record phone conversations too.

Colette comes downstairs without hearing her. "Wow, isn't it great Harrison is sleeping in on a Saturday?"

Jack jumps. "What?"

"What are you doing?"

"Just getting caught up on some work. I am sorry, what did you say? Can I get you a cup of coffee?" Jack shuts down his laptop.

"Yes, and I said, 'Isn't it nice Harrison is sleeping through the night?' Do you miss getting up at night with Harrison?"

Jack laughs. "Like I miss IRS Audits."

"Come-on, isn't it nice to hold a little baby in your arms?"

"Of course, but it is not exciting at four a.m. when the little guy is crying."

Colette frowns and changes the subject, "So, are you excited about tonight?"

While they are making their dinner plans, Harrison gets up and the three of them enjoy a nice morning together. Jack states, "I need to run some errands, and I will take Harry with me to give you a break. Is there anything I can get for you?"

"Thanks, and it is Harrison. Where are you going?"

"The Home Depot near the mall." The reason he chose the mall there is a Radio Shack inside the mall. At Radio Shack, he gets advice from the high school salesperson on the recording devices. He buys two telephone recorders and three voice activated listening devices.

When Jack gets home, Colette is out running errands. He puts Harrison down for a nap and goes into his home office to test the devices. The telephone recorder is so simple. You simply plug the recorder in the phone jack in the wall and push the phone jack into the device. The device looks like a pack of gum and is barely noticeable. Even if you saw it, it looks like it belongs. He calls Billy and records their conversation.

After a quick update on golf, Jack jumps to, "I still do not believe you will not let me contact Bunar directly. I need you to make one more bet for me." Billy gives his usual sermon but as usual, Jack still convinces Billy to take the bet. "Hey I won two out of my three bets this week, and I only owe Bunar six grand. I know I have taken a beating but I am close to getting out of this. I simply need you to place a bet for ten grand on the Celtics against the Atlanta Hawks for tomorrow's game, and. win or lose, I am done with Bunar."

"Okay but are you sure this is your last bet with Bunar?"

"Definitely!" Jack pauses, "If I win."

"Win or lose, this is the last bet… I take."

"Hey, do you place bets for anyone else with Bunar?" Jack does not want to get Billy ensnarled in his Bunar plans.

Lucky for Jack, "No, why do you ask?"

"Just curious. Hey I need to run." Jack starts listening to the conversation he recorded. He can hear both of them clearly, editing and copying the audio files on his laptop. He is listening to the conversation, when he hears Colette come in the house. He is very tired but is getting close to the end with the FBI and Bunar. He could cancel the dinner with Colette so he can get some sleep but knows it is not fair and not right.

Jack and Colette get ready for dinner. They head into Boston's North End for dinner. The North End is world famous for the Italian Restaurants and the Old North Church where Paul Revere started his famous ride through the streets of Boston during the Revolutionary War.

Colette picks her favorite restaurant, 'Daily Catch'. The place is so small there is no restroom and only eight tables. You have to use another restaurant's bathroom across the street. Jack orders a bottle of wine when Colette interrupts, "I do not feel like drinking tonight." He says okay and orders himself a beer. Colette announces, "I have some big news."

Jack figures she is about to announce they are re-landscaping their back yard, "Great, what is up?"

"I am pregnant."

To his surprise, he immediately breaks down crying and squeezes out, "Wow, awesome, I am so excited." The pressure of dealing with the FBI and Bunar, trying to win two big sales, stealing from his wife, the platonic relationship with Michelle, and now being a father for the second time is just too much for him to handle. Wiping his eyes gives Colette a big hug. With the size of the restaurant, it is impossible to not notice them. With Jack still weeping and smiling, he squeezes out in between the tears, "I just found out we are having our second baby."

The small restaurant claps. Colette is shocked, "I am blown away. I knew you would be excited but I had no idea you would cry. You did not cry when we found out about being pregnant with Harrison."

Jack is starting to calm down, "When we had Harrison, we were really trying. I did not even see this coming. I should have known when you talked about staying up with babies this morning, you were sick the other morning, and you did not order wine tonight. I have just been so wrapped up at work I did not see it. I guess I started crying because I am so excited."

Jack starts asking the normal questions. When is the baby due? When did Colette find out? What names does she like? Does she want to find out the sex, like they did with Harrison?

When the euphoria wears off, Jack realizes he is going to have another mouth to feed while he battles his gambling losses, the unknown future of his work, the danger of not paying Bunar, and the threat of the FBI. He may have to look for another job. They are having such a good time, he forgets about his troubles for a couple of hours and enjoys dinner and an evening with his wife.

48

Starting the Plan

"Let our advance worrying become advance thinking and planning", Winston Churchill

Jack gets up Sunday morning and goes for a run. He typically does not run on days he plays basketball but today he needs to think. Colette being pregnant and Bunar helping Colette, accelerates the timeline to make some very tough decisions. He decides to keep Colette in the dark for now. *With Colette being pregnant she does not need to worry about my self-induced gambling problems and my company-inflicted accounting troubles.*

Even with Bunar helping Colette, he needs the FBI out of his life. *Can I give Bunar to the FBI without incriminating myself and without Bunar ever finding out it is me?* He is going to continue to gather the information on CM, but hold off on telling CM's CEO, Catherine Corbett, until after the Memorial and Reno Regional deals. This way he has a chance to earn $200,000 in commissions. If he wins both deals, he can anonymously report the accounting fraud, quit CM, and find another job.

Jack decides to leave a bug in McCracken's. He is going to stick one of the voice activated devices under Bunar's table. He will call Billy to set up a lunch meeting with Bunar tomorrow at McCracken's. This should give the FBI a full day of conversations on the listening device.

Jack is also going to bug Kevin and Dennis's office phones at CM in addition to his own office phone. Jack will need to go to CM today to bug the phones.

He feels invigorated after his run. He will go after Kevin, and get the FBI off his back without Bunar knowing. Besides getting caught placing the bugs, if either CM or Bunar finds the bugs, they will never know where they came from. He showers and tells Colette he is going into the office for a few hours.

At the office there are only a couple of cars in the parking lot and none he recognizes, which is a good sign. Going into his office, he practices unplugging the phone jack and putting in the listening device. It literally takes 10 seconds. Testing out the device, he calls Billy to make sure he has placed the bets with Bunar and to set up the lunch tomorrow at McCracken's. Jack tells Billy he is more than welcome to join them. Billy would love to, but is unavailable. After they hang up, he unplugs the device and listens to the conversation. *Perfect.*

Down the hall is Kevin's office. As usual, it is unlocked. Jack is in and out in less than 15 seconds, now for Dennis' office. Dennis' office is on the first floor in Accounting, which is made up of a group of offices with a reception area. He has not seen anyone in the accounting office, which is a good sign. He scans the area and goes into the reception area. He still does not see anyone.

Jack tries to get into Dennis' office and the door is locked, *"Shit"*. He jiggles the door but it definitely is locked. He starts to walk into the accounting reception area when he sees someone walking down the hall. Running over to the reception desk, he hides under the desk. He is listening to see if he can hear the person walk by the accounting office. He did not have enough time to get a look at the person. The hair on the back of his neck stands up as he hears the person coming into the accounting office. As quietly as possible for someone six feet four inches, he squeezes himself into the area where the receptionist's legs would be and slides the chair in front of him. He is facing towards the far wall versus the hallway running between the reception desk and the other offices in accounting.

Jack is trying to listen, but all he hears is himself panting, so he slows down his breathing, as if shooting free throws. The person walks by the desk. He swears to himself because the person has stopped right in front of him. Waiting for someone to move the chair when he hears a door open but not close. *How can I be trapped again on a Sunday inside of CM.* Last Sunday it was in Kevin's office this week accounting. *Can I turn around without making much noise?* He needs to see if the person walks by the reception desk on the way out. He slowly pushes back the receptionist's chair when he notices a hook under the desk with a set of keys. *My luck could be turning around.* He is willing to bet the keys open doors in accounting including Dennis's office.

I can't spend another minute trapped. He slowly slides back the chair. *Can I tiptoe out of the accounting office into the hallway?* Quickly he pops up from under the desk, walks around the desk in the reception area heading for the door. He is almost out of accounting, when he hears a familiar female voice, "Hey, what are you doing?"

Jack has no idea how much she has seen. Turning around, Maureen O'Shea inquires, "Fitzy what are you doing in accounting?"

Quick on his feet, responds, "I was hoping Dennis was in the office on a Sunday."

Maureen laughs. "No way, only his lackeys, like me, work on Sundays."

Jack laughs too. "Then what are you doing in on a Sunday?"

"With the end of the quarter coming, I am starting to do the prep work on the financial numbers."

"How are the numbers looking?"

"You should know more than me. I just take your sales and put them in the right accounting column."

Jack is trying to decide he if should take a risk and ask Maureen about the books. *It is too risky after getting lucky Maureen did not ask me why I was looking for Dennis by walking out of the office versus into it.* "How long are you going to be here?"

"At least a couple of hours. Why are you in today and how are your sales looking for the quarter?"

Jack goes positive. "Looking good. That is why I am in today. I am trying to get caught up too."

Jack heads up to his office to pack up and go home. Nothing he can do now with Maureen in the office. He will come back by CM on his way home from basketball.

On his way home he gets a small gift for Colette to celebrate her getting pregnant. As usual, Jack has no idea what to get her. He stops at the supermarket and gets her a plant and a cheap congratulation card on getting pregnant.

At home he talks Colette into letting him take a nap before his basketball game. At basketball, his team easily wins the game. The team they play is weak so Jack does not play much and does more passing than scoring when he does play. His team will be the number one seed during the play-offs, which start next week. After the game, asks Chip if he can see him for a few minutes.

Chip says, "Easy win tonight. You coming out for beers?"

"No can do, but I need another favor?"

Chip laughs, "Don't tell me you want to re-borrow the five grand you just paid me back?"

"Nope, but…," Jack pulls Chip's shirt and drags him over to the corner of the gym. "The FBI is putting some real heat on me, and I need a legal favor. I am going to send you some documents this week that I need you to keep in a safe place in case something happens to me."

Chip gets serious. "Fitzy, the FBI does not physically hurt people. Why do you need me to put something in a safe place?"

Jack says, "I am not worried about the FBI hurting me. I am worried about the guy the FBI is trying to take down hurting me."

"I think it is time you get a lawyer. Why don't we set up a meeting this week with one of my firm's attorneys?"

"I appreciate the offer, but I am going to take care of this all by myself."

"Jack, you are not smart enough to take on the FBI. What is a good day for you next week?"

Jack lightens up the mood. "Come on man. I am smarter than the FBI."

"I am serious. As your friend, who is an attorney, you need an attorney. At a minimum you can lay your case on the table and you can get some real legal advice."

To get Chip to get off his back, "I will think about the attorney, but until then can you hold onto the packages?"

"So now it is packages versus a package. What are in these packages?"

"Not telling, just need you to hold onto them."

Chip frowns. "Okay but I am not guaranteeing I will not open them."

"Thanks, and we both know you will not open the packages, and, as usual, do not tell your wife."

"What are you up to? You are going to cost me my marriage. Why do I keep doing you these favors?"

Jack starts walking towards the exit of the gym, "Because, I have a great jump shot. Tell the guys I said 'sorry' and I will have a beer with them after we win our playoff game."

Chip yells, "Sure, and I will drink another beer tonight just for you."

Pulling into the CM parking lot, *'Shit'*, as he sees Kevin Blair and Kim Savard's cars in the parking lot. He just wants to get in and out. *Kevin is still probably pissed at me from Friday. I don't want to see him but I really need to bug accounting.* Jack parks on a different level of the parking garage in case Kevin and Kim leave before him, he then sneaks through a back down into accounting without anyone seeing him.

The accounting office is dark. He walks into the reception area. Smiles because no one is in the office and the darkness will cover him if someone looks into accounting. He grabs the keys from under the reception desk and starts trying them on Dennis' door. The first three keys fit into the lock but do not open the door. The fourth key opens the door. Jack quietly slips into Dennis' office and closes the door behind him. *If my CM sales career goes down the toilet I may take up a new career as a private detective. Shit,* Dennis has the shades drawn in his office and it is almost pitch black. He did not bring a flashlight. Risking it, he turns on the lights. It takes his eyes a second to adjust before quickly installing the telephone listening device.

He is out of the office in under a minute and puts the keys back under the receptions desk. He will use them tomorrow night to pick up the recorder. He now heads back to the parking lot and hopes neither Kevin nor Kim sees him. Just to kid Kim, he will thank her for coming in Sunday night.

To put the finishing touches on a very successfully day, he learns the Celtics won and Bunar now owes him four grand. To put a cherry on top, Colette is excited

Jack did not go out for beers after basketball. He is rewarded, after a shower, in the bedroom. *My luck is definitely turning around.*

49

Lunch with Bunar and getting the bugs

"Believe me! The secret of reaping the greatest fruitfulness and the greatest enjoyment from life is to live dangerously!"
Friedrich Nietzsche

Getting into work, there is only one new voicemail, "Fitzy this is Bunar. I bet you are looking forward to our lunch today. Congratulations on your win."

After being out of the office for a week, Jack starts getting caught up on paperwork. The first thing he does is his expense report for last week. Including flights, hotel, and entertainment he spent over nine thousand of CM's money, which is about what he expected. He works on his follow-up from last week and what he needs to do to get the deals signed. Busy working, his phone rings with a Boston number, the number is the FBI.

"Agent Stephenson good to hear from you. You are on my call list today."

"Well, I guess I should ask you why you were going to call me today?"

Jack is in a good mood, "No this is your dime. Please, you go first."

"I just wanted to let you know I am working on the paperwork to indict you in the Bunar gambling ring."

Jack pulls back. Getting indicted is not in his plans. *Maybe Agent Stephenson is bluffing but no way to tell.* He still moves forward with his plan. "Agent Stephenson, I am not sure if you can delay your indictment but the reason I'm calling is to let you know I am having lunch with Bunar today at McCracken's and to see if you could meet me tomorrow morning."

"So are you going to help us?"

Just what Jack wanted, "Are you going to promise you will go away and I will not be indicted if I help you?"

Jack is surprised, "Yes, I promise you will not be indicted, if you help us."

'Bingo' He is recording the conversation. "Great, where do you want to meet tomorrow morning?"

"Your pick. I will even come down to Bridgewater."

"Obviously, I do not want anyone to see us. How about we meet at the Exxon station off exit 23 in Brockton at seven-thirty?"

"I will be there."

Step one complete. Jack closes his door, disconnects the telephone recorder and plugs it into his computer. He now has Agent Stephenson on tape saying he will not be indicted. He saves the message to add to his Bunar file.

Listening to the recorded Agent Stephenson's conversation is a major disappointment. Jack can only hear his side of the conversation. Agent Stephenson's side of the conversation is all static, "Damn it." The FBI must have some kind of scrambler on their phones. His second failure at trying to get Agent Stephenson on tape. Just like at the airport. He wonders, *Can Agent Stephenson tell I was recording the conversation?* He gives the FBI more credit. *Maybe I should go see Chip's law firm. Nope.* He pushes forward with his plan.

Jack does some more work before heading into Boston for his lunch with Bunar. Driving into Boston he reviews his plan. He bought some special two sided adhesive tape, which he is going to stick the FBI's voice-activated recorder under Bunar's table. He is going to do this when he is done with lunch so he does not record his gambling conversations but instead conversations of other transactions.

It is a beautiful sunny day in Boston and Jack finds a parking spot near McCracken's. He is thinking about Bunar saving his wife last week, but he also reflects on the times Bunar slashed their tires. Even though Billy says Bunar would not hurt them, Jack is not so sure. Although sunny outside, it is very dark inside McCracken's.

Jack walks over to Bunar's table and sits down. They exchange some friendly barbs when Jack states, "Before we do anything, I want to thank you for helping my wife and son last week."

"I am glad I could help."

Jack gets back to business, "So are you going to pay me my four grand now or after lunch?"

Bunar laughs, "Nope. You are not getting paid today."

"What? This is Bullshit. I won and you are not going to pay me?" *Is Bunar not going to pay me because he helped Colette this week?* He must have said "Bullshit" louder than he wanted, because Stevey walks over to their table.

Bunar laughs and says to Stevey, "Fitzy wants to get paid today." Jack looks at Stevey with his confused look. Bunar continues, "Stevey, after all your trips to Bridgewater to get paid when Fitzy owed us money, he expects us to pay him the first day. That is very funny." Stevey starts laughing. "We are fine Stevey, go sit back at the bar."

Bunar has taken the wind out of Jack's sails, "Come on man." Jack starts grasping at straws, "I thought bookies had to pay on time to keep up their good reputation."

Bunar keeps laughing, "Fitzy, sometime I think you are a very bright guy and other times I think Stevey is smarter than you. Yes, I will pay you but not today. I pay on Wednesdays and get paid on Wednesday. I made exceptions because you are new and you wanted to make more and larger bets. I just figured you wanted to take me up on my generous offer of lunch and wanted to make some bets because by my math even with your win yesterday you are still down over $30,000." Bunar slides over today's sports page with the games and betting lines.

Even though Jack did not plan on betting he is tempted. Jack refocuses. "Okay, is there any way I can get paid tomorrow?"

"Fitzy, I like you, and, even though you were a few days late with your payments, you did come up with a good amount of money in a short period of time. Additionally, I am hoping to build a long and mutually profitable relationship." Bunar pauses, "Okay, you can come back tomorrow and I will have your money. A day early. You can still make some wagers if you want."

Jack does not want Bunar to think he is not ever coming back, "I took a beating the last two weeks and I just need a little breathing room. I will definitely make more wagers with you once I get my cash situation back in order."

"Enough business. Let's enjoy a little lunch." They have a great lunch. They tell funny stories about Billy. Jack wants to get a feel for Bunar's business, so he gets Bunar to start telling about the crazy bets he has taken and what he has taken for payment. When lunch is over, Jack is thinking about not leaving the FBI's listening device. Bunar is a good guy, he helped Colette but Jack needs to get the FBI out of his life and Bunar did slash their tires. Just before Jack stands up, he clicks and sticks the bug under the table.

Making sure he gets his four grand tomorrow, as he is leaving, "Thank you in advance for paying me tomorrow."

On the drive back to the office, Jack wonders if he is doing the right thing. Bunar really seems like a good guy and they just had a great lunch. *Bunar is a big boy and his problems with the FBI are his not mine. The plan must go forward.* Bunar not paying Jack does put a big wrinkle in his plans, so Jack decides when he gets back in the office to call Agent Stephenson and reschedule their morning meeting to Wednesday morning at the same place.

Jack does not need to wait until he gets into the office, because Agent Stephenson calls his cell phone.

"Jack, you better not be screwing with us. I know you just left McCracken's."

Jack makes up a story. "Bunar did not have time for me today. I am going back to meet with him tomorrow."

This statement is a huge risk and a good test. If the FBI has cameras, bugs, or agents inside of McCracken's they will know Jack is lying but if they do not, he will also confirm the FBI needs his help. "You were inside McCracken's exactly 57 minutes, I am surprised you did not meet with Bunar."

Jack keeps it up, "I waited, but Bunar was unavailable."

"The restaurant was pretty empty for lunch today with only his usual associates, so I am surprised he did not see you."

"Sorry, I do not keep his schedule. He said he will see me tomorrow."

"Was he agitated today?"

Jack feels comfortable the FBI is not inside of McCracken's. "A little I guess. He was on his cell phone most of the time."

"I will meet you Wednesday morning and this better be good. If you are screwing me you will get indicted and I will make sure all of Bridgewater knows including your wife and employer." Jack is about to push back but Agent Stephenson has already hung up.

As he walks into the building, Kevin sees him in the lobby atrium from the second floor. Kevin sprints down the stairs to meet Jack. Kevin screams, "Come up to my office now."

"I just got back from lunch, can I check my voicemails and e-mails. I will call see you in five minutes.

"Nope, get your ass in my office now." Based on Kevin's recent erratic behavior, Jack does not know what to expect. He is confident it will not be good.

Jack wishes he tapped Kevin's office in addition to his phone line because he would love to record this conversation. Kevin continues right where he left off on Friday. "What kind of bullshit was that on Friday?"

"What are you talking about?"

"You are inches from being fired."

"Are you serious?"

"Damn serious"

"Okay, well at least tell me why you are going to fire me."

"Because you disobeyed me last week. When I said we were going to see Memorial and you just left me in Reno. Your job is to close deals and you are behind quota. Plus you fell asleep during our meetings last week."

"I am leaving this meeting."

"If you leave this meeting you are fired."

"You are not being reasonable. I disagreed with your ridiculous request to get Reno signed this quarter. I am 60% of my quota, and the two deals on my plate can put me at 130% of my number in the next 90 days. You are a big boy, so I figured you could get back to Boston on your own."

"I noticed you did not address falling asleep."

Jack pushes back, "Write me up if you want but it is not a fireable offense because it did not affect the deal, and we both know it. I will state I stayed up all night getting ready for the meeting, as you requested."

"If you get Reno Regional signed this month, I will let you keep your job."

Jack knows most of this is just a show to push him to sign Reno Regional this month because Memorial is not going to sign. "Go ahead. You have been in this business a long time. We just did the demos last week, and our competition is on-site today. Your requests are not reasonable."

"Get out of my office, while I decide your fate. If you are lucky, I will figure out how to make our number this quarter so you can keep your job and keep your stock options above water."

Jack does not say anything going back to his office. As Jack walks back to his office, he sees Kim following him. She asks him a question about Reno Regional. Jack does not hear her, and walks into his office. Jack is tempted to quit and pack up his stuff. He tries to focus but is still shaking after the conversation with Kevin.

Kim follows Jack right into his office. "Hey Fitzy, I got a question on Reno Regional?"

Jack is just on the edge of rage, "Sorry, now is not a good time. Let's connect in an hour or two."

"You okay?"

Jack mumbles, "I will be okay." Jack walks her out of his office locking the door behind her.

Jack feels like crying but what he really wants to do is go back into Kevin's office and beat the shit out him, *Shove this job and the Reno deals up your ass.* Jack really needs the commission checks on both deals. He is trying to figure out if there is a way he can get Kevin fired and win the deals. He decides his first job is to get Kevin fired and getting the commissions are secondary.

Jack is so frustrated, he calls CM's CEO, Catherine Corbett, directly. "Catherine Corbett's Office, this is Sandra."

Jack gathers himself, "Sandra this is Jack Fitzpatrick in Sales. How are you doing today?"

"I am fine. What can I do for you Fitzy?"

"Is Catherine available? I would like to meet with her today."

"Catherine's schedule is booked until Wednesday. How about 4p.m. on Wednesday?"

"I will take it."

"Okay, what should I tell Catherine this meeting is about?" Jack pauses. He obviously cannot tell her 'To get Kevin Blair fired.' Jack is still thinking when Sandra says, "Are you still there?"

"Ah yes. Please tell her the meeting is a Northwest sales update." Jack hangs up. In retrospect, not getting to see Catherine today is probably good, because it will give Jack time to get the telephone recordings from both Kevin and Dennis's offices. *Kevin is going down for cooking the books.* It hits Jack. If Catherine is cooking the books too, Jack is going down. He decides it is worth the risk and can always cancel the meeting if necessary.

Jack's caller ID shows the call is Michelle with Reno. "Hey, how are you doing? Shouldn't you be in the middle of the MacroHealth demos?"

"I'm great, I just got a few minutes but I want to give you a call. MacroHealth is bombing."

"Wow, why are they doing so badly?"

"They are not following Cheryl's instructions, which is pissing her off, and they did not bring a doctor, so they are not doing a good job of answering our doctor's questions. It is looking good for you, Fitzy. Well, I have got to go. I just stepped out during a break. I will give you a call tomorrow with more information."

"Please do and I will be working late tonight if you want to call me after the meetings."

"I will try, but we have a dinner with MacroHealth tonight. Bye."

Jack spins in his chair. It now looks like he could win the twenty-eight million dollar deal sooner rather than later. It was a lot easier to put a $140,000 commission behind ethics when you do not think you are going to win. Jack now has until four o'clock on Wednesday afternoon to make a decision. *I can always cancel the meeting.*

Jack decides to head home for a few hours and will come back to the office later in the evening to get the bugs. Jack tells Colette he has some follow up work from the Reno trip and is going to go back to the office.

He gets back into the office around 8:30p.m. There are only a couple cars in the parking lot. Because accounting is on the first floor, Jack walks towards accounting first. There are lights on. Being the end of the quarter, Jack is not surprised. He goes upstairs to Kevin's office. The sales department is empty, as usual, and Kevin's office is unlocked. Jack very quickly unplugs the recorder, and heads towards his office.

Jack can listen to Kevin's phone conversations then check back on accounting. Jack plugs the device into his laptop. He blushes because he feels weird listening to Kevin's personal conversations, but then refocuses on Kevin wanting to fire him.

The device tells Jack there are 37 calls for a total of 5 hours. *Wow, I will be here until 2 a.m. if I listen to the whole thing.* Jack starts going through the calls. Kevin got in early on Monday around seven a.m. The first call is to voicemail. There are only a couple of calls, nothing exciting. At, eight a.m. Kevin has a call with

Catherine Corbett. Jack gets his answer as to whether Catherine is in the know of the accounting fraud. Very quickly it is obvious she is not.

Kevin starts the call with Catherine by bullshitting her with how good the meetings went last week in Reno and that Memorial will sign this quarter. Kevin mentions three other clients who are signing multi-million dollar add-ons. Jack writes downs these client names assuming they are fake deals. Right after the call with Catherine, Kevin leaves a message for Dennis Hintz to call him.

To Jack's surprise and disappointment Kevin's next call is to Kim Savard. "Holy shit!" The two of them are having an affair. They talk about how much fun they had in Reno together. Jack had no idea. Another decision for Jack. He can blackmail Kevin because he is married and having an affair but he would be taking down his friend Chip Savard. Jack cannot listen anymore. He pauses the tape before clicking to the next message. Shaking his head debates, *If I tell Kim or Chip, would Kim tell Colette about my platonic relationship with Michelle?*

Jack takes a deep breath and re-starts the tape. The next call to Kevin is from Dennis Hintz. Kevin changes his tone from the conversation with Kim, and jumps on Dennis, 'You got the numbers ready to make our numbers for the stock market?' Dennis timidly tries pushing back, 'Are you going to close forty million in new deals by Monday, June 30th?' Kevin stays on him, 'I am trying but either way we need to make our stock market numbers, you hear me?' Dennis squirms, 'We need to tell Catherine what we are doing?' Kevin yells, 'You listen to me, we are not telling Catherine anything. And we are making our quarterly numbers.' Jack can tell Kevin angrily hung up. From the time of the call, Jack can tell this was just before his meeting with Kevin.

The next few calls are a combination of business and pleasure. Kevin has an hourly contract call with a prospect, which Jack skips. Kevin calls a friend, and has him buy a hundred thousand dollars of CM stock for him. Jack writes down Kevin's friend's name, Dave. Jack can research later. He shakes his head. *I really liked Kevin and now I find out that he is cheating on his wife; cooking the books; and making illegal stock trades. Man what you can learn about someone when you tap their phone.*

Kevin calls Maureen O'Shea in accounting. By now Jack is not surprised to find out Kevin is having an affair with her too. Jack is expecting more dirt but the rest of the calls are an uneventful combination of personal and business.

He will grab the other bug from Dennis' office before going home. He is surprised to find the lights are still on in the accounting office. He debates finding out who is in accounting but decides he does not want to push his luck.

50

Follow up lunch with Bunar

"Take time to deliberate; but when the time for action arrives, stop thinking and go in."
Andrew Jackson

The next day, Jack stops at Radio Shack on the way to the office to buy another voice-activated listening device. He plans on swapping this device with the one he left at Bunar's yesterday. He sees Kim Savard on his way into work and his stomach turns, as he gives Kim a fake hello walking into this office.

For his lunch with Bunar today, Jack is planning to get his four grand from Bunar, switch bugs under the table, and get out. He needs to get ready for the FBI, and giving them evidence on Bunar, without Bunar knowing, to get the FBI out his life forever.

Jack's morning goes by quickly as he gets ready to drive into South Boston. Getting ready to leave, he receives an e-mail from Catherine.

From: Catherine Corbett
To: Jack Fitzpatrick
Cc: Kevin Blair
Subject: Meeting on 6/25 @ 4pm
Sent: Tuesday, June 24th 11:18am

Jack:

I am looking forward to meeting with you tomorrow and Kevin is going to join us.

Thanks,
Catherine

Now Jack has two problems, Kevin will be in the meeting and two he will probably have to deal with Kevin before tomorrow at four. He leaves the office to meet with Bunar.

Every time Jack sees Bunar at McCracken's something happens he does not anticipate, and now he is really at risk because he is picking up a bug and dropping one off. As usual, McCracken's is dark and Bunar is sitting with Stevey at the usual back table. The bad news is Stevey is sitting where Jack sat yesterday, right where the bug is. Jack wonders if they know he planted the bug. Bunar jokes, "If it is not my favorite gambler?"

Jack sits right next to Stevey so he can get the bug. When Jack sits downs, Stevey stands up, "Why so close, Fitzy?"

"I thought we had assigned seats." Stevey shrugs and walks back to the bar to sit down. As soon as Stevey stands up, Jack makes the quick decision of grabbing the bug he stashed yesterday and sticking a new bug under the table. Jack tries to wipe the sweat off his brow before Bunar sees it.

Bunar says, "Get up!"

Panicking, "What? What's wrong?" Jack does not stand up.

Smiling, "Get your ass up! What is wrong with you today?"

Slowly he stands up not sure what is going to happen next. *Do I confess?*

"We are going for a walk."

This can't be good. "W-w-w-where?"

"Fitzy, what is wrong with you. I need to go get the money I owe you." Bunar lets out a big laugh, "What did you think I was going to do?"

Jack relaxes, "Nothing, I just figured you would give me the cash." Trying to be cool, "So where are we going?"

"Just a short walk over to TJ's on K Street." They walk out the back door then down a narrow alley lined with black garbage bags. At the end is a rusted chain link fence, that Bunar athletically and effortlessly hops. Not to be outdone Jack mimics the move, and then they take a left heading towards the ocean.

Bunar is casually talking about the Red Sox, how he hasn't been to Fenway Park in years, and one of his gamblers wants to pay him in season tickets down the third base line.

They are one street from the ocean, when Bunar takes a right and they enter a skinny one story cinderblock building with faded green paint and a sturdy old brown door. There is a half lit neon sign, TJ's. As they walk in Bunar says, "Stay close, don't say much, and we will be out of here in ten minutes."

Jack nods thinking, *Man this fun.* The place is emptier than McCracken's. On the way out, Jack plans on asking, 'How do these bars stay open with no customers?'

As two of them are walking up to the bar along the side of the building, the bartender says, "Bunar, you are early but I got your money." Then he looks Jack up and down, "What are you drinking and I hope this skinny guy isn't replacing Stevey?"

Bunar laughs, "Nope but he is our guy if we start a Southie Basketball team and I'll take a Guinness. Fitzy what are you drinking?"

When in Rome, "I'll have one too."

The three of them take a seat towards the back at a worn round table. As they are sitting down, the guy hands Bunar an envelope. If Jack wasn't looking that way he wouldn't have seen the transaction. Bunar doesn't acknowledge the transaction nor introduce Jack. The bartender is talking about some guy from Providence.

The door opens and three guys walk in. Jack is staring at them as they walk towards them. The guy in the front's face lights up when he sees Bunar, "Surprise, Surprise, Surprise, if it isn't the asshole who ain't going to store my dope." He grabs a chair and spins it around and sits down facing Bunar with Jack on his left and the bartender on his right. The other two guys stand behind him. To Jack's total surprise he takes a small black gun and points it right at Bunar saying, "You ain't so tough wit out Stevey."

Bunar just stares at him

"That's right keep you damn mouth shut." Still Bunar says nothing.

The guy then looks at Jack, "What are you looking at asshole?" Waving the gun in Jack's direction, "Maybe I should pop you first."

Jack tries to look away, but his body tightens up and his insides feel hollow. Bunar calmly responds, "Carl you are not going to shoot anyone today."

The bartender interrupts, "Carl, what do you want?"

Carl looks at the bartender, "I was going to have you to store my dope but now I am going to put a cap in Bunar's buddy's ass just for fun."

Carl starts to look back at Jack, when Bunar suddenly lifts up his side of the table. The beers go flying, drives the table into the unsuspecting Carl's chest, knocking him over his chair. Then Bunar steps on Carl's arm taking the gun from him. Standing over Carl, "Should I shoot one of your guys or just as you say put a 'Cap in your ass?'" The two guys look at each other but don't move. In less than one second, Bunar has the situation in control.

Carl pushed the table off himself with his free hand but can't stand up with Bunar's foot still on his forearm. Squatting down with the gun in his right hand, "Carl, this has got to stop. Skinny is going to get involved soon if you keep this up." Bunar looks at Fitzy, still frozen in his seat, "Lets go."

The two of them walk back to McCracken's. Jack is in shock and does not say anything until Bunar is about to jump the chain link fence back to McCracken's back door. "Thanks man, I thought that guy was going to kill me."

"That guy was not going to kill. He just wanted to scare you and I was sick of his shit."

"You saved my life."

"Fitzy, I didn't save your life but you will have a great story to tell the guys at the country club." Bunar then grabs the envelope from his back pocket and counts out forty hundreds for him. Jack wants to hug Bunar or at least tell him he doesn't want the money but Bunar easily hops the fence and walks down the alley back to McCracken's.

Bunar offers lunch but he isn't hungry, and with his hands shaking, he is not sure he could find his month. He shakes Bunar's hand, thanks him again and is off.

Putting the four grand in the glove compartment, he takes a deep breath trying to relax, and realizes he has the recorder. Jack turns on his laptop to listen to

Bunar's conversation on the way to the office, while he is still parked on a side street near McCracken's, he plugs the listening device into the USB port on his laptop.

'Crack, Crack' the sounds of knocking on Jack's windshield. Jack jumps and looks up, its Agent Stephenson. Putting down his window, Jack begs, "Agent Stephenson, please, please, get away from my car. If Bunar or Stevey see you, I am in deep trouble."

"So, how did your meeting go?"

Holy Shit, he knows what happened at TJ's. "What?" *I need to get out of here.*

"How did your meeting go with Bunar?"

"Fine, fine, I really need to get back to the office."

"You better be at our meeting tomorrow."

I will be there."

"I am watching you. Do not screw with me."

"No worries, I will see you tomorrow morning." Jack shuts the window and drives off. *Agent Stephenson is going to get me killed.*

The cell phone caller ID says Kevin. Jack figures Kevin has seen the e-mail from Catherine. Too much going on and not wanting to get into an argument, he sends the call to voicemail. Seconds later cell phone flashes a new message. Listening to the voicemail, "Fitzy, I just stopped by your office. What the hell are you doing setting up a meeting with Catherine behind my back. What are you up to? Call me as soon as you get this message." Two minutes later Kevin calls his cell phone again with another aggressive voice mail, and then multiple texts messages. *Maybe I should cancel tomorrow's meeting with Catherine.*

He stops for lunch, a #9 pocket without onions from D'Angelos, to calm his nerves and avoid Kevin. Finding an empty spot in the parking lot, backs into a spot. He locks his car and scans the parking lot, looking for something but not sure what. He reboots his laptop and plugs in the device from McCracken's.

The overview says there is a full eight hours on the tape. Unlike Kevin's phone recorder, it looks like Jack is going to have to listen to the full eight hours, and it will be hard to fast forward. The recorder starts with Bunar speaking right after he left. The tape is not nearly as clear as the phone recorder, so Jack turns up the volume to the highest setting. 'Stevey, that Fitzy guy is all right. He is a little arrogant, but I like him.' Jack can barely hear, 'Then why did you have me slash his tires?' *The guy just saved my life, but just incriminated himself.* 'Stevey, I may like Fitzy, but this is business and it is good for him to be afraid of us. Anyway no harm no foul.'

They have twenty minutes of small talk about sports scores, who is sleeping with who, and what Stevey had for dinner last night. Jack is getting bored when he hears Stevey say, 'Who do we meet with next?'

Bunar, 'Carl D'Auria from the Providence gang.' *Must be the guy from TJ's.*

Stevey, 'The same guy who pulled a gun us three weeks ago?'

'Yup and I need you to be alert, Carl always carries that damn Baby Glock gun with him and he likes to point it at people.'

'Why are you meeting with him?'

'We all have bosses even when we don't have bosses. I am your boss even though you can, for the most part, do whatever you want and I have Skinny to report to.' Jack laughs out loud when he hears Bunar's bosses name is Skinny. The tape continues 'and Skinny asked if I would meet with Carl.'

Jack's cell phone rings. Again it is Kevin. He looks at his watch, he has been out of the office for almost two hours. *It is time to take my medicine.* Jack shuts off his computer, "Jack Fitzpatrick."

"Where the hell are you?"

"I went out for lunch. I'm heading back to the office."

"How far from the office are you?"

"Ten minutes."

"Okay. As soon as you get back to the office get your ass into my office."

Jack enters CM's office through the back way because he wants to drop off his laptop and the Bunar tape. He knocks on Kevin's door. Kevin is on the phone and waves Jack into to his office, and to shut the door. Kevin has his nice voice on. He is smiling on the phone. The second he hangs up, a deep growl comes over his face. "Fitzy! You are fired!"

"I thought we went through this yesterday?"

"I thought we did this yesterday too, when you said you would be on your best behavior. Why are you setting up a meeting with Catherine?"

There it is. Knowing the question was coming, Jack is prepared. "Because both Catherine and Cheryl Scharff at Reno Regional are women and nurses, I thought it would make sense for Catherine to give her a call."

Kevin calms down a little. "Good thinking, but you do not go directly to our CEO. There is a chain of command and the chain of command goes through me." The Catherine story worked. If not he was going to try and blackmail Kevin with Maureen and, if that didn't work, Kim.

"You told me to think of ways to win those deals, and this is what I came up with. Based on our conversation yesterday, I was not coming back to you and did not want to waste any time."

Kevin pauses, "Get out of my office. And in the future never go around me to Catherine or next time you will be fired. Clear?" Jack nods his head and walks out of Kevin's office. Knowing he dodged one big bullet, hopefully he will be able to keep Kevin off his back until four tomorrow.

Jack has ten new office voice messages. It's no surprise the majority of them are from Kevin. One is from Agent Stephenson saying he is lucky he did not arrest him when he drove away and he better be at their meeting tomorrow morning. Another message is from Michelle saying MacroHealth is still bombing on day two of their demos. The last is from Colette asking when he will be coming home tonight after working late last night. It is almost five and Jack needs to get ready for both the FBI and CM CEO meeting. Jack calls Colette, and tells her he will be working late. She is extremely upset but right now she is the least of his worries.

Because the FBI meeting is first he gets all of the FBI info together. He documents Bunar's cell phone number, his bets without writing down his name, both of the times Stevey slashed his tires, Stevey's visit to CM, and his trips to McCracken's. He listens to the Bunar tape. *The guy saved my life but as he said, 'This is business.'*

Restarting the tape where he left off, picks up where Bunar was talking about Skinny. Jack rewinds fifteen seconds hearing, 'and Skinny asked if I would meet with Carl. If Skinny asks to meet with someone I meet with them. I do not have to do what Skinny says but I do have to listen.'

Stevey, 'Why do you think Carl is meeting with you? Is he going to try and shoot us again?'

Bunar, 'I have no idea but I hope it is a large wager on the Yankees. With everyone betting on the Red Sox this week, I will take a bath if the Sox win. I want the Sox to win but financially I need the Yanks unless Carl makes a large wager.'

Stevey, 'Hey, he is walking in now and with two guys.'

Bunar, 'I will have his two guys wait outside and you wait inside near the door in case they come back in.' There is a pause before Bunar says, 'Have your two guys wait outside.'

In a voice with a strong New York accent, which obviously is Carl, 'Getta outta here.'

Bunar responds, 'The three of you can have a couple of beers before your drive back to Providence because we are not going to talk any business unless your guys wait outside.' There is a pause and Jack assumes Carl gave some kind of signal for his guys to wait outside of McCracken's because Bunar says, 'Okay, why are you here?'

Carl, 'No chit chat Boon?' Jack quickly figures out Carl calls Bunar, Boon. There is silence. Carl continues, 'Okay I will get right to it. I should be putting bullets in you but I got a truckload of marijuana and I need a place to store it. The heat is on me big time in Providence, and I need a place to store it for a few weeks.'

Bunar, 'I was hoping you wanted to bet on the Yankees?'

Carl, 'Getta outta here. I hate the damn Yankees. So are you going to store my dope?'

'Sorry man but I am not in the dope business, not buying, not selling, and definitely not storing.'

'Getta outta here. Skinny said you would do it.'

'Skinny may of set up this meeting but he does not make decisions for me.'

'Skinny is the boss. He says you are storing my dope.'

'Get out and I am not storing your dope.' There is a pause, before Bunar continues, 'Carl you are not going to scare me with your baby glock. We both know what happened the last time you pointed a gun at me. You shot Mullane. By the way how is Mullane doing?'

'Boon being a cocky bastard is going to bite you in the ass. One last chance, you storing my dope?'

'Carl you got problems and I got problems. There is a rumor the FBI is watching me to get to Skinny. I am a simple bookie and I do not want to get involved in drugs. Skinny and I have a working relationship, I run book in his territory and that is it. If my relationship with Skinny changes he will tell me, not some punk from Providence carrying a small gun.' There are some shuffling noises.

Bunar, 'Carl put your gun away. Go see Skinny directly and see if he can store your dope. For all I care, rent a damn locker at the airport and store the dope there.'

'I have never liked you Boon. And for your airport locker comments, this is an eighteen wheeler full of dope that I need a place to stash and slowly start distributing.'

'I definitely do not want to get involved. This meeting is over. Carl, to show there is no hard feelings, you and your guys are welcome to have some drinks and a meal on me. At five o'clock we have an Irish singer.'

'Asshole, no way am I eating your dog food, and I would expect a call from Skinny. If I were you I would not be surprised if you see me in a couple of hours with a direct order from Skinny.'

There is silence before Stevey says, 'So boss, what did he want? He seemed pretty pissed when he left?'

Bunar, 'I am going to call Skinny and you can listen in.' Jack can hear the tones of cell phone dialing. 'This is Bunar is Skinny available.' Silence, 'Skinny, Carl D'Auria just stopped by here asking me to store a truckload of dope and I told him no way. He said you told him I had to store it. Is this true?' Silence, 'Skinny we have a good working relationship and you have treated me very well. I am not your guy for storing dope. Please find someone else.' More silence, 'You can send him back here if you want, but I am not storing his dope. I have got enough problems of my own and Carl will cause problems for both of us, because after he stores it, he wants to start dealing.' More silence, 'Okay, your call.'

Jack has been taking notes the whole time. He cannot tell what Skinny is going to do in regards to the marijuana truck but it's not his problem.

A woman comes over to the table because Jack can hear a female voice and a conversation about where they are going for dinner. The female voice says, 'The singer is about to start.' All Jack can hear is 'Wild Rover' Irish music. After shutting off the tape he makes a copy of just the cell phone beeping noise when Bunar called Skinny. Jack makes three copies of everything.

It is almost seven, Jack walks toward accounting to see if there is a chance to get the recorder from Dennis's office. Jack has already decided he doesn't need Dennis' tape, and is going to focus on taking down Kevin. Dennis appears to be a pawn and Catherine does not appear to be in the know, but Jack still needs to get the device back. There are people in the accounting office, and Jack heads back up to his office.

Jack now starts working on the accounting fraud at CM. As with Bunar, he gets all the information together and makes three copies. *Should I be doing this at home?* He feels comfortable doing the FBI work at the office but if anyone catches him doing the CM stuff and takes it, he could lose all of his information. *I am just being paranoid,* but he still gets up and locks the door.

It takes about two hours just to cut up the tape recording on Kevin. Jack deletes the useless calls, puts the accounting frauds on one flash drive, and the infidelity calls on another flash drive. It is after eleven, the packets are all set.

One complete set goes in a FedEx box addressed to Chip Savard at this office. The cover letter says do not open unless something happens to The Fitzpatrick Family. The letter inside of the sealed package has an overview of CM, the FBI, and Bunar. If something does happen to him or his family, suspect Bunar, CM, and then the FBI. Jack will put the box in a FedEx mailbox on his way home. The second packet is for his files at home, the he divides the last packet into one for the FBI and one for CM.

It is after midnight and his last stop is accounting to get the last bug out of Dennis's office. If Jack plays the tapes for Catherine tomorrow they may sweep the offices to see if there are bugs. "Damn it", there is a light on in accounting. He sneaks into the office, hoping it has been left on by accident as there is no way anyone is here after midnight. He puts his boxes on the couch in the waiting room and walks behind the receptionist's desk and grabs the key to Dennis's office. Looking around, the office appears empty. *No way is anyone else here at midnight.*

Grabbing the keys from under the desk, he quickly goes up to Dennis' door trying several keys until he is able to open the door. The light is on in the office. Jack is surprised he did not see the light from the hallway, but with the hallway light on, he did not see the light. He waits to hear something hoping Dennis left his light on by accident too, seeing as the door was locked. *No turning back now,* he peaks in and the office is empty. He walks over to the phone jack.

"Hey, what are you doing in here?"

In one motion he jumps and turns around, it is Maureen O'Shea. "Hey Maureen, I thought Dennis might be working late."

"Fitzy, what are you doing in here? It is midnight and there are keys in the door. You scared the crap out of me."

"Let's get out of here first, then I will tell you." *I need time to think of a story.* "Do you want to come up to my office?"

"We can just go to my office across the hall."

He locks up the office and puts the keys into his pocket. "Fitzy, you know I like you but this does not look good with you breaking into the CFO's office at midnight." *What do I say?* Does he try to blackmail Maureen with the Kevin affair? At least it is Maureen. He has options. Maureen continues, "Jack the longer it takes you to respond, the bigger the lie. Come on, spit it out." Jack laughs. Maureen stays on him, "We may know each other, but I am serious. What are you doing in Dennis's office?"

Pausing, "Maureen, I know this does not look good for me, but can I ask you for another favor?"

This time she laughs, "You are kidding right?"

"No, can you keep this quiet until Thursday? After Thursday, I will tell you everything." This will all be out by then and either Kevin is going down, maybe her boss Dennis, him, or even all three of them. If he is fired, he will not have to worry about telling her. If this doesn't happen by Thursday he will have time come up with another lie.

Now it is Maureen's turn to pause, "I need more information than this. I could call your boss or even the police."

There it is, the opening to Kevin, "Maureen, I know this is hard but I really need you not to tell anyone, including Kevin, until Thursday." *When to play the Kevin card*? "Then you can tell whoever you want."

"This is not fair."

Begging, "Please no one until Thursday."

"I don't know. Especially with no information about what you are doing." She switches gears, "Hey does this have anything to do with you asking for that contract last week?"

Staying on her, "Yes it does, but I really need you to promise not to tell anyone tomorrow." Playing his ace card, "And that includes", he gives her the I know look, "your boyfriend, Kevin."

Maureen's whole body language changes and she blurts out, "How do you know?"

"All I need is a promise you will not tell anyone, including Kevin."

She bows her head. "I promise."

He tries to pick her up, "Maureen, it is only until Thursday and this has nothing to do with you. Thank you." Unless she is cooking the books with her boss and lover. *But why would she give me the contract? She is not involved.* He grabs his stuff out of the accounting lobby heading off to FedEx, drops off the package, and home to bed.

51

FBI Meeting

"In politics... never retreat, never retract... never admit a mistake." Napoleon Bonaparte

At five a.m. Jack is still staring at his ceiling trying to get some sleep. *Can I get the FBI off my back without giving them Bunar?* Going into his study, he rearranges his paper work.

As he drives to meet Agent Stephenson, he reflects on what he has gotten himself caught up in, *a very dangerous game,* with dangerous outcomes. One reason he likes gambling so much is the adrenaline rush, this FBI stuff has pushed his adrenaline to the max. He is ready for this to be over.

Getting off the highway, he pulls into the non-descript Exxon station. Instinctively he is looking for a Ford Crown Victoria. The only car in the lot is a large white full-size van. As soon as he pulls into a parking spot, the van pulls behind him, blocking his exit.

Agent Stephenson comes over to the BMW, "Get out." Getting out, Jack grabs only the recorder and his notes on Carl D'Auria. He leaves the other paperwork on CM in the car. When Jack gets into the van there are four agents, one driving, one in the front passenger seat, Agent Stephenson next to Jack, and one in the rear seat. As soon as Jack gets in the van they drive off and get on the highway heading back into Boston.

Jack is outmanned four-to-one. He is evaluating how the FBI is using a selling technique on him. In sales there are times when you want to outnumber your prospects. This way you can show strength. In sales, there are also times when you want your prospects to outnumber you so they can feel their strength. He smirks, realizing most likely the FBI never lets their criminals or snitches outnumber them. In Jack's case, they want him to be a snitch and scare him with the threat of being a criminal. *The scare tactic is working.*

Agent Stephenson introduces everyone in the van. Jack does not listen to their names but does nod. Agent Stephenson seems to be in charge and the decision maker. "So Jack, what do you have on Bunar?"

The numbers are not in his favor and for his plan to work he needs to speak with Agent Stephenson alone, "Agent Stephenson, yes I am prepared to give you information on Bunar's operations, but, no offense to your other agents, I would like to speak to you alone. Bring me back to my car. We can sit and talk there."

All of the agents look at Agent Stephenson. "Okay but not in your car. There is a diner off the next exit in Randolph where we can get some breakfast while the van goes for a short ride."

Jack nods. The silence is scary but he knows not to speak. *Man this feels like a contract negotiation.* There is a human urge to fill silence. Using silence is a great sales technique. Ask a tough question and wait for the prospect to answer. Inexperienced sales people will either try to fill the void by answering the question for the prospect or will ask an easier question. Jack sits in silence. Obviously the FBI has used this tactic because the four of them say nothing even when they arrive at the diner.

Sitting in the booth, Agent Stephenson breaks the silence, "So what do you got, Jack?"

"First, I need you and the FBI to leave me alone for good. Do I have your word after I give you the information you will go away?"

Stephenson smiles, "Now Jack, this depends on what information you have for me."

"Okay." He takes a deep breath, "I got the personal phone number for Skinny, I know about a truck load of marijuana floating around Boston, and I know about a shooting."

Stephenson smiles, "So you want to barter but you do not want to give up your friend Bunar. Well, I am sorry but no deal. I want Bunar."

Jack reads he is bluffing, "I am disappointed. I thought you are after Skinny and not a small time guy like Bunar."

"Watch yourself, Jack. I read you as basically a decent guy in the suburbs who likes to lay down some big bets, and to do this you need a Boston Bookie versus a little one from Bridgewater. From what you just told me, I need to be more worried about you being part of Boston's Organized crime. Maybe Bunar is the pawn and you and William Nestler are running him?"

Jack may know how to negotiate contracts, but it looks like he may have over played his hand. *Back to basics,* "My original question, if I give you Skinny's personal phone number, a truck load of marijuana, and a shooting will you guys forget about me and delete me from your database?"

"No deal. I want Bunar."

If Agent Stephenson is bluffing, bluff back. "Disappointing, my attorney says you cannot charge me with anything and you are correct I do not want to give up Bunar." Jack decided last night to not give up Bunar for saving both his and his wife's lives.

Agent Stephenson looks at his watch and slightly backs-off, "Well, show me what you got, and I will tell you if it is enough to get me off your back."

Agent Stephenson just blinked, "I need your agreement you will leave me alone and never call again."

"Are you positive you have Skinny's private phone number, where a truck load of marijuana is, and who shot who?"

Negotiating in good faith, "To be exact, I have a recording of someone dialing Skinny's phone number and have information on who has the marijuana, but I do not know where the truck is. And I know who shot who."

Stephenson's face lights up, "You bugged McCracken's?"

"I simply want out, and I want you to go away forever."

"Give me Bunar and I will go away. Tell me about bugging Bunar?" Agent Stephenson pauses, "To be honest with you, we have been trying to bug McCracken's for the past three months, but the court approval has been hung up because McCracken's is a public restaurant. When we send our agents in there, they are watched like hawks, because it is a local place where, if they do not know you, you are the police. We have even tried breaking in but Stevey lives in a back room."

Jack stays focused, "So do we have a deal?"

Agent Stephenson is thinking when his cell phone rings. He gives a one word response, "Okay." After another minute he looks back at him, "Yes, we have a deal."

He slides the FBI's listening device across the table with his one-page note of on Bunar's conversation with Carl D'Auria. The notes do not mention Bunar, McCracken's, nor himself.

"Jack, this is good police work. You should think about joining the force if the sales thing does not work out. Let's get out of here. The van is on its way back."

Agent Stephenson pays the check, and the two of them walk outside to the waiting van, "So how did you bug McCracken's?"

Jack does not directly answer the question, "Desperate men will do desperate things. All I want is for this to be over."

"I should really push you on Bunar, but I am going to let you off the hook."

No one says anything in the van on the ride back to Jack's car. Shaking hands with Agent Stephenson, Jack wishes him luck getting Skinny and Carl D'Auria. When he gets into his car, he pats the recorder in his breast pocket. He has the FBI on tape saying he will leave him alone. Now he just needs to take care of Kevin Blair and things should get back to normal.

Something in the car is not right. His seat is not in the normal position. It is not off a lot but enough. First he checks the glove compartment and the four grand from yesterday is still there. Looks in the back seat and all of the notes and tapes on CM are gone, "*Shit*". It all makes sense. Getting him to ride in the van, not going back to his car, and the call at the diner. *No wonder Stephenson let me off the hook.*

Slamming his fist on the steering wheel, now the question is whether they know what they have on CM, can they figure it out and what will they do, will he get the information back? There is nothing on Bunar in the files, so will they give it back?

Screw the FBI, they lied to me, I will mess up their stake out of Bunar's. Jack drives to McCracken's. *Will telling Bunar about the FBI get me killed?*

He parks around the corner and walks into McCracken's. During the drive he puts together his partial truth strategy. After his eyes adjust, there is Bunar, Stevey, and the female bartender at McCracken's.

When Bunar sees him, "Fitzy, I should say I am surprised but I knew you would be back to make more bets. Come on over." Bunar doesn't get up. They sit down at their usual spots. Reaching under the table, Jack grabs his bug. Bunar continues, "So what three games to you want to bet on?"

Whispering, "Bunar, I wish I was here to bet. You and I have bigger problems. Is it okay to talk here?"

"What the hell are you talking about, Fitzy?"

Jack looks around the empty bar, "I was contacted by the FBI this morning." He waits for Bunar's response, hoping Bunar does not have a temper.

Bunar aggressively says, "And ......" Bunar rolls his hands in a motion for Jack to spit the rest out, "You did and said what?"

"I told them I did not bet with you I simply went to McCracken's. They must have done some research or something, because they know you and I are friends with Billy."

Bunar rolls his hand again, "And?"

"I kept telling them I was not betting with you, but they must have been tailing me because they know every time I met you here." Jack's purpose in the leading statement is so Bunar will not think he knows too much.

"And?"

"That is it. I wanted to let you know the FBI is watching you and, now me."

Bunar is listening close to every word, "So why are you here? Are you wearing a wire?"

Shit, did I grab the bug to soon, if I get stripped searched? "No, I am not wearing a wire. I am here because I want you to know the FBI is watching you, and I was hoping you have a way to get both of us out of this."

"Have you contacted a lawyer?"

"No."

"Thanks for coming to me. I have heard rumors the FBI is watching me, and now I know they are."

"Are you running drugs and prostitutes?"

Bunar laughs. "Why?"

He is nervous but feels comfortable when Bunar laughs. "The FBI told me you were a very bad person, pushing drugs, women, and even murder."

"Fitzy, I am simply a bookmaker providing a service to the public."

"I was really nervous about coming to you about the FBI but you are very relaxed."

"We both will be okay. No more talking to the FBI and if they do contact you, just let me know."

"How can I contact you?"

"As always, go through Billy."

"Agreed," Jack asks, "I have to ask. Am I safe?"

Bunar answers with a question, "From me or the FBI?"

"You have slashed my tires."

"I was just sending you a message to pay your debts, you personally were fine. Just make sure you pay your debts."

They shake hands. Jack feels good for getting back at the FBI. He does not need the CM paperwork back from the FBI because he has another copy at the house. He is assuming the FBI will not know what they have, because they are looking for Bunar versus accounting fraud at a public company.

Walking into the sunlight with a spring in his step, though not perfect, the first part of his adjusted plan seems to be working. Jack turns the corner to his car. He clicks his car door opener and is opening the door when an aggressive forearm pushes him against his car. He thinks is Stevey but before he can turn around, hears "Jack Fitzpatrick you are under arrest for racketeering and undermining an FBI investigation."

He turns around to see Agent Stephenson is pointing a gun at him. *Two days a in a row a gun is pointed at me.* "Are you serious?" Before he even has time to answer the same white full-size van from this morning pulls up next to them and the FBI agents push Jack into the van.

"Jack, I am very disappointed you met with Bunar."

Feeling energized, "I am very disappointed the FBI broke into my car and took my personal paperwork. Especially after I thought we had a deal."

"Well, the FBI would not do this without a warrant because it would be illegal." Agent Stephenson looks at the agent in the passenger seat of the van. "And if we did, we sure as hell would not have confused office paperwork with a Boston bookie."

"So when I return to my car, can I assume my paperwork will again be in the back of my car?"

"Not so fast. I want more."

"We have a deal. What I gave you is great information."

"It is up to me determine what is and what is not great information."

"What about our deal?"

"You broke our deal when you went back to Bunar's. Did you tell him about us?"

"All I did was have lunch with a friend."

"No way, you were only in McCracken's two minutes." Stephenson pauses, then grins, "You have the right to remain silent."

Jack interrupts, "You are kidding?"

"I am arresting someone in connection with Boston Organized Crime and the person is you." Agent Stephenson puts Jack in handcuffs.

"Come on, I will be out of jail in five minutes and I assume your bosses would laugh at you for arresting a business guy from Bridgewater."

"I am very serious." Jack does not respond. They all sit in silence. Agent Stephenson says, "However, I am willing to give you a chance to avoid jail and to end this once and for all." Jack still does not say anything, "Can you get me more information on the marijuana truck?"

"We had a deal and I stuck to my end."

"Okay, if that is your decision. Let's go to FBI headquarters where you will be charged with the very serious crime of undermining a FBI investigation."

Jack is confident they have nothing on him and they are only bluffing but he does not want to push his luck and have to call Colette to tell her he is arrested. This will lead to a whole set of questions from Colette and will only put his marriage even more at risk.

"I will ask you one more time. Can you get me more information on the marijuana truck?"

"How do I know you will keep your word? Just this morning we had a deal you would leave me alone and here we are back in the van."

"This morning I was frustrated with our conversation because you weren't giving me detailed information on Bunar. Once I had a chance to digest your information, I realized you had some good information, just not enough of it."

"I do not trust you because I thought we had a deal." They pull up in front of One Center Plaza, FBI Boston Headquarters.

"Your call, it will take about an hour to book you, including calling your wife."

He pleads, "You have all my information on the marijuana truck."

"Not enough", they pull him out of the van. *How can I save myself and Bunar?*

"Hold on, how about I give you guys a whole new case?"

"I am listening."

"You had it this morning but you did not understand what you had." Jack explains the evidence he has against CM, "So are you interested in accounting fraud?"

It is a warm June day in Boston and he is sweating profusely even with the air conditioning from the van. His hands are shaking. Assuming the FBI goes ahead with the deal, after the CM meeting, he is going to go to the Charlie Horse Bar and suck down a truckload of Miller Lites.

"Nope, I want the marijuana and Bunar."

Bluffing, "As far as I am concerned, we are done. Either arrest me or bring me back to my car." Jack strategically pauses, "But before you arrest me, I want you to know I recorded our conversation in the diner."

"You think you are pretty smart." Jack says nothing. "All you have is a federal agent working on a case." Jack does not blink and stays silent. Finally Stephenson continues, "Well, tell me more on why I should I listen to your accounting fraud."

Kevin is going down and what is better than getting Kevin fired and arrested by the FBI? Jack goes into greater detail on the evidence including the stock price.

"I am not going to arrest you for now. We will take you back to your car. I guess it will take our investigative and accounting teams a couple of weeks to figure out what we have, but I will need you to keep working at CM and I will be in touch. No more trips to Bunar's or you will be arrested."

52

CM Meeting

"The time is always right to do what is right."
Martin Luther King

By the time Jack gets back to CM it is almost four o'clock. After leaving the originals with the FBI, he had to stop at home to get the extra copy of the CM files. When Kevin sees him, "Where have you been, we are meeting with Catherine in five minutes."

"I am almost ready. Just give me a minute."

Jack grabs Kim Savard and pulls her into his office closing the door. "Kim there are some major things going on at CM right now. I cannot go into detail but I will cut to the chase with you. I discovered you are having an affair with Kevin."

Kim starts to tear up, "Have you told Chip?"

Shaking his head, "Nope, but I had to tell you."

Kim crying, "What are you going to do?"

"Nothing for right now. Even though you work for me, I consider you and Chip friends, this is between you and Chip. I strongly recommend you stop seeing Kevin, and, if you are having any thoughts Kevin is in love with you, you should know, he is also having an affair with another CM employee too."

Kim just sits there crying. She spits out "Thank you for not telling Chip." Leaving his office, "You can stay in here as long as you want to collect yourself."

He meets Kevin, and they walk to Catherine's office. On the walk, Kevin is empty handed, not even holding a notebook. "Fitzy, why are you bringing your briefcase and computer?"

Jack excitingly says, "I have never been in Catherine's office and I wanted to make sure I have at my fingertips any, information she wants."

Smugly answering, "Catherine is a pushover. I will take care of this meeting. You just keep your mouth shut."

Jack is wowed how spacious Catherine's office is. She has a huge corner office with modern dark mahogany furniture. Looking out a floor-to-ceiling window, Jack can see the large Japanese koi fish in the pond shaped in the CM logo below. Catherine has the three of them sit at a glass conference table in her office.

The three of them start out with some talk about the weather. Jack smiles thinking, *Both of them, especially Kevin, doesn't see this coming.* Catherine is obviously in the dark, and Kevin has bought his story. When the talk turns to business, Kevin does all the talking. He starts by giving an overly optimistic update on the Reno Regional and Memorial deals. He then asks if Catherine will call Reno Regional's CFO. *Man Kevin is good. The bastard is snowing Catherine. It sounds so good, I am starting to believe him.*

Kevin wraps up with more bullshit. Before Jack knows it, the meeting is over. He has not said one thing. Catherine thanks both of them and asks, "Is there anything else?"

Jack has a chance to get out and wait for the FBI to do the dirty work in a couple of weeks. Also, it really is a good sales idea to have Catherine call Cheryl Scharff. Jack is just standing there, when Kevin states, "Come on Fitzy let's get out of Catherine's office. She is busy." Kevin throws a low blow, "Are you falling asleep on me again?"

"You arrogant bastard," Jack blurts out, "Catherine, Kevin is cooking your books!"

Kevin stares at Jack, "Fitzy you must have fallen asleep because you are dreaming. Let's go before you get fired for incompetence."

Jack says to Catherine, "Call up Dennis Hintz and ask him about the books. The two of them are cooking your books."

Catherine asks Kevin, "Is this true?"

Kevin smirks, "Of course not. Jack is crazy. If it will make you feel better, I will meet with Dennis and give you an update after I have spoken with him."

Catherine now asks Jack, "This is a very big accusation. Do you have proof?" Jack quietly nods. Catherine quickly asks, "Well, let's see it."

Jack grabs his briefcase and pulls out his documentation. He is not going to use the tapes unless he has to. Kevin screams, "This is preposterous. Fitzy you are fired. Stop wasting Catherine's valuable time."

Jack says to Catherine, "Fine. To show you how serious I am. I resign."

Kevin yells, "You are fired, you bastard, for lying to our CEO. Good luck finding work."

"Don't call me a bastard and a liar. You are the one who is cooking the books and sleeping with the CM staff." Kevin quickly gets up and stands over him. As Jack stands up, Kevin tries pushing him. With Jack being six feet four inches tall, younger, and in better shape, Jack quickly tosses him to the ground.

Catherine yells at them, "Stop it. Now!"

Kevin is sitting on the floor looking up at Jack, "You cannot bully me" and tries standing up.

Jack stands over Kevin and does not let him up, "Are you sure you want to get up?"

Catherine says with a calm voice, "Let's all calm down. Jack please get off Kevin and let him stand up. I am going to get Dennis Hintz up here right now so we can figure this out."

Jack points at Kevin, "You accuse me of bullying you, wait until we hear Dennis' story about how you are bullying him."

Kevin stands up and changes tactics, "Fitzy, you sure know a lot of information. Are you sure it is not you and Dennis, who are cooking the books?"

Jack stands up, "Nice try, you are going to jail."

Catherine gets in the middle of them, "Please calm down."

Jack and Kevin do not listen, "Not me, you."

Jack repeats himself, "Maybe you did not hear me. You are going to jail. I gave the FBI the information on you."

Catherine shakes her head, "You what?"

Jack is shaking from the physical exchange and emphatically says, "That's right, I gave the accounting fraud information to the FBI."

Catherine yells to her secretary outside of the office, "Get our legal counsel in here right now too. Tell them to stop whatever they are doing and to get them in here now."

Catherine asks, "Are you two done with the macho bullshit so we can get to the bottom of this?" They both nod.

Kevin says, "I need to go to my office to set some paper work." They both look at him with reservation. "I am not going anywhere, he is the one who is cooking the books. I will be right back."

Sure enough, Kevin comes right back and the three of them, Dennis, and the attorney sit back down at the table. Catherine takes control of the meeting. She tells her secretary to get some water. Catherine takes a minute to update Dennis and CM's attorney on the meeting. Catherine leaves out the physical confrontation between Jack and Kevin. Jack is only watching Dennis. Kevin is giving Dennis the 'Go with whatever I say look.' Catherine says directly to Jack, "So Jack, what did you send to the FBI?"

Jack, staring at Kevin, explains what he found on the Memorial and Kennesaw accounts. Kevin interrupts, "Catherine this is all bullshit. The little weasel is just trying to keep his job."

Catherine tells Kevin, "Please be quiet!" She asks Dennis, "Before Jack continues, is what he is saying true?" There is complete silence in the room. Kevin is about to say something, when Catherine stares and points at him. They are all waiting for a response. Jack was feeling strong coming into the meeting that Dennis would confess to the accounting fraud based on the way he has been pushing back on Kevin, but is not sure. *Did Dennis change the books back, and if he did, the only guy left to fry will be me?* The room is staring at Dennis.

Dennis nods in simply agreement and bows his head.

Kevin pulls a gun. "This is all bullshit." Pointing the gun at Jack, "I am not going down."

The situation is eerily similar to yesterday at TJ's. *How did Bunar get the gun?* Catherine says, "Kevin, please put the gun away."

Kevin states, "This is a witch hunt."

Catherine keeps begging, "Please put the gun away."

Jack is studying Catherine's table. *This table looks a lot heavier. Do I push or lift?* Kevin screams, "This job is all I have." Kevin switches from pointing the gun at Jack to Dennis.

Now is my chance. Jack tries to lift and push the table but it is too heavy. He does push it enough for Kevin's chair to violently knock back. The gun fires. Jack jumps across the table. The gun fires a second time. Tackling Kevin square in the chest, the gun goes off a third time.

Jack is on top of him and successfully grabs the gun. Jack pops up holding the gun with two hands. The room is frozen. Catherine slowly walks over to Jack and gently puts her hands on Jack's forearms, "Please put the gun down."

Jack looks around to see if anyone is shot. Somehow everyone is okay. Security finally makes it into the room, taking Kevin with them.

Catherine asks them to sit back at the table. "The police will be here in a few minutes and I want to get some details." Jack is disappointed she does not thank him for saving her life. "Kevin is obviously fired. Now, Jack what did you send to the FBI?"

Jack's adrenaline is flowing and he rapidly tells everything except the phone taps. He tells them about Betty's accusations at Memorial to Reno Regional and the discrepancies with the CRM software, the accounting software, and their contracts. Catherine asks, "Why?"

Jack assumes the question is for Dennis. Catherine asks again, staring at Jack. He is not prepared for this question, and his sales reflex kick-in to ask another question, "Why what?"

"Why did you turn this information over to the FBI?"

Jack pauses before throwing Kevin under the bus, "As you saw today, Kevin has been coming down on me very hard. I was able to find out Kevin was pressuring Dennis too, and, for all I knew, you were in on it too. I did not know where to turn, so I sent the information to the FBI."

He is hoping there are no more follow-up questions for him but Catherine asks, "Who at the FBI did you send the information to?"

Lying, "I do not remember."

Catherine glares, "Do you know I could go to jail in addition to getting fired?"

"Catherine, if you did not know anything, why would you go to jail or get fired?"

Catherine actually smiles, "Jack you are being naïve. I am the CEO. I signed the Sarbanes Oxley Act. I am responsible for my employees. I should have controls in place to not allow this kind fraud to take place. I can go on and on."

CM's attorney interrupts to explain The Sarbanes-Oxley Act was signed into law in July 2002 following the series of high profile corporate scandals. Its objective is to protect investors by improving the accuracy and reliability of corporate disclosures made pursuant to the securities laws. Sarbanes-Oxley imposes stiff penalties for company officers who fail to ensure the accuracy of their financial reports and further penalizes anyone who obstructs fraud investigations by destroying or altering records for publicly traded companies.

Catherine interrupts the attorney, "I think that is enough, Jack gets it."

Jack doesn't apologize, "I am not going to say I am sorry. I almost got killed today."

"Thank you for catching Kevin and saving our lives." Jack thinks, *Finally*. Catherine continues, "I wish we could have handled this internally, but it is not an option now, especially with the shooting." Pausing, "Do you want to help this company?"

Jack nods, half expecting the next question to ask him to try and get the information back from the FBI.

"Okay, we have a lot of work to do. First, I need a copy of everything you sent the FBI including the contact." Jack gives a very sad nod. "CM will survive this but it will not be easy. For right now, I need you to go back to your desk and not say anything to anyone. This will all come out in the next couple of weeks. I will call on you where needed"

Jack asks, "What can I do to help you?"

Catherine encourages him, "Win legitimate deals. I will do whatever I can to help you win the deals, including Reno and Memorial."

Jack asks, "Even after all this, I would still like you to call Reno Regional's CFO to help me win the deal."

The police arrive and question all of them. It is after seven when Jack heads home. He has one last big thing to do to complete his plan.

53
Epilogue

"Life would be infinitely happier if we could only be born at the age of eighty and gradually approach eighteen." Mark Twain

Colette has dinner waiting in the stove for Jack. He needs to tell her about his day but he decides to wait until Harrison goes to bed. Jack asks Colette to come into the dining room.

Colette nervously, "Oh my God you are having an affair."

Shaking his head, "No but I have a lot to tell you. There are reasons why I have been 'acting weird' lately."

Jack tells Colette everything, including the guns. When he gets to stealing the money from her, she is in tears and asks Jack to move out, screaming, "I will never trust you again". He begs for forgiveness.

Eight months later.

Kevin Blair pleaded not-guilty to attempted murder and accounting fraud but is still awaiting trial.

Dennis Hintz got fired the day after the meeting with Catherine. He pleaded guilty to accounting fraud. Because he made a deal with the Feds by giving more evidence on Kevin, he got a $50,000 fine with a suspended sentence, no jail time, and one thousand hours of community service.

CM Solutions got a $5,000,000 penalty from the Security Exchange Commission. Catherine Corbett was able to save her job after a 50% drop in CM's stock following the announcement of the accounting fraud. She now has the company back on track and the stock is starting to rise again.

Agent Tim Stephenson received a promotion after finding the truckload of marijuana but was unable to get Bunar nor Skinny.

With a lot of hard work, Jack was able to win the twenty-eight million dollar Reno Regional deal. With Reno Regional installing CM products and no longer buying products, Michelle Parks no longer hears from Jack. Memorial ended up de-installing CM and choosing MacroHealth.

Jack and Colette have a healthy baby girl, Emerson. Jack is able to save his marriage by joining Gamblers Anonymous. With his commissions from the Reno Regional deal, he puts the money back in Colette's account and is working on getting out of debt, and paying the marker at Foxwoods. Jack is learning he has a lot of extra money since he gave up gambling.

"Hi, my name is Jack and I'm a compulsive gambler."

About the Author

Shaun Priest is a senior executive who lives in Atlanta, Georgia with his wife and two children. He grew up in Massachusetts and graduated from Providence College in Rhode Island. Currently he is Senior Vice President, of a web technology solutions company. His hobbies include reading, blogging, recreational gaming and a multitude of sports including running, basketball, golf, and tennis. When not busy, Shaun is busy working on his next novel.

To learn more, visit Shaun's website www.shaunpriest.com, his business blog www.closerq.com, or send him an email at shaun@closerq.com.